Praise for Patrick Hoffman

'Patrick Hoffman's intricate, hallucinatory second novel is a thrill ride of noir pleasures.'   *—Irish Times*

'This violent, twisting tale by a former private eye is gripping and feels 100 per cent authentic.'   *—The Sun*

'A highly entertaining high-octane and exceptionally violent Donald Westlake–like crime caper told with real verve and wit'   *—Irish Independent*

'Astonishing . . . a mind-bending, attention-demanding narrative as full of shocks and surprises as an LSD party'   *—Wall Street Journal*

'Patrick Hoffman's second novel . . . crackles with authenticity'   *—San Francisco Magazine*

'Filled with epic twists and savage turns, the pace is relentless, and Hoffman's drive sets fire to the pages as he crawls across the sinister black underbelly of the Californian dream . . . Exhilarating and powerful.'   *—Daily Mail* on *The White Van*

'My favourite debut of 2015 so far . . . His careful, pared-down prose is a delight . . . *The White Van* is a caperish delight, channelling Elmore Leonard and Donald Westlake to exhilarating and unexpected effect.'   *—Guardian*

'A nifty bit of noir set in the mean streets of San Francisco . . . a juicily d︎︎︎︎︎ *White Van*

About the Author

Patrick Hoffman is a writer and private investigator based in New York. He recently moved from San Francisco where he worked as an investigator, with the last five years spent at the San Francisco Public Defender's Office. His debut novel, *The White Van*, was shortlisted for the CWA Ian Fleming Steel Dagger. *Every Man a Menace* is his second novel.

EVERY MAN
A MENACE

Also by Patrick Hoffman

The White Van

EVERY MAN
A MENACE

Patrick Hoffman

Grove Press UK

First published in the United States of America in 2016 by Grove/Atlantic Inc.

This paperback edition published in 2018.

First published in Great Britain in 2017 by Grove Press UK, an imprint of Grove/Atlantic Inc.

1 3 5 7 9 8 6 4 2

A CIP record for this book is available from the British Library.

Paperback ISBN 978 1 61185 533 3
E-book ISBN 978 1 61185 955 3

Printed and bound by CPI Group (UK) Ltd, Croydon, CR0 4YY

Grove Press, UK
Ormond House
26–27 Boswell Street
London
WC1N 3JZ

www.groveatlantic.com

For Kathy Coyne

Part I

Getting out of prison is like having a rotten tooth pulled from your mouth: it feels good to have it gone, but it's hard not to keep touching at that hole. Raymond Gaspar served four years this time. He served them at a placc in Tracy called the Deuel Vocational Institution, DVI. The only vocation he learned was making sure the drugs kept moving. By the time he was done, he'd become something like a football coach. He told the players where to stand, what to do. He wasn't the head coach. That would be his boss, a man named Arthur.

Raymond fell in with Arthur because one of his uncles used to associate with him. As soon as Raymond got bounced from San Quentin up to DVI, his uncle told him to find a man named Arthur. *Don't worry,* he said. *There'll only be one Arthur on the yard.* That ended up being true. Arthur smiled big when he heard who Raymond was.

It turned out Arthur was a good man to know at DVI. He was big business, and not just there either; he kept a low profile, but his fingers stretched well beyond the yard. He associated as white, but he dealt with blacks and Latins, too; as far as Raymond knew, Arthur was the only man in the

California Department of Corrections who could make a call to the Black Guerrila Family or the Aryan Brotherhood and get action from either group. That's how he was.

Raymond had been locked up for trying to sell a stolen boat to a man in San Francisco. He had walked right into a police investigation that didn't have anything to do with him. It was simple bad luck. They wrapped him up outside the garage on Sixth Street. When the cops searched his car they found an ounce of crystal meth. It was a bad day. They had him on tape talking about the boat, which led them to the boat itself, back in a garage in Richmond, and they had the drugs. Two months later, his public defender, a good lawyer, lost a motion to suppress at the preliminary hearing, and Raymond was forced to take a deal: four years.

Arthur must've thought that stolen boat made Raymond something of a businessman. He kept him off the front lines, didn't use him as muscle, and right off the bat made him a supervisor. It was a fine thing to be doing: make the rounds, see where things were with the supply, let Arthur know that everything was good. He didn't have to touch the dope, and he didn't have to play rough either.

Raymond swore he saw a shine in Arthur's eyes when he reminded him that his release date was approaching. It was uncharacteristic. "I got a little situation you could help me with," the older man said. They were sitting near the handball courts in the south yard. A few of Arthur's men sat near them. Arthur was a big man, with a big head and big shoulders; he sat hunched over with his elbows on his knees. In his country accent—he'd been raised on a horse farm in western Colorado—he explained that he had a little side thing going in San Francisco.

"I got this lady that buys a little pack of Molly every month and sells it to this other dude. Thirty, forty, fifty pounds a month. Real weight. I set it up—everything's good. She cuts me a little percentage off the deal each time." He made a gesture like he was flicking water off his hands. Raymond wanted to ask what kind of percentage, but he didn't. Arthur told him anyway.

"Thing is, that ten percent is not enough." He looked at Raymond like he was confirming his level of interest. Raymond nodded.

"What I'd like to do is replace at least one of these two parties with you. I mean, unless you're planning on going straight or some bullshit? Accepting the Lord into your heart?" Raymond shook his head.

"It's a complicated situation, though," Arthur went on. "We can't just go and push a motherfucker out on this one." He made his face look like the very idea was distasteful. "Nah, you can't just push 'em out. I want you to go there and—acquaint yourself with the situation. It's hard for me to see everything from here." He pointed at the walls, turned, and looked at Raymond.

"Go and look?" Raymond asked. He felt a sense of uneasiness come over him.

"That's it," Arthur said. "Just go and look around, get to know these two skunks, see wassup. Do some of that fancy bullshitting you do; make sure this next deal goes through. I'll cut you half of my ten, put you at thirty thousand or something around there, let you land on your feet. After that, if we gotta do the same shit the next month, we'll drop it to a quarter of the ten, two-point-five, put you at fifteen or something. It's not bad." He smiled; Raymond did, too. Fifteen thousand a month was good.

Arthur continued: "Even if we don't make a move, it won't hurt to have you on the ground. You did your thing in here, man. And I still owe that fucking uncle of yours, so . . ."

He held his fist out. Raymond bumped it.

It felt good to step off that Greyhound bus and put his feet down on Mission Street. It was late in the afternoon, cold and damp around the bus station, but the air smelled clean to Raymond. He walked all the way to the Prita Hotel, on Nineteenth and Mission. He always stayed there when he was in the city. The Prita was the kind of place where you needed to get buzzed in at the front door, then buzzed in again at a second door at the top of some filthy stairs. You talked to the clerk through a dirty Plexiglas window. The hallways smelled like cigarettes and crack smoke. They charged by the day, the week, or the month. The rooms consisted of a bed, a small TV, and a locked door. Raymond paid for a week.

When he'd gotten his room, Raymond lay down and thought about the situation he was about to get into. Arthur had outlined the arrangement. Gloria Ocampo, a Filipina woman, was bringing the ecstasy in. Every month she got a shipment from some Israelis and sold it to a guy named Shadrack Pullman. Arthur had set the whole deal up, hence the 10 percent cut. "But you gotta watch this chick," he'd said. "She's paranoid, nasty, and smart." He tapped the side of his head with his pointer finger. "A capital-G Gangster, you understand? Don't let her looks fool you."

Raymond had asked about Shadrack next.

"Served his time right here," Arthur said, pointing out at the yard. "He's all right—you know—a little on the eccentric side. He's got a little Pomo in him, you know? Indian, Native American. He's the type of character gonna let you know what he thinks, one way or the other. He don't keep it close to the chest, but he's all right." Arthur waved his hand like Shadrack was nothing to worry about.

"Truth of the matter is, if we do end up having to move someone, it's gotta be Shadrack first, 'cause trying to get rid of Gloria would be like kicking a damn hornets' nest." He shook his head like he wasn't ready for the idea. "You never know, though. Her time might come, too."

Raymond asked what he was supposed to say he was doing there.

"I talk to Gloria somewhat regularly," Arthur said. "I check in, thank her for her timely payments. Last time she made mention of Shadrack turning eccentric—that's her word, she called him eccentric—I said, 'All right, I'll send someone, have a little talk with the boy, straighten him out.' She said, 'No, don't worry.' She got a Pinoy accent. I said, 'No, it's fine.' Bottom line, you know, it's grounds for entry. But you just gotta say your lines, man. Say you're there watching over my interests, making sure the deal keeps clicking. She'll probably ask you, you can tell her you getting two-point-five on my ten."

Raymond asked if his showing up was going to cause any kind of concern.

"Maybe so, maybe not," Arthur said. "But what the fuck they gonna do about it? You're working for me. Those two aren't about to make a move on me."

Lying there on the bed, Raymond pictured the whole thing. He could handle it. He could make a threat, or follow through on one. But, the way he saw it, the ideal thing would be to let these two carry on. Collect his two-point-five and stay mellow. He didn't want to kick a hornets' nest if he didn't have to.

A few hours later, Raymond walked up Mission Street and bought himself a prepaid cell phone. The sidewalk was crowded, but he felt tense and lonely. The city had changed. It seemed richer. When he got back to the Prita, he sent a text message to Gloria Ocampo.

She texted back right away. Said she'd come by at eight. For a brief moment, Raymond wondered what he was getting himself into.

He had vague plans of using the money he'd make from this job to start something straight. Buy some tools, start working carpentry or something like that. But he wasn't about to go fully clean. He didn't really want to leave the grimy life behind. He liked making money from drugs, from illegal shit. It made him feel high. He'd been doing it most of his life, and he wasn't about to quit now. He didn't really care for carpentry all that much.

Gloria Ocampo showed up exactly at eight. She was slightly plump, nothing like Raymond had expected. He had pictured a club girl: skinny, with tight jeans. Gloria was probably in her fifties. She had dark circles under her eyes that made her look tired. But she was still pretty; she dressed nice, and she smelled good, too.

When she came in she looked the room over like she was making sure nobody else was there. Then she walked to the one window and looked out into the light well.

"You just got out?" she asked, turning back around. She had a strong accent, just like Arthur had said.

"Just today," Raymond said, feeling a wave of embarrassment at the poorness of the room. He wiped at his face.

Gloria dug into her inside jacket pocket and pulled out a folded sheet of paper. When she handed it to Raymond he saw that there were three hundred-dollar bills inside—crisp and clean, the faces up.

"That's all I have now, but I give you more later," she said.

Raymond shrugged and put the money in his back pocket. He realized he was thirsty, and licked his lips. He wanted to ask Gloria if she was Arthur's girlfriend, but he worried that she'd think he was hitting on her. He looked at her body instead, imagined having sex with her, then looked away, aware of the silence. He could feel his heart pumping in his chest; it occurred to him that he might already be in over his head.

"How's Arty?" Gloria asked. Raymond had never heard anyone call him that before.

"He's fine."

"What he say you doing here?"

The curiosity on her face, the intensity of it, struck Raymond for a second. "He wants me to look in on one of your partners," he said. "Make sure everything stays clicking."

She nodded. Then she walked back to the door, which was still cracked open, and closed it. "Don't say anything stupid," she said, pointing at her ear and then at the ceiling. "But what'd he say about this partner?"

"He said the boy was acting reckless," Raymond said.

"Shadrack's not a boy," Gloria said, shaking her head. "And he's not acting reckless. He's acting crazy. He's acting like one of these homeless men that shouts at walls. You know this kind of crazy? A lot of people are not happy with him, Mr. Gaspar." She looked at Raymond for a moment, made sure he was listening. Then she continued.

"These people, they want to know if you're the right man to take care of this. You know what I mean? They don't want you to start something and then decide that you can't finish it."

This wasn't what Raymond had been expecting. He'd thought Gloria would meet him with resistance, say that Shadrack was fine, that she didn't need his help. Raymond hadn't heard of any other people. He didn't know what to think of this news, but he felt his interest tick up. He watched her for a second and reminded himself not to get too eager. *Sit, breathe, wait.*

"I'm worried about it," Gloria went on. "I'm worried he's going to ruin the entire arrangement. You fix that. You come at the right time." She raised her eyebrows and looked into Raymond's eyes searchingly.

He felt his neck get warm. "Well, that's why I'm here," he said. He prided himself on his ability to read people, and right at that moment his bullshit detectors were sounding.

"Tell me now," Gloria said. "Why'd Arthur send you?" She turned her head, worked at removing something from her teeth with her tongue, and turned back to him. "As opposed to that other guy?"

Raymond didn't know who she was talking about. "I guess he thinks I'm a people person," he said. "I guess he thinks I got a gift for fixing problems. Truth of the matter is I couldn't tell you. You should ask him."

Her face did something resembling a smile when she heard this. "Tomorrow's Sunday," she said. "On Monday I take you to get a new ID." She raised her finger like Raymond had protested. "I take you to get an ID. Arthur told me to. On Tuesday you go to Shadrack's house and we'll see what kind of people person you are." Her face transformed itself into a friendly thing. She said good-bye, and left.

As soon as she was gone, Raymond sent a text message to Arthur. An inmate named Duck held a phone for him in prison.

New number. Met your girlfriend. She on one.

On Monday, after checking in with his parole officer, Raymond went back to his room and texted Gloria. She picked him up in a tan minivan driven by a silent young Asian man with a thin mustache. The driver barely looked at Raymond when he got in. There were crumbs on the floor of the van, like someone had been tearing up loaves of bread. Raymond sat in back, feeling stressed by all the activity around him.

They drove to an industrial neighborhood lined with barbwire in South San Francisco. A few semitrucks sat parked and quiet on the shady side of the road. When the van stopped, Gloria handed him an envelope and said it contained seven hundred dollars. She told him to give it to a man named Javier.

"Don't worry," she said. She pointed at the building. "Go on."

There was a garage door open. The place looked like an auto-body shop. Inside Raymond noticed a bank of security monitors within an office on the right. He saw himself in black and white on one of the screens. Farther in, two men stood hunched, working on the door of a car. One of them sensed Raymond standing there, and turned.

Raymond said he was looking for Javier. The man said something in Spanish to the other man, who walked over to a doorway toward the back. *What the hell am I doing this for?* Raymond thought.

The man who'd spoken stood there smiling and nodding like they'd shared some kind of joke. Then he shifted his eyes toward the lot. Raymond told himself to calm down. He took a deep breath, let his shoulders relax.

After a short time another man came from the back with his eyebrows raised. He wore blue coveralls, like the other men. He had the look and walk of a convict. Raymond pulled out the envelope and handed it to him.

"Who sent you?" the man asked, in a casual way. He opened the envelope and counted the money with his head tilted.

"Gloria," Raymond said, pointing without conviction over his shoulder.

Javier walked Raymond into the back room and had him stand against a blue backdrop. A camera was already set up on a tripod. Javier looked through the viewfinder, adjusted the tripod, adjusted the camera, and snapped three pictures of Raymond. The flash from the camera popped with each shot.

"Real cards with holograms," he said. "We'll call you when it's ready."

As Raymond walked back out to the car he realized he hadn't given Javier his number, but he kept going.

"What the fuck was that for?" he asked when he got back into the van. He felt genuinely angry.

"Got to have a backup plan," said Gloria. She was using the passenger-side visor mirror to apply wine-colored lipstick. She didn't stop what she was doing to look at him.

They rode without talking all the way back to the Mission. Raymond had an uneasy feeling in his gut; it felt like a test of wills. He didn't like having his picture taken. He didn't like being told what to do, either. He remembered Arthur saying how crafty Gloria was and he wondered if he'd just been played.

Before he got out, she handed him another envelope, this one holding a thousand dollars. His silence suddenly felt immature, but he realized that's exactly how she wanted it. "It's from Arthur," she said.

"Well, thanks," Raymond said. For a moment, he felt, inexplicably, like crying—but it passed.

"Fifty-six Colby," Gloria said when he got out. "Five-six Colby, C-O-L-B-Y. Got it?"

"Fifty-six Colby," he said.

"That's Shadrack Pullman's address. Go see him tomorrow evening."

* * *

Colby Street was off Silver Avenue. Raymond took a taxi there, which, after four years in prison, felt luxurious. He arrived about an hour before the sun set. The house was plain, a box on a block filled with similar-looking ones. He stared at it for a moment and then made his approach. There was a garage on the bottom, with a gated front entrance beside it and stairs leading up to the living area. Plastic blinds covered the windows on the second floor. The walls were dirty; even on a rundown block, they stood out.

Raymond felt nerves swimming in his stomach as the doorbell buzzed upstairs. After a few moments, he heard the metallic sounds of locks being unbolted, chains being undone, and finally the door—around a corner and out of sight, at the top of the stairs—being pulled open.

"Who is it?" called an angry voice.

"It's Raymond Gaspar," he said. "Arthur's friend."

Silence. Raymond studied the stairway, noticing dust and hair on the ground, dark smudges on the walls. He felt his heart speed up a little.

"What's the password?"

Gloria hadn't mentioned any password. "Arthur," he said, trying his best to sound confident.

During all the talk about Shadrack Pullman, Raymond had never been told how he looked. The man coming down the stairs now must have been about six feet four, 180 pounds. He wore loose jeans and no shirt, and he had long hair, though the hair up top was receding a little. He was white, Raymond thought, but there was something Asian-looking about his face. No, not Asian, Raymond remembered. Native.

He was angry. Raymond couldn't tell if he'd heard what he'd said, so he repeated it once the man had reached the bottom of the stairs.

Shadrack came right up to the metal gate and looked down at his visitor. Raymond took a step back.

"Arthur's not the password," Shadrack said.

His eyes seemed speedy; he was looking at Raymond wrong, focusing behind him. He held his face tight, scanning the block to see if Raymond had come alone before settling his eyes back behind Raymond.

"They call you Ray, Raymond, or Raymundo?" he asked.

"Well, Ray, or Raymond."

"Shit, then come on," he said, opening the gate. "Get on up."

Raymond walked in past Shadrack and up the stairs, then turned and waited. Shadrack waved him forward. In his mind, Raymond pictured throwing an elbow at his host's throat if the man tried anything. The doorway led to a living room. The lights were off, but a huge television played a nature show with the volume muted. As Raymond's eyes adjusted, he saw that the room was cluttered with stacks of books, with boxes and newspapers. A female mannequin leaned against the wall in one corner, bald and white. She had been drawn on with a marker; it looked like a child had scribbled out her breasts and face. The house smelled dirty.

"Shh—turn," said Shadrack.

Raymond turned. The man held a pistol in his hand. Raymond felt a pulse of fear, but he stayed still, and as he focused on the gun he saw that it wasn't real, that the barrel was solid. Still, he didn't like it; his heart beat hard in his chest.

"Give me your driver's license."

Raymond reached into his front pocket, felt for the rubber band that served as his wallet, separated his state ID from his money, and handed it over. Shadrack stepped back into the doorway so he could use the daylight to see it. He looked from the card to Raymond's face and back again. The gun hung loose in his hand.

"Raymond Gaspar," he said. "You're the one Arthur sent?"

Raymond nodded. "He told me to check in on you," he said. "Make sure everything was cool."

"Do I look like I need help?"

"No, not you," said Raymond. "You seem all right."

"What'd you do? You was his bodyguard, in Tracy?"

"Something like that."

"You don't look like a bodyguard, though," Shadrack said.

"Well, I'm more gifted at thinking than fighting, if that's what you mean."

"So you're a deep thinker?"

"Just as a way of saying that I'm not a great fighter."

Shadrack raised the gun toward Raymond's head and pulled the trigger. A burst of water hit him in the neck.

Anger spread through Raymond's stomach and chest. Where he'd been for the past handful of years, that was grounds for a fight. He was ready to rip the man apart. In the darkness, he felt his face turn red.

"I'm just playing, boy," Shadrack said, tossing the gun to Raymond. "Shoot me if it make you feel better." He stepped in front of Raymond, holding his hands wide in surrender.

Raymond could smell the man's underarms. He turned away, and set the gun down on the TV.

"Take your shirt off," Shadrack said.

Raymond waited.

"You gonna take your fucking clothes off before we talk about anything. You heard me?"

The door clicked, and the room lit up. Raymond turned in time to see Shadrack lock two dead bolts, then set a metal police lock at a 45-degree angle to the floor. Raymond's eyes swept over the room. A real sawed-off shotgun lay on a table against the wall, closer to Shadrack than himself.

"Let me tell you something," said Shadrack. "Where I'm from, a stranger show up at your house, it's the stranger's duty gotta prove who he is, not the other way around." His voice dropped down to a whisper. "I'm sure you understand if your shyness is outweighed by my need for caution."

Raymond watched the man breathe, watched his chest fill up with air and empty.

"I already got my shirt off," said Shadrack. "Shit, you might be wearing a wire, boy. Feds, Gloria, they all listening. Now take your hands and pull out your pant pockets."

Raymond did as Shadrack said.

"Pull your pockets out, good. Turn around."

Raymond turned, and Shadrack stepped forward to pat the back pockets of his pants.

"Put that shit down on the floor."

Raymond took his room key and money from his back pocket and dropped them onto the carpet. Shadrack reached into his jacket pockets next, then opened the coat and fingered the breast pocket.

"Take off your coat. Drop it there."

Raymond did as he was told. He moved slowly.

"Now, take off your shirt. Set it with your coat."

Raymond turned and looked at Shadrack's face. The man's expression seemed to say that he just wanted to get this over with, too. Raymond pulled his shirt off and dropped it.

"Take your boots off," Shadrack said.

Raymond bent down, keeping his eyes on Shadrack, and untied his boots.

"Socks, too."

"Come on," Raymond said.

"You're a stranger, boy. I don't know who the fuck you are. Said you're Arthur's friend, you know me, you know my reputation. You think I'd let you in off the street? Like y'all don't know who the fuck I'm talking to? Y'all don't know the fuck I'm dealing with? Shit, don't make me worry about how dumb you are."

Raymond felt a little stab of shame when he said this.

"Before I talk to you about anything that me and Arthur *might* want to talk about, I gotta know you're not coming in here wearing a damn microphone. Not because"—Shadrack paused and looked up at the ceiling like he was addressing a listener somewhere else—"not because I'm partaking in any kind of criminal conspiracy, mind you, but because I respect Arthur's privacy. Get it? Now take your fucking pants off. Let's get all this bullshit over with. We gonna do this, or you gonna turn out."

Raymond took his clothes off. He felt sick. Shadrack looked his body over—made him raise his arms, raise his balls—told Raymond he should be used to it coming out the pen. Raymond felt himself slip into the kind of trance necessary to get through this type of thing. After a few minutes

Shadrack went down the hall and returned with a brand-new white T-shirt, still in plastic, like he kept them around especially for these occasions. While Raymond unwrapped it, Shadrack found some used blue sweatpants, held them up to check the measurement, and handed them over. He didn't give him anything for his feet. Raymond's own clothes went into a black trash bag while Raymond eyed the shotgun.

Having knotted the bag, Shadrack cleared off a space on a dirty couch across from the TV and told Raymond to sit down. Then he pulled a radio out from under the table, turned it on so that static filled the room, and found a station playing Mexican music. He pointed first to his ear and then to the ceiling, just as Gloria had, as if to say, *They listening*.

"Tell me exactly now. Why'd Arthur send you to see me?"

Raymond's stomach knotted up. He thought about it for a moment and then said, "The man's happy with the situation you and Gloria got going here. It's a good relationship, works good for everybody. But Arthur's been hearing things from certain people." Shadrack's eyebrows shot up and he began to speak, but Raymond raised a finger and quieted him. "He's been hearing that you've been acting a little on the strange side." Raymond paused for a moment, let it sink in. "Not the fun kind of strange, either. Strange enough that people are starting to worry. That's why I'm here. He sent me to check in on you. That's it. See what your status is, nothing else. Make sure you stay on track, just for the week. Get everything taken care of—let me tell him everything's fine. He's just worried that if you keep making everyone nervous . . ." He left the sentence unfinished.

"And he believes you can communicate with the Seven Gods because of what?" asked Shadrack.

"I don't know what that is," said Raymond. The stereo continued to blast its Mexican music. The nervous feeling in Raymond's chest had connected to his breath and grew with each inhale. He felt scared. Shadrack stood over him, his face angry. The energy in the room had shifted.

"You thought you could come in here and communicate with me using human words?" Shadrack said. He pointed at his chest and tapped at it a few times, a gesture Raymond didn't understand. Then he mumbled a few indecipherable sentences. It sounded like he was speaking backward, talking in tongues.

"You don't speak Seven-L, do you?" asked Shadrack. He stood there, rocking from one foot to the other.

"I'm afraid not," said Raymond. He felt nauseous. His forehead started to sweat. Shadrack was looming over him, blocking his way.

"And you're just a boy, too," said Shadrack. "How old are you? Fifty-five?"

"I'm thirty-two, now."

"So, the—the—the—" Shadrack stuttered and then seemed to change tracks. "Are we friends?" he asked, looking truly concerned.

"I'd like us to be friends."

Shadrack sat down beside him. Raymond noticed a sheen of sweat on the man's face. He took a few deep breaths, like he was trying to steady himself.

"Remind me one final time," said Shadrack. "What services are you offering?"

"I'm just a friend. Someone to help, help make sure every-thing goes smooth."

"Like a helper?"

"Exactly," said Raymond.

"Oh," Shadrack said. "I see. Hold on." He jumped up and left the room. Raymond looked at the door, then at the shotgun; he thought about walking out, but something told him to stay. He took a deep breath and tried to relax.

Shadrack came back into the room. He stood in front of Raymond and held out a bottle of Visine. "Open your mouth," he said.

"Nah, I'm good," said Raymond.

"Open up, friend!"

"What is it?"

"It's LSD. Come on. Open up."

"I got a piss test next week," Raymond told him.

"They don't screen for acid," Shadrack said. "Come on, punk." He was smiling now; Raymond saw his teeth. They were gapped and pointed, the molars capped in gold.

"Look, it ain't nothing," he said, squeezing a few drops into his own mouth. "Now open your damn mouth. We gotta celebrate your ass getting sprung."

Raymond opened his mouth. Shadrack squeezed the bottle so that a solid squirt hit Raymond's tongue. He tried to spit it out.

"No, don't spit it out!" Shadrack yelled. He jumped around, laughing. He jumped on Raymond and hugged him. "You a crazy son of a bitch!" Shadrack said. "You're fucking crazy!"

* * *

Shadrack wanted to go to a party after that. He let Raymond put his own clothes back on, and then he got himself dressed: black pants and a wrinkled black suit coat over a white V-neck T-shirt. He sprayed some hair spray into his hair, ate gum, gave Raymond gum, grabbed a black doctor's bag, and led them downstairs to the garage.

"You sure you should be driving?" Raymond asked.

"Sometimes I am, sometimes I'm not," he answered.

Shadrack's car, a silver Toyota, was so normal looking that Raymond's mind was put somewhat at ease. He couldn't feel the drugs yet, but despite his nervousness he felt somehow happy, too. They were getting along. They were friendly now. He would be able to handle this job after all. Shadrack pulled the garage door open and the outside world—cold air, concrete, and street light—was suddenly right there.

They got in the car and fastened their seat belts. Shadrack slowly backed out, watching carefully to make sure the mirrors stayed clear of the door. Raymond asked again if he was sure he could drive, and Shadrack said he could do it with his eyes closed.

They worked their way down Mission Street. Raymond was still just nervy, not high, but the neighborhood had taken on a more festive atmosphere. The people looked happy, dressed up; bright colors and music seemed to be coming from everywhere. Even the bums were laughing. Shadrack was driving with a focused expression on his face. It seemed, to Raymond, like a perfect way to celebrate getting released from the penitentiary.

The party was right off Dolores Park. "This man you're gonna meet is a true child of the Seven Gods," Shadrack said, once they'd parked. Raymond couldn't tell if he meant it or not. They walked up a steep hill to reach the house, which to Raymond seemed like a pleasantly odd thing to do. He breathed in deep. His chest felt open. The drugs were setting in.

He hadn't taken acid since he was a teenager. The house looked like a palace, looming straight up from the sidewalk three stories high, its surfaces new and clean. Shadrack rang the bell and pointed at a camera above it. Raymond felt a shyness pass over him.

A voice came on the speaker. It sounded like a man pretending to be a woman.

"Who is it?"

"Special delivery," said Shadrack, looking into the camera.

They stood there and waited. Shadrack set his bag on the ground, ran his hands through his hair, took a deep breath.

The door swung open so fast that Raymond almost had to jump back. A regular-looking guy, a businessman, stood on the other side. He wore a blue button-up shirt, tucked in like he was at an office. He had a softness around his cheeks and gut. He smiled big at Shadrack.

"The Doctor has come!" he said. He was in his forties, white.

"We're both doctors," said Shadrack, flicking his thumb toward Raymond. Then he stepped forward and the two men hugged and slapped each other's back like a secret handshake.

When they'd separated, the man turned to Raymond. "How are you? Brendan Moss," he said, holding out his hand to shake. His eyes were wide open, like he was playing around. Raymond shook his hand and flinched—it was soaking wet.

"I was washing dishes!" the man yelled.

"Come on," said Shadrack, waving them up the stairs. When Raymond passed him he whispered, almost like a preemptive reprimand: "Handle your high, brother."

They stepped into a large room. Raymond gawked at the height of the ceilings, the glass windows, everything clean and modern. He'd expected some kind of biker party, not this. People turned their heads and stared, and Raymond froze until the heads swung back, the noise of conversation resumed. Moss grabbed him by the arm and pulled him toward a bar. "Get this guy a drink," he yelled out. People smiled as they passed. Raymond felt gripped by the realization that just three short days earlier, he'd been wearing a blue uniform, living in a packed gymnasium, eating canned tuna on special occasions.

The bartender, an Asian man, was wearing a white shirt and black tie. They smiled at each other and Raymond was briefly certain he knew him from somewhere. When he tried to admit this his voice sounded strange in his ears. The bartender's smile faded a little, and he turned toward Moss for help. But Moss—his hand still on Raymond's arm—was looking somewhere across the room.

"Get him a drink," said Moss.

Raymond looked back at the bartender. He seemed annoyed.

"What can I get you, sir?" he asked.

"Budweiser?" Raymond couldn't think of anything else.

"We only have Peroni, sir," said the bartender.

Raymond nodded, uncertain. He could still feel the heat of Moss's hand on his arm, but when he looked, he saw that Moss had left him standing there alone. He searched the room for Shadrack, but he couldn't see him either. The lights had been turned down, and the room felt candlelit now. Everyone's clothes looked beautiful. It was a costume party, Raymond thought. He took a breath and turned back toward the bartender, who was holding a bottle of beer out for his examination. It looked fine. The man poured it into a glass.

Raymond's hands were sweating. His ears popped. Where had Shadrack gone? Where was Moss? There was a fireplace at the other end of the room, and he walked toward it.

He had been lost in the blue and orange tangles for God knows how long when someone grabbed his arm. He turned, expecting Moss, but instead found a young woman asking if he'd walked there.

"Did I walk here?"

"Do you work here?" she said again. She had a foreign accent. She looked over his shoulder as she talked.

"In this building?" Raymond asked.

The floor below his feet seemed to be moving in small circles. The woman he was speaking with looked, suddenly, elderly. Her makeup was thick, Raymond realized; she was much older than he'd thought. At some point he understood that they were standing in the middle of a group of people. He stepped back from the older woman; there were chairs set around them, people sitting and talking. To his right, a woman with long blond hair held a dog in her lap like a baby. It looked cute until he noticed she was breast-feeding it. She saw Raymond watching and stopped; she pulled up her shirt to cover her breast and gave him a nasty look.

The place had become crowded. He was still holding the beer, he realized, and he drank it. He started trying to move a little, in time to the music, but he felt strange, like a bear dressed in clothes, and then he kicked over a glass and red wine spilled out. The glass had broken. People were clapping at him. A short man with makeup all over his face pushed toward him and began to chant, "Enemy, enemy, enemy." Raymond stumbled back to the bartender to ask for a rag. A beautiful woman with dark hair stepped out of his way. Raymond, for a moment, became transfixed. But someone grabbed him before he could talk to her.

It was Moss. "Don't worry, friend!" he said. His long eyelashes looked fake. He pulled Raymond in and hugged him tight. His body was soft, Raymond thought, like he was wearing some kind of padded suit. But he was wet, sweaty.

"Where's Shadrack?" Raymond asked.

"Come on!" said Moss. "He's been looking for you." Other people were dropping their drinks now. Raymond heard glass shattering. Someone had smeared shit or mud all over one of the walls. Everyone seemed to be talking at once. The white dog the woman had been nursing followed behind Raymond's feet. Its mouth was stained red and looked bloody. They passed a homeless man in the hallway. He had long dreadlocks, and piercings covered his face. "Sorry, inmate," the man said.

"Come on!" Moss said again. His face, now, resembled a loose-jawed puppet. "He's in there," said Moss, pointing at a door at the end of the hallway. A red glow the color of fire leaked out from beneath the door. Moss put his hand on Raymond's lower back and pushed him forward.

They found Shadrack sitting on a chair that looked like a throne. Two women sat on a bed to Shadrack's right, regarding Raymond with peaceful expressions. They seemed friendly. Graceful.

"Found him," said Moss, who had now taken on the appearance of an angel, wise and gentle. Shadrack's hair flowed down over his shoulders, his posture straight. He seemed philosophical. *Impossible*, thought Raymond. This wasn't the same man he'd met earlier.

"Where you been, old friend?" asked Shadrack.

"I spilled wine," Raymond said.

"Well, you know what they say," he said, gesturing for Raymond to sit down next to the two women. Moss sat on a bench across from them.

"Don't cry over spilled wine," one of the women said, moving over to make room. She had a mirror in her hands, and after sniffing some powder off of it, she offered it to Raymond. She looked Japanese.

"Exactly," said Shadrack.

"I can't," Raymond said. "I'm on parole."

"Parole?" said the woman, leaning forward to look at him. The other woman leaned forward, too.

"He's a good old boy," said Shadrack. "Don't worry. He just stole some boats."

Raymond hadn't told Shadrack anything about his old case. He looked to him for an explanation, but Shadrack just stared, a smile blooming across his face. Then he closed his eyes and put his fingers near his temple. Raymond closed his eyes, too, and in his mind, as clear as day, he heard the sound of Arthur, his boss, stuck in prison, singing: *Every man gonna help each other, help your sister, help your brother.*

"Help your brother," said Shadrack.

Raymond opened his eyes. The man was smiling. The woman next to Raymond took his hand in her own and squeezed it.

"Ladies, let Mr. Gaspar lie down on the bed," said Shadrack.

The women stood up.

"Take his shoes off," said Shadrack.

The women untied his boots and pulled them off. Raymond felt embarrassed in his socks; he felt naked. He watched from the bed as Shadrack opened his doctor's bag and pulled out what looked like a large green emerald. It was the size of a small plum. He pulled out other stones, too; they were all different sizes. Purple, yellow, orange, brown.

"I need you to take your shirt off again," said Shadrack.

Raymond pulled it off, and lay down flat on the bed. There was a thrumming in his head. *Every man gonna help each other.* The women took his hand again and started massaging it. Shadrack sat down next to him, and the bed sank a little.

"Bless this child, in peace and heaven; he's been delivered out," Shadrack said. He put a stone on Raymond's forehead, and Raymond closed his eyes.

"Bless this child in function and form; he's a Seventh Son."

He placed a stone in the hollow of Raymond's neck.

"Bless this child of truth, this child of danger, this child of courage."

Raymond felt three stones fall across his chest.

"Bless this child of nourishment. Bless him with rest," Shadrack said, setting one final stone on Raymond's belly.

In his mind's eye, Raymond saw emeralds cut into shapes that couldn't be described in human language. He saw the universe and all its workings. He saw the cosmos as veins in a body. He saw the insides of stars like rooms in a house. He saw all things combined into one being. And then he disappeared.

The next day, Raymond woke to the sound of knocking on his door. He didn't know where he was; he looked around his room and tried to make sense of it. The knocking continued. His body, as he lifted himself from the bed, felt wrecked. As he moved from dreamless sleep to wakefulness he realized he was still high.

"Who is it?" he called out.

"Gloria," said a voice from outside. He pulled on his shirt, his pants, flattened his hair.

"It's two p.m.," she said, when he'd opened the door. Her face showed concern.

"I was resting," he said, stepping back. "Just resting." He watched the way she entered the room, the way she walked, and concluded that she was afraid. He could see it in her posture. Shadrack's voice played in his mind: *You're filled with fear*. He couldn't remember if he'd actually said this.

"You met him?" Gloria asked.

Only one day had passed since he'd last seen her, but it felt longer than that. Raymond nodded his head, tried to act casual. *We met.* He felt his cheeks and collarbones get hot. He wanted to be outside.

"He welcomed you?" she asked.

Raymond nodded. "Took me to a party," he said. He felt tongue-tied and dumb, dry mouthed, disorganized, dirty. Gloria had left the door open and he moved to close it, sticking his head out into the hall first. He saw the young Asian man who had driven Gloria's van standing about ten feet away. He had been text messaging, and now he looked up and stared. Raymond closed the door.

"Who is that?" he asked.

"He's my driver," she said.

Raymond shook his head. "He made me do acid."

Gloria smiled, looked at the ceiling. "Of course he did."

"I think I'm still high."

"I see," she said, as though everything had fallen into place. "When I leave, go to the store. Get a gallon of milk. Drink it. Sober up."

He nodded.

"I need you to go back to his house today," she said. "This is what you tell him. Tell him: 'The boat has shipped.' No—tell him: 'The ship has sailed.' That's it. The ship has sailed. You know, it's good news. Deliver it like good news and he'll be happy. Let's keep him happy, okay?"

She gave Raymond another three hundred dollars and left him standing there in his room.

When he was a teenager in Santa Rosa, Raymond's mother had lost her job at a restaurant. The manager accused her of stealing forty dollars from the till. She didn't do it—she'd never stolen a cent in her life—but a few things happened after she lost that job. She fell behind on rent, which made her cut back on other spending. It was just Raymond and his mother living alone, then. His father had died of a heart attack when Raymond was two.

The summer she lost that job, right before his sophomore year, Raymond had a little growth spurt. When school started he felt embarrassed in his too-small clothes, but in the first week he became friends with an acne-faced boy named Couchi Ortiz. Couchi was a stoner, an outcast, but he liked Raymond. It was Couchi who got Raymond into stealing cars. They would go to Marin County and find Toyotas they could unlock with a shaved down key. Couchi knew a man in Vallejo who would buy the cars for five hundred dollars apiece. It was good money. Raymond started buying his own clothes after that: brand-new 49ers Starter jackets, Girbaud jeans, Nikes, everything.

One day after school a rich kid named Vance Mueller walked up to Raymond and punched him square in the nose. Then he jumped on top of him and kept punching. He was a nasty kid, sick in his head, and he beat up Raymond's face real nice.

Two months after that beating, Raymond, Couchi, and another one of Couchi's friends were riding in a car they'd stolen earlier that week, listening to Mac Dre and teasing each other in the way that teenagers do. They were in the hills between Novato and Vallejo, on Highway 37, when a highway patrolman saw them. He pulled them over with no cause, claiming they were speeding, and ran the plate.

That was Raymond's first arrest. But sitting there in that dirty hotel room in San Francisco, Raymond wondered whether things would have worked out the same way if his mom hadn't been accused of stealing that money. He might have had some better school clothes. He might've never fallen in with Couchi. Wouldn't have done any of it.

Raymond returned to Shadrack's house later that day. The same nervous feeling spread out in his chest and belly. Shadrack, fully dressed this time, came down the stairs with a look on his face that expressed a combination of suspicion and humor. It felt confrontational. Raymond's heart beat hard in his chest.

"Gaspar the guilty," said Shadrack. "King of all the spies."

"What the fuck happened to you last night?" Raymond asked, trying to sound friendly.

"That was a good old party," Shadrack said, stepping to the gate and surveying the street the same way as before. "You were acting crazy, man. Shit."

Raymond smelled marijuana before he got to the top of the stairs. Inside, he saw a black man sitting on Shadrack's couch. The man was dressed fancy, in a button-up shirt, slacks, nice shoes. Forty years old, maybe. He was a little overweight, with a thin mustache and goatee. He barely nodded at Raymond before turning back to the blunt in his hand.

"Ray, John, John, Ray," said Shadrack, introducing them. John nodded again, then started to get up, like he was going to leave.

"No, no, stay there, John," said Shadrack.

Raymond scanned the room. It seemed even dingier than he remembered; the clutter made it feel dangerous. He wasn't sure if this was the drugs, still, making him paranoid.

"Get 'em up," said Shadrack, motioning for him to raise his hands. When Shadrack went into his pockets he found the three hundred dollars.

"What kind of money is this?" he asked.

"Just money."

"John, see that gun?" said Shadrack. "Hold it on him."

John leaned forward, putting the blunt down, and picked up the sawed-off shotgun. He shifted in his seat and pointed it at Raymond. The room swung. Shadrack walked over to a lamp near the wall and held the bills up to the light.

"Who gave this to you?" he asked.

"A friend of mine," said Raymond. He was so scared he couldn't think straight.

"Was this friend of yours a Filipino woman, about yea tall?"

Raymond nodded his head.

"I see," said Shadrack. He walked back over toward Raymond, got right in his face. "I don't like her," he whispered.

"She's different than us," Raymond said. "Less interested in having fun."

Shadrack smiled. "Put the gun down," he said. Then he pushed the three hundred dollars back into Raymond's front pocket.

"We good?" Raymond asked.

"Oh, we good—me and you—we good," said Shadrack. "I read you last night, clear as day. You are worthy, Raymond.

You a worthy bastard, but—and I told you this last night—you are filled with fear, more fear than anyone I've ever read. It's gonna kill you."

"Nothing I can do about that," said Raymond.

"Well, there is," said Shadrack. "For one thing, you can stop being a slave. Stop acting like this man, this King Arthur, is your God Jesus. You know: *Yeah, yeah, yeah, yes sir, Arthur, sir*." He paused, shook his head. "You could run away, right now, never see the man again. Let me ask you something straight up, no bullshit. How much is he paying you?"

"He's not paying me anything," Raymond said. "You know, down the road, another job, that kind of shit."

"You believe him, John?" asked Shadrack.

"Don't know, don't know the man. Don't know Arthur either, hard to say," John said.

"Well, I do know Arthur," said Shadrack. "I been knowing him. He ain't the type to send a man to do a job and not pay him. How much is he paying you?"

"Twenty," said Raymond. "If it all goes through."

"He tell you they planning on ripping me off?"

"That ain't Arthur's way," Raymond said. Everything was moving too fast. "Respectfully," he added, "I don't know this man." He pointed at John. "I don't talk business in front of someone I don't know."

"Again, boy, you missing the damn point," said Shadrack. "John here, he belongs. You don't. You can say anything in front of him. He's my partner. Now listen: if Arthur is paying you twenty—and that sounds about right—but if he is, I can pay you a lot more than that."

34

"For what?"

"For letting us know how he's gonna do it."

"You're paranoid," said Raymond. "We gotta stay on track, man. The ship's sailed."

"Gloria already told us that," said Shadrack, dropping his head like he was disappointed.

Raymond felt outmatched. The air smelled stale.

"Listen," Raymond said. "I've been doing this kinda shit for a while. I know how things go. I'm gonna ask you one time: Can we work together? Get this job done? Make sure it goes smoothly? I'm not here to play games. Let's stop all that. Nobody's gonna rip nobody off. You gonna get your shit, like always. That's it. Can we just slow down? You keep doing you, but just be a little more normal? I'll get paid my little chunk of change. You'll get paid. Arthur's happy, everybody's happy?"

"I told you he was wise," said Shadrack.

"You sure did," said John.

"That's your word? Nobody ripping nobody off?" said Shadrack.

"That's my word," Raymond said.

"So, when you do hear that they're gonna rip me off, you'll at least listen to my offer?" asked Shadrack. The smile was gone. His face was deadly serious.

Raymond looked at John: he was staring at the floor, holding his eyebrows up, looking like he was contemplating an answer of his own. A clock ticked somewhere in the room.

"If that happens, I'll hear you out," Raymond said.

Shadrack snapped and pointed his finger at John like a gun. "He sings in seven tones, and feels as much as you," he said. "Feels it right in his chest. He's filled up with feelings. He's filled up like a poet in a love story."

They took Raymond along with them that day. They rode in John's car, a black SUV. John drove, and Shadrack sat in front, with Raymond in back. They took Silver Avenue over to Palou, crossed Third Street, and headed up the hill to Hunters Point.

When they got to Harbor Road, they told Raymond to wait. He watched them walk to an old, flat, two-story housing project with a group of teenagers standing in front. John talked to them briefly before the door opened. The streets were quiet. Laundry hanging on a line between two buildings flapped in the wind. Trash blew here and there.

When they came back, Shadrack said, "Goddamn, she got him on a tight line, though."

"It is what it is," said John.

They went to Oakland next. John drove the speed limit, stopping at every stop sign. He held the wheel with both hands and kept his eye on the rearview mirror. He was a professional. In Chinatown, an Asian man stood waiting on the corner of Seventh and Harrison. He jumped in the back, looked at Raymond, and asked, "Who the fuck is he?"

"He's with us," said Shadrack. John pulled back out into traffic.

"He looks like a fucking cop," said the man.

"No, no, you don't want to say that," said Shadrack. "Huang, meet Ray. Ray, this is Huang." Huang looked to be about thirty-five years old; he was losing his hair. He dressed like a rapper, in a tracksuit, a gold chain, and a gold watch. He shook Raymond's hand disdainfully.

"Why you say my fucking name?" said Huang.

"He's with us, boy," said Shadrack. "Calm down."

"Bullshit," said Huang. He sat blinking for a moment, then unzipped his jacket and pulled out a baby blue envelope from his inside pocket. When he handed it forward, Shadrack looked out the window, confirming nobody was observing them, and then opened the envelope. He fingered his way through a stack of bills, his lips moving as he counted. It took a long time. Huang's knee tapped up and down while he waited. Raymond noticed that he had long fingernails, like a woman.

"Y'all good?" said Huang.

"Perfect," said Shadrack. "We'll see you in a few days."

Huang snorted. Raymond stayed silent. The car bumped along the road. Thirty seconds later they returned to Seventh Street and Huang jumped out of the car.

"He's touchy," said Shadrack. "Full-fledged United Bamboo, though. You ever heard of them?"

"No," said Raymond.

"Shit, they Taiwanese, man. World's bigger than your little prison gangs." He turned to John. "Head over to the lake," he said.

At Lake Merritt, John parked on the street. People walking alone or in couples passed by on the sidewalk as they sat in silence. Raymond watched the back of Shadrack's head and waited.

"What time you got?" asked Shadrack.

"They're not late," said John.

"So you said that family's as big as—"

"Biggest in Hunters Point. They've got about forty or fifty of them over there," said John. "Cousins, aunts, uncles, all of them. They're in the Fillmore, too."

Raymond measured his breaths and waited. It was a beautiful day in Oakland; the sun was out. Seagulls flew and landed.

When the car pulled up next to them, Raymond's first thought was that they were looking for parking. He shook his head at the passenger. But the woman cocked her head, held her hand up, and waved her fingers.

"There they are," said John.

Shadrack got out and slammed the door shut. He walked to the other car, opened the back door, and got in. Raymond bent forward to look at the driver. He could tell it was a white man, but that was it. The car pulled away.

"Should I get in front?" asked Raymond.

"Nah, you're good," said John.

"Who're they?"

"Just more people."

"Everybody pays first?"

"Certain types do."

"He's got them paying before they even see it?"

"That's how he is." John shook his head. "Not normal, but as you're probably starting to see, he gets away with a lot more shit than a normal man could." He adjusted the rearview mirror and looked back at Raymond. "Like having you come along."

Raymond nodded a little and looked across the lake to see if the car was circling back.

"The man does have a strange sense of humor," said John.

Raymond measured John from behind, imagined reaching over the seat with his left hand, locking John's head against the headrest, and cutting his throat. The car felt hot. He pressed the window button, but nothing happened.

John leaned forward and turned the car on. Raymond lowered his window a few inches and asked, "How come he lives in that filthy house?"

"Shit, it's just some people's nature to be dirty."

Raymond closed his eyes for a moment. He was tired as hell. Just before he drifted off, Shadrack came back and opened the door.

"She had on all white!" said Shadrack. "Head to toe. I said, 'You on your way to get married?' She said, 'I'm already married. It just makes me feel more spiritual.' She's the kind of person you wonder if it's bad luck even talking to."

"Where next?" asked John.

"We good, for now," said Shadrack. He turned in his seat and looked at Raymond. "You saw her? Head-to-toe white like a damn Latter-day Saint."

They drove Raymond back to his hotel. It was dark outside by the time they got to the city. A man was selling crack to another man on the sidewalk. Shadrack rolled down the window and spoke through it as Raymond stepped out.

"Better to be dumb and have friends, than smart and alone," he said. The car pulled off.

Raymond had just drifted off to sleep when he was woken by Gloria knocking on the door. It was almost like she was timing her visits to keep him awake. As he let her in, he peeked down the hallway and saw a different young man this time.

"Why don't you invite him in, too?" he said.

"He's not with me," she said. Her anger took Raymond off guard. He'd come to realize that she had all kinds of different moods, and they changed fast.

"Where'd you go?" she asked. "I've been calling you."

Raymond found his cell phone and saw five missed calls; the ringer had been turned off.

"Where you been to?" she asked again.

"I went to Shadrack's house. Like you said."

"From there. Where did you go?"

"You been following me?"

"If I was following you, would I ask where you go?"

Raymond felt anger boil up in his guts. This woman, he thought, needed to learn how to interact with people. Basic conversational skills. She was getting on his nerves. "We went to Oakland," he said.

"I know that. I'm asking who did you visit there?"

Raymond didn't want to tell her who they'd seen. For the first time, he wondered if Shadrack's fear of getting ripped off was well founded. "We went to a place in Hunters Point, don't know who he saw there. They left me in the car. Then we went to Oakland. Met a Chinese guy with a fat envelope, name of Hung, or Wong, or some shit. Then they saw some white lady dressed in white. That's it. They didn't tell me who anyone was, didn't tell me nothing."

"Who's they?"

"Shadrack and John."

"Who's John?" she asked, her face looking like she was finally closing in on some kind of truth.

"He's a black dude. I thought you knew him. They work together."

"A black dude named John," she said, mockingly. Raymond sensed hatred coming from her. He was so tired he felt feverish. This job was becoming more and more difficult.

"It's too much back and forth between y'all," he said. "I just need some sleep. My mind's not working right."

"Come here," said Gloria. She stepped closer to him and put a comforting arm around his shoulder. He could smell her perfume. For a moment, he felt a sexual energy run between them. It scared him, and he stepped back. Her eyes looked damp.

"You need to keep your phone on," she said. "I'll pass by later." She turned and looked at the bed for a moment. "Rest. You're confused," she said.

"I know," he said.

She left him after that. As soon as she was gone, he tried to call Arthur. Duck answered the call and told him Arthur had been thrown in the hole. There was a new guard who'd caught him with dope. Thirty days. Duck cursed the guard up and down, said they were thinking of acting on him. He asked Raymond if he was good, and then asked if he'd had his dick sucked yet.

Thirty days in the hole, Raymond thought. *Better to be dumb and have friends than smart and alone.*

A few hours later, he woke up to the sound of knocking again. He assumed it was Gloria, but when he opened the door he saw four plainclothes cops. They wore hoodies and nylon jackets, with badges hanging from their necks and guns on their hips.

"Raymond Gaspar?" said one of them.

"Yeah?"

"Parole sweep," the cop said. "Give me your ID."

He did as they asked. They searched him and then sat him down in the hallway. He didn't have anything in the room, but they weren't leaving. They turned his bed over, searched under the sink. They turned out each pocket of his pants a second time. Eventually two of the cops left, but the other two kept him sitting in the hallway. Finally, after an hour and a half, they called it a night. It was almost one thirty in the morning by that point.

The cops didn't answer any of his questions. The way they'd searched him, though, it looked like someone had given them a tip.

He couldn't sleep after that. He tossed and turned and when he finally fell into something like sleep, he was woken again by hard knocking. This time he asked who it was. The person on the other side wouldn't answer. When he finally opened the door, there was a young black guy there, sober seeming, dressed in black. He looked Raymond dead in the eyes, then told him he was sorry, must've had the wrong room. It was four in the morning. Somebody didn't want him to sleep that night.

His cell phone started buzzing before nine. The only numbers he'd saved were Gloria's and Duck's, and this wasn't either of them. He answered it.

"It's your old friend," said Shadrack. Raymond didn't remember giving him his number. "Got a little situation. I'm 'bout to pick you up in thirty minutes. Wait outside for me. You check in with your mother yet?"

Raymond told him he hadn't. He hung up the phone and sat there wondering what the hell Shadrack was talking about. Then, with nothing else to do, he called his mom.

She went on and on about how happy she was, about him needing to get a job, a fresh start, all that. He said he'd come visit as soon he got settled in; maybe he could get his parole moved up north. Before he hung up, he asked if anybody had come by looking for him. She told him no, but the damnedest thing had happened. Somebody had broken all four of her garage windows last night. Raymond felt his blood pressure rise.

Shadrack picked him up a half hour after that. He wore his hair wet, combed and pushed behind his ears. He'd shaved, too, and Raymond noticed a dark spot of blood where he'd nicked himself above the lip. The man's eyes still looked like he was on speed; he kept working his mouth around like a crackhead. Everything about him made Raymond nervous.

"Man, you look tired. Wassup, you went out last night and got your rocks off?" Shadrack asked.

"Parole sweep," Raymond said. "Middle of the night." He watched Shadrack's face for a reaction.

"No shit."

"Then some black dude woke me up."

Shadrack turned the car off Mission and headed up Seventeenth toward Folsom. "So what'd the black fella want?" he asked, smiling a little.

"Don't know. Didn't say," Raymond said. "Let me ask you a question: Why'd you want me to call my mother?"

"'Cause that's what you're supposed to do, when you get out the can," Shadrack said. "Call your mom, make sure no windows were broken, no doors kicked in, that kinda thing."

"Pull the fuck over."

Shadrack kept driving. Raymond reached for the steering wheel and the other man slammed on the brakes. They stopped in the middle of Seventeenth Street. A car honked behind them.

"What the fuck you playing at?" Raymond asked.

"I didn't do it." The honking grew louder as other cars joined in. "Your bitch boss of a friend, the Filipino bitch—she did it."

"Bullshit. How'd you know about it?"

"She told me."

"Y'all don't even talk." He felt like he was about to hit the man.

"That don't mean we don't got ways of hearing what she says."

"Pull the fucking car over, man," Raymond said, pointing toward the curb. "What the fuck you think you're playing at?" He felt violence balling up in his right hand.

Shadrack swung the car toward the curb and pulled out a cell phone. Raymond thought he was going to call somebody, but instead a recording started coming out of the speaker: it was Gloria's voice. There were some muffled words, some static. Then he could hear Gloria saying his mother's address, 1407 Spruce Street, Santa Rosa. After that the recording stopped.

"You're pissing me off, man," Raymond said. "I swear to fucking God."

"It's me they want," Shadrack said. "They gonna try to tell you I did it. You'll see."

"How'd you get that?"

"Shit, I might look poor, but I got ways and means."

"Bullshit. She wouldn't mess with my mom like that. Come on."

"Don't know what she'd do," said Shadrack. "But I do know she's the type of bitch that'll do something. She won't even act on it. She'll just hold it like a damn ace up her sleeve, use it if she wants. But watch, she'll use this one, next forty-eight hours—mark my words, you try and stand up for me, she'll make you think I broke the fucking windows. You get it?"

"I'm done playing," Raymond said. "What do you want out of this?"

"I want help," Shadrack said. He stared out the window for a moment. "I'll pay you. Just tell me how she wants you to do it."

"I don't know what you're talking about."

"But you will. I promise. You will."

"I ain't crossing nobody," Raymond said. "Get that through your head."

"Just keep an open mind," whispered Shadrack. "Stay focused, I'm saying. Think critically. Keep your eyes peeled."

Raymond was too tired to deal with any of this. His head hurt. His shoulders ached from holding his neck tight.

"Now don't go and get all dark," Shadrack said. "I know you feel like you're at the center of a shit storm right now, but it ain't all about you. Think about it, you know Arthur—this deal gotta be one of seven decisions on his plate today. It seems big to you, but it's just one of many for him. Same for Gloria. Shit, she's got her hands in so much shit she should look like an Indian goddess with eight arms. You know what I'm talking about?"

"I guess so."

"Don't be so stiff. Look at me," he said. "I'm the Molly Man. I made it from the bottom to the top. Shit, I'm from the fucking trailer parks, man." Raymond watched him as he spoke. It seemed absurd to be sitting in a beat-up Corolla listening to this speech. "I'm the king of the 415, you understand that?" Shadrack went on. "I've sold more pills than there are people here." He seemed to be getting angry as he spoke. After another moment he pointed down near Raymond's feet.

"Open that bag," he said. His black doctor's bag, the same one he'd brought to the party, was sitting there; Raymond hadn't noticed it when he'd gotten in. He pulled it up to his lap and unlatched it.

The bag was filled with gems—cut sapphires, rubies, emeralds. There must've been half a million dollars' worth of jewels, all of them loose, just cut rocks. They were beautiful. Raymond put his fingers in and pushed them around. Cold like glass, they clinked around like marbles.

"What are you showing me this for?" asked Raymond.

"I don't believe in money," Shadrack said. "I don't believe it's worth anything. Except you can trade it for them stones. Them stones'll tell me who to trust, and they told me to trust you."

46

Shadrack's face looked serious, but his eyes were smiling. Raymond had the distinct impression that just under the surface, the man was laughing at him.

"You're bullshitting me," Raymond said.

"Stones don't lie. Very first night we met, they said you were a Seventh Son."

"I don't know what the fuck you're talking about."

Shadrack watched him for a moment. Then he said, "Listen, time out, man," forming the signal with his hands. "No bullshit, I think you should maybe consider just walking away from this whole situation. I'm telling you the truth. Shit's gonna get ugly. Maybe you should just pack up and leave."

The car felt cramped. Raymond didn't say anything.

"Don't tell her I said that," said Shadrack.

"Don't worry about me. I ain't saying shit to that woman," Raymond said.

"She's fucking crazy," said Shadrack. "She probably got this whole city wired, you know that? Probably got this damn car wired. She's about the nosiest person in North America. She probably got her bedroom wired, hear what she says when she's sleeping."

Raymond squinted at him. *Weren't you the one just playing me a tape of her voice?* he thought. He reminded himself not to argue. "Over-the-top crazy," he said, nodding. "But tell me for a second: What do *you* want to happen?"

Shadrack's eyes went distant. "I want—I wish it was just the way it was before you came, you know," he said. "Do it the old way, the way it was supposed to go, nobody ripping nobody off. We done all kinds of deals, me and Gloria. There ain't no reason to stop now."

"Well then, everyone's finally on the same page," Raymond said.

"Until Gloria puts her witchy little fingers in the soup," Shadrack said.

"That's true," Raymond said. *Humor this man,* he thought. "That's true."

Raymond had a meeting with his parole officer after that. Shadrack dropped him off there, underneath the Central Freeway. Said he'd call later that afternoon, pointing his finger at Raymond like a gun.

"Don't snitch," he said.

Raymond shook his head as he watched the car pull away. Then, before he went inside, he called his uncle Gene. Told him he'd been sprung and asked him to pick up his mother and take her to his house for a bit. He said that everything would be fine, but he had to move her. When Gene asked what was going on, Raymond said he was doing something for "that guy." Gene didn't ask any more questions.

Forty-five minutes later, his parole officer finally came out into the cramped reception area and called his name. They went into a meeting room, where the PO opened up a file and started asking questions. Where was he staying? What had he done to find work? When he'd gone through his checklist, he looked up and said he'd gotten a call from an Officer Bierdeen, a Mission District cop, who told him they'd searched Raymond's room the night before.

"Now why would they do that?" he asked.

"Don't know," Raymond said. "But they didn't find nothing."

"No they didn't," said the parole officer. "Not this time."

Raymond started to get up to leave, but the man stopped him. "Give me another address for my file, in case you leave the Prita," he said.

"I'm not planning on moving."

"Where would I find you? Your mama's house? Is she still up in Santa Rosa?"

Raymond stared at the man for a good five seconds. "Yeah, my mother lives there," he said. "But I wouldn't be staying with her. I'd probably go down to Sixth Street, the Auburn or something."

The PO nodded his head and made a notation in his file. Raymond walked back to the Prita, keeping his head down. The city seemed filled with ugly faces. All kinds of people were smoking crack, and he was damn near tempted to join them.

It occurred to Raymond when he was back in his room that Shadrack could have gotten any old Filipina lady to say his mother's address. Sure, it had sounded like Gloria, but how could he know it was really her voice? Any jail-house lawyer would tell you evidence like that wouldn't hold up in court.

The more he thought about it, the crazier Shadrack seemed. There was no conspiracy to rip him off. Raymond hadn't seen any sign of anything like that. The man had gotten some woman to say Raymond's mother's address. That was all. He would just sit back. Let things work themselves out.

His thoughts were interrupted by knocking on the door. It was Gloria this time. When she came in, the smell of perfume filled his room. There was no sign of her driver in the hall.

"You saw him?" she asked.

"I did."

"And he what?" She held her chin up, so she was looking down her nose at Raymond. She looked like some kind of pissed-off teacher.

"He told me that you broke my mother's windows."

Raymond watched her face undergo a series of transformations. She smiled slightly, and then the smile disappeared, her eyes filling with anger. She looked hateful. Raymond couldn't tell if she was guilty or not.

"This man," she said, "has gone too far." She held her hand in the air like she was brandishing a poisoned dart.

"He's crazy," Raymond said.

She looked him dead in the eyes, like they were finally understanding each other. "A crazy man," she agreed.

"He thinks y'all want to rip him off."

"No," she said, shaking her head. "Why would we do that?" Her face still looked angry. "I have a prediction," she said, then paused for a few seconds as though planning her words. "Tomorrow he will say, 'Only Raymond. I only deal with Raymond, now.' This man is going to wash everything down the drain."

Something about this felt scripted. A lonely feeling settled over Raymond. He wanted to be done with these people, their world. He wanted sleep. His shoulders hurt. His head hurt. He was hungry, thirsty, dehydrated.

"One thing I don't understand," said Raymond. "How's he get to say anything, if he's the one doing the buying?"

"Because of your boss," she said. "Your boss says I can't cut him out. So, for now, he stays," she said. "It's that simple."

She left after that. Raymond, for the first time since he'd gotten to San Francisco, started to consider what it would mean to replace Shadrack.

He bought a pint of whiskey and wandered downtown. The only people out were bums. He walked under the tall buildings. At one point, he felt someone following him, but when he turned around he saw a beautiful woman about thirty feet away. She reminded him of a girl he'd seen before, but he couldn't remember where. He thought about talking to her, but she went into a Walgreens and disappeared. The wind had picked up. He kept walking.

He thought about getting a hooker, or some pills, but he was feeling too unsettled to do either. Something bad was coming. There was nothing nice in San Francisco.

It was one in the morning when he finally lay back down on his bed. It barely surprised him when at three o'clock, the young black man with the blank face came by and knocked on his door. Said he had the wrong door again. When he came back at five, Raymond tried to fight him, but he ran.

Raymond's heart was beating hard after that. He tried to cry into his pillow. He tried to force sobs, but nothing came, so he just moaned and moaned and let the bad thoughts ride through his mind.

At a quarter to seven, his phone buzzed. The sun had just come up; his room was covered in dust. Shadrack had texted him: *Godz blezzed uz with wizdom and sin.* Raymond didn't know what the hell the man was talking about.

A couple of hours later, the knocking returned. He figured it was the black guy again, and anger spread through his whole body. He wanted to get the jump on him this time. He got out of bed as quietly as he could and snuck over to the door. Then he reached for the handle, grabbed it, and pulled the door open.

Shadrack was standing on the other side. He had his doctor's bag with him.

"Jesus, what's wrong with you?" he asked.

Raymond shook his head. "I thought you were that black guy."

"What black guy?"

"Never mind. What do you want?"

"*What do I want?* What kind of greeting is that? I brought you coffee." He held out a cup of coffee, and Raymond took it.

Shadrack scanned the room as he stepped through the doorway. "You living like a damn homeless man," he said.

"Your place ain't no fucking mansion."

"Come on, get dressed."

Raymond pulled his clothes on, went to the bathroom down the hallway, brushed his teeth, and rinsed his face. Tired as he was, he didn't even stop to wonder where they were going. When he came back to the room, Shadrack was sitting on the bed. He seemed to be in the middle of some kind of deep rumination. His face glum, his shoulders hunched. He looked lost. The man was dreading something, Raymond thought.

"You got your ID on you?" Shadrack asked, looking up.

They walked to the car, the sun shining down on both of them. Shadrack said he'd had to park on South Van Ness because he didn't have any change for the meter. No change, but a bag filled with jewels. He had an errand they had to do, he said. Before Raymond could ask, he cut him off, said he'd tell him when they got there.

They drove south on 101, Shadrack leaning toward the wheel, Raymond slumping in his seat, trying to catch some sleep. As they got closer to South San Francisco Raymond realized that Gloria had never taken him to collect his ID. He felt sweat on his forehead.

"I'm sick of playing," he said. "Tell me where we're going."

Shadrack pointed at the airport. "Right there," he said.

"You better stop fucking with me," Raymond said. "You ain't letting me sleep. You and Gloria both, you keep messing with me. I'm tired of it, man. You get it?"

"Well, we're reaching the end of this little journey," said Shadrack. "Soon enough you'll be able to sleep all you want." He looked at Raymond and winked.

"I'm not flying."

"I'm not asking you to fly. Now shut your damn mouth."

Raymond looked at the doctor's bag near his feet and swore that if he had the chance he would take a handful of Shadrack's precious jewels. He would take the whole damn bag. It was time to push this motherfucker out, he thought.

They moved to exit the freeway, joining a stream of taxis floating toward the airport. Raymond resigned himself to whatever was coming. He sat back and looked at the sky, watching the planes cut through it.

Shadrack stopped in front of the United Airlines terminal. It looked like a prison for rich people. After making sure they were unobserved, he pulled an envelope from his breast pocket and handed it to Raymond. It was stuffed full of traveler's checks.

"Need you to buy me a ticket," he said.

"Shit, man, you can do this shit online now," Raymond said. "Do it on your damn phone. You don't need me to do this."

Shadrack's eyes searched Raymond's face. A female voice announced something about passenger pickup on the intercom. A cop walking by bent his head and looked at them.

"I need you to buy me a ticket," Shadrack said again, when the cop had passed. "Go in there, go to the desk, and buy a ticket to Mexico City. Make it for three days from now, Friday. You hear me?"

Raymond shook his head. "And I'm supposed to pay with these?" he said.

"With those. Make it in your name."

"My name? I'm not flying anywhere, man! I'm on parole, I can't go—"

Shadrack raised a finger to silence him. "I didn't say you flying. Just buy it in your name. It'll hold a seat for me. You can't get violated for conspiring to leave a damn state. You only get violated if you leave the state. Go on. We'll cancel yours and change it to mine on the day of, but I'm on the no-fly watch, all right? I put it in my name today, the FBI'll be here waiting. So we'll come in together, switch the tickets right before the flight. Nobody gonna know, and I'll be gone. It's how I do it every time, dummy."

Raymond squinted at him. It didn't make sense. But the image of Shadrack on a plane, soaring far away, certainly intrigued him.

"Just do it," Shadrack said. "Stop asking so many damned questions."

"Friday?"

Shadrack nodded.

"First class?"

He thought about it for a moment. "If there's enough money in them checks right there, yeah, first class. Go on, I'm gonna circle around. I'll be back."

Raymond went to the desk and bought a one-way ticket to Mexico City. It was the first time he'd ever bought a ticket at the airport. The traveler's checks made the woman helping him smile mechanically. She muttered to herself while she counted. Tired-looking people shuffled by pulling bags. Raymond's own weariness had faded. He was wide awake.

Outside, he waited for Shadrack. The man's face, as he pulled up, looked so serious it almost seemed funny.

"You did it?" he asked, when Raymond was back in the car.

Raymond handed him the ticket. Shadrack took it out of the envelope, examined it, then folded it up and stuck it in his pocket. Raymond felt a brief wave of fear. He didn't like putting his name on paper, didn't like the idea of Shadrack holding this over him somehow, but arguing seemed impossible; instead, he sat there and felt doomed. Shadrack looked around for a moment, then pulled out into traffic.

"I knew this dude once," he said, when they were back on the freeway. "Back when I was still just a kid selling weed in Eureka. He was one of those dudes with a wide face. You never wanna fight one of them; they're liable to head-butt you. He used to scare everyone. There wasn't a single tweaker on the street wouldn't cross over when they seen him coming. Matter of fact, they called this wide-faced dude—"

"You saying *wide* or *white*?" Raymond asked.

"Wide—*wide*," said Shadrack, waving his hand in front of his face. "They called him Pan Face, or some shit. I'll tell you a story, though, he got cut in the arm with a knife by a girl one time, and they took him to the hospital and he got one of them staphs, one of them MRSAs. He ended up dying from that shit. The point is, the girl that cut him, did it just 'cause she was crazy. She didn't have no reason to do it. See? You had the scariest boy in town, shit, scariest boy in the *area,* get cut by a girl, and dies from a fever." He shook his head. "My question for you is: When you were in prison, you ever thought Arthur was the scariest boy on the yard?"

Raymond didn't like the question. He felt his stomach knot up. "Yeah, he's a scary old boy," he said.

"Yep, and Gloria's a scary old girl."

"So what are you saying?" Raymond asked. "Gloria's going to stab Arthur in the arm? He gonna die of a fever?"

"She gonna stab somebody. She always do," said Shadrack, shaking his head side to side like a man unhappily speaking the truth.

You are in the hands of a crazy man, thought Raymond. "We gonna finish this deal tonight?" he asked.

Shadrack turned and looked at him. "Sure as a song is sung by a singer," he said. "This deal will be done. Don't you worry, Mr. Deal Broker. Look at that van," he said, pointing at a white van that had veered in front of them, out of its lane. They drove in silence for a moment. Then, after taking a deep breath, Shadrack said, "I wish I could just do the deal with you, though. No Gloria, none of them Filipinos."

Raymond glanced over at Shadrack and watched his head bump up and down with the road. He thought about that stolen boat. He thought about his mother, hidden away at Uncle Gene's. When Raymond was twelve years old, she had tried to get him into the Best Buddies program. She thought he'd needed a positive male influence. Raymond was a sullen boy, and he'd told her he didn't want to do it. Maybe his life would have turned out different. He might be working in a bank now, or be a paramedic, or some bullshit. You never know: he might have ended up with a child molester for a mentor.

Shadrack dropped him back at the Prita. Said he'd call him later, told him to shower and shave—get cleaned up.

"Since you been out," he asked, "you go and get yourself a good meal? Steak, or some shit?"

Raymond said he hadn't.

Shadrack looked him up and down. "My advice is make sure you get yourself pretty and fed," he said. "It's gonna be a long night."

On his way upstairs, Raymond walked past a prostitute: a black girl wearing jeans with her hair pulled back. She nodded, and when he passed she called out, "Five-oh." She thought he was a cop. Normally he would have felt insulted, but he was too preoccupied to care.

He half expected to see Gloria waiting for him, but there was nobody. The hallway was dark and empty. It smelled dirty, like old cigarette smoke. A handwritten sign had been taped to the door directly across from his own: DON'T BOTHER ME.

Raymond lay down and tried to clear his head. His socks, damp and itchy, felt dirty on his feet. The muscles of his shoulders wrapped in painfully on themselves. Gloria would be calling any minute now. He closed his eyes and the image of a snake, black and yellow, its tongue hissing out of its mouth, jumped into his mind. When he drifted off he had a short dream about Shadrack burning his hands and holding them up, and yelling. The man's teeth had turned shiny black. The dream was interrupted by his phone vibrating in his pocket.

It was Gloria. "Hold on," she said harshly when Raymond answered. "Are you there?"

"Yeah, I'm here," Raymond said, sitting up. He was covered in sweat. His room seemed even smaller; the walls suddenly looked like they'd been painted with dirt. A car horn blared outside.

"He'll only do the deal with you," she said. Raymond shook his head. "Listen to me," she said. "We called him, and he said the deal was off, unless it was *you*. He said, 'I only do it with Raymond Gaspar.'"

Raymond wondered why the hell Gloria would accept Shadrack's damn orders. It didn't make any sense. She told him she'd pick him up at seven that night.

He ended the call and looked at his hands. "Surprise, surprise," he said to himself. What would they say at DVI if he came back after a week outside? *Well, you can take the prison out the man, but you can't take the man out the prison. You're supposed to buy a one-way ticket, not round-trip! Blah, blah, blah.* He felt then that life was sitting in dirty rooms being scared all the time. Men would continue to knock on his door while he slept for years to come. Every last one of his mother's windows would be broken. People all around him would have their teeth kicked in. The world was rotten to its core.

At two minutes after 7:00 p.m., Gloria texted and said she was there. When Raymond stepped outside he could've sworn he saw the same young black guy that had been keeping him up at night walking away from Gloria's van. He couldn't tell, though; he didn't see the man's face. The van's back door opened. Raymond walked to it and looked in.

"Who's that black dude?" he asked.

"The black dude?" Gloria said, turning. "He's asking for change. We told him we didn't have nothing." She shrugged.

There were three men with her, this time. The driver was the same one he'd seen with Gloria before, the man with the mustache. Next to him, in the front seat, sat another Filipino man. Gloria—dressed like she was going to a business meeting: black pantsuit, pearls, heavy makeup—sat in the middle row. Another man, older than the rest, sat in the very back. Gloria didn't introduce any of them.

"Only Raymond," she said, shaking her head, as he got in, apparently imitating Shadrack. "I'll only do the deal with Raymond Gaspar." She scooted over so he could sit next to her. "If it wasn't for Arthur, I swear to God I would feed Shadrack to the fish."

"Where we going?" Raymond asked. The van pulled into traffic. Gloria's perfume smelled like flowers. He closed his eyes and breathed it in, picturing a different place.

"We don't know," Gloria said. "He said he'd pick you up at a restaurant in Emeryville."

"I still don't understand how this motherfucker gets to set the terms."

"He pays a high price," Gloria said. Raymond waited, but that was all she offered by way of explanation.

"Let me ask you something," he said. "How much we dealing with here? How much is it? How much you selling? How much he paying? You never told me any of that."

Gloria chewed her gum and looked at him like she was trying to understand some deeper meaning to the question. Raymond could recognize her habits now, the way she tilted her chin up and gazed down at him when he spoke. She liked to pause before she answered his questions.

"We're selling four hundred and forty pounds," she finally said.

Raymond felt like he'd been hit in the gut. It was a lot more than he'd expected. Ten times more. Arthur had said forty, fifty at the most. Raymond had to stop himself from reacting. Ten times more? Did Arthur know? "For how much?" he asked, trying to sound unimpressed.

"He'll give you five-point-six."

"Five million?"

Arthur should be getting half a million on the deal. His own little cut should be almost three hundred thousand, instead of thirty. Raymond's heart was threatening to beat out of his chest.

"Five-six, yes."

"I gotta count it?" he asked, still trying for indifference.

"No, no, no. Just look at it. Examine it. Leaf through it. Make sure it's real. He's crazy, but he always pays."

"And then what?"

"After he's given you the money—you make sure it's after—you'll give him the address. The pack is in a storage locker in Vallejo." Her accent made her pronounce it *Ballejo*. "Also, the key. That's all."

She handed him a slip of paper and a silver key. The paper had a handwritten address on it: *556 Lemon Street #342. Vallejo.*

"After they pay you, they'll give you a ride back to the restaurant. We'll wait for you there. That's it. That's all. Deal done. Time for everyone to go home until we start all over again."

They bounced along the road for a moment. Then Gloria said, "He's a racist, too, you know. He called me a Chinese bitch. That's why you're here, Mr. Repair Man."

Mr. Deal Broker. Mr. Repair Man.

They got onto the freeway at South Van Ness, looping around the ramp. Raymond looked at the frosted windows of the jail as they drove past. He pictured all the men sitting in there, dressed in orange, breathing stale air, kicking themselves for stupid moves. Traffic was thick, but moving. His belly felt racked with nerves. *Ten times more!* Arthur was sure as hell going to want to know about that.

Quietly, almost to herself, Gloria was singing what sounded like an old disco song: *Something in the way you make me feel, it feels so good to me.* For a moment Raymond wondered if she was high. He pivoted in his seat so he could take a look at the man behind him: a skinny, older Filipino man with pockmarked cheeks who met his gaze and smiled. They were coming off the Bay Bridge now.

"Exit there," said Gloria.

The driver pulled off the freeway and pulled into a parking lot alongside a Denny's. They backed into a spot with a view of the entrance. The driver cut the engine.

"Now we wait," said Gloria.

Raymond scanned the lot. He looked for occupied cars, looked in the restaurant windows, searched for groups of men that looked like cops. The driver of the van was sending text messages. He should've had his eyes up, Raymond thought, ready to move.

His mind cycled through a series of strange thoughts. He hadn't eaten, and he imagined what Gloria would say if he got out of the van, went to the counter, and ordered pancakes. That thought was pushed out by a memory of a childhood friend of his, a boy named Rusty, who had once shit his pants in a parking lot much like this one. The boy had started to cry afterward.

The phone in Gloria's hand lit up. She looked at it, then looked at Raymond.

"Five minutes," she said.

Raymond's forehead was damp. He breathed deeply, trying to relax. Underneath all his nerves and dread, though, he recognized a new kind of feeling: optimism. The end was near.

The man sitting behind Raymond said something in their language and the man sitting in front turned around. Raymond expected to see a cool look on his face, but what he saw instead—sadness—made Raymond feel ashamed. The man looked right at Raymond, then answered the man.

"What are they saying?" Raymond asked, trying to sound good-humored.

"He said," said Gloria, pointing her thumb over her shoulder at the man in back, "that you are a very important person. And that man," she said, pointing to the front, "said he feels honored to have ridden in the same car with Mr. Repair Man."

The man in back and Gloria both laughed. Their laughter seemed fake, almost violent. It sounded like barking. "Nothing," said Gloria, as though Raymond had accused her of something. "They didn't say anything important. They say, 'You owe me this, you owe me that.' They always argue, these two." The man in front didn't join in the laughter. "Stupid," said Gloria.

All five of their heads turned as a police car sped past. Gloria organized her face into an expression of unworried confusion. Raymond looked at her pearls and thought about snatching them off her neck; then he imagined grabbing her face and kissing her. He thought about the last girl he'd kissed, a girl from the Tenderloin named Emily. A man walked out of the restaurant with a phone pinned between his ear and shoulder, carrying large paper bags filled with food. He was muttering something. He looked like a trucker. As Raymond watched, he dug in his pocket, his eyes locked on the van, and a car alarm chirped. He got into the car beside them and drove away.

"Here," said Gloria, pointing toward the entrance. John's black SUV was pulling into the lot, heading for a space across from them.

"Hold on," said Gloria.

They watched as the driver's door popped open. John, standing tall, his chest puffed out, walked toward the door of the Denny's. The way he carried himself, calm and slow, made Raymond appreciate him. He went to the cash register and spoke to a redheaded waitress.

"Is Shadrack with him?" Raymond asked.

"He'll take you to him." They watched John for a moment. Gloria said, "When he comes out, walk with him. Walk right behind him. Get into the front seat. Don't talk until you're in the car."

John came out with a coffee in his hand. He walked back toward his car.

Raymond opened the door and stepped out. He and Gloria exchanged one final look; her eyes stayed flat and calm. Then he slid the door shut and walked after John.

For some reason, right then, he remembered that Gloria had claimed not to know John. The thought unsettled him, but it was too late to do anything about it. A moment later he was in the SUV.

The inside smelled sweet, like pipe tobacco. John was already turning the car on. "Buckle up," he said, fitting his coffee into a cup holder.

Raymond watched Gloria's van—its engine and lights still off—until he couldn't see it anymore. Then he turned to John.

"You good?" Raymond asked.

"I could complain, but it won't do nothing," John said.

Raymond touched the key in his pocket, nodded his head, and looked at the road coming at them. The lights of the dashboard glowed blue. John did something to the steering wheel and the radio switched on; the sound of an announcer providing play-by-play for a basketball game filled the car. *Draymond Green is having an MVP-type night,* the voice said. They were back on 80, heading away from San Francisco.

"Where we going?" asked Raymond.

"Gonna go meet the man."

Raymond had a habit, when he was nervous, of working his tongue over each tooth in his mouth. He was doing it right then. He looked in the side-view mirror to see if Gloria's van was following them, but all he could see was yellow headlights.

"They're not following us," John said.

The basketball game continued. John would occasionally react to a shot with a slight shake or nod of his head. When it went to commercial, he turned the volume down almost all the way. He kept the car on cruise control, driving exactly the speed limit, in the middle lane. Every few seconds, his eyes went to the rearview mirror.

"You ever do one of those pills?" Raymond asked. Maybe he'd take one tonight, he thought, after the job was done. Celebrate new beginnings. He hadn't done that in a while.

"Hell no," said John, quietly. "It ain't pills, either. It's powder."

The man was acting grumpy. Raymond turned and looked at his face. John knew he was staring, but he kept his eyes on the road. Something about the way he refused to return his look rubbed Raymond the wrong way. He wanted out of the car.

"When we gonna get there?" he asked.

"We're getting close," John said.

Different things that Shadrack had said passed through Raymond's mind. *I read you the very first night we met. Sure as a song is sung by a singer.*

John switched his turn signal on and guided them onto the Hercules exit. Raymond suffered through a quick moment of thinking he'd forgotten his phone before his hand patted it in his left pocket. Then he touched the pocket that held the key and note. John turned left onto a road Raymond had never been on before. They headed up a windy suburban street filled with beige houses set back at intervals, blinds drawn. Raymond became more and more nervous with each turn they made.

Eventually, John pulled into a driveway. The house looked the same as all the surrounding ones. A light on inside made the blinds glow orange. John opened his door and stepped out. Raymond let himself have one second alone before he took a deep breath and opened the door.

For the first time since he'd been released, Raymond looked up at the stars in the sky. He turned and scanned the block again: no sign of anyone else. Everything was silent. There was a chill in the air.

"Come on," said John, walking toward the house. He pulled open a metal screen door, then turned and looked at Raymond. His face was shaded; Raymond couldn't see his eyes. It seemed like he was waiting for someone to let them in. Raymond's nerves grew more raw by the second.

"Who is it?" Shadrack called from inside.

"It's us," said John.

When the door opened John placed a hand on Raymond's back and nudged him forward. Shadrack stood just inside, his face looking either bored or distant. Raymond had to squeeze by him to enter. As he passed, Shadrack pulled his head back like a man avoiding bad air.

The room was empty, the carpet dented where a couch had once sat. Raymond smelled cigarettes. He walked to the center of the room and turned to face Shadrack. The man's face was unmistakably sad; there was a weariness in his eyes, and his mouth hung flat and loose. Raymond's chest flooded with dread.

"Go on down that way," Shadrack said. He pointed down a hallway that led away from the front room. Raymond's mouth went dry. He wanted to ask Shadrack what was wrong, but he couldn't. He waited for Shadrack to lead the way, but the man waved him forward.

An orange glow leaked from under the door at the end of the hall. The hall itself was dark and carpeted. Raymond could feel Shadrack and John behind him; he wanted to turn back, to run past them and get back outside, but he felt suddenly powerless. Something was drastically wrong. He decided to pray—it was something he rarely did, but right then, walking in that hallway, the darkness all around him, he prayed to God to deliver him from this situation. His fear had become complete.

"Go on," said Shadrack, when Raymond paused near the doorway.

He reached for the door—it was cracked open—and pushed it. Shadrack and John stepped up behind him and forced him into the room. Raymond's eyes settled immediately on the floor, but it took him a moment to process the fact that it was covered in plastic. It was one big sheet, the kind a painter lays out before a job.

Shadrack, standing in the doorway, said, "Sorry, man. I liked you, I really did."

Movement came from Raymond's right side. He looked that way and saw Gloria's boy, the one with the mustache. He held a gun at Raymond's head. "No, no, no," said Raymond.

Raymond heard the shot, felt his head swing like he'd been punched. He felt the ground pulled to his chest, saw his blood and brains thrown on the floor.

Part 2

Part 2

"Hello friend," said Mr. Hong, his mouth a few inches from Semion Gurevich's ear.

Semion sat at a table in the back of a club he owned in Miami. The table was raised up on a tier, overlooking a crowded dance floor. The bass from the speakers rumbled. The lights turned everyone red.

"Join us," he said, leaning back in his seat.

He gestured at the table. There were two women and another man sitting with him already. They were all dressed and tanned for a night out. Semion watched Mr. Hong glance at them, smile shyly, and say he couldn't. Mr. Hong looked, Semion sometimes thought, like the kind of man who always wins at the horse tracks. A perennial winner.

The older man bent down to Semion's ear again. "Usual," he whispered. "Fish market, sometime now until one week. Have your boy bring the documents to my office." Semion understood *fish market* to mean a warehouse outside Chiang Mai, Thailand. He understood *documents* to mean money. *My office* meant Mr. Hong's lawyer's office, in Miami.

Mr. Hong pulled his head back and looked at Semion. "Good?"

"Yes, good, you old bastard," Semion said. "I love you, you know that? I love the way you dress!"

"Good," said Mr. Hong. He nodded to the other guests at the table, gave Semion's shoulder a final squeeze, and walked away.

Semion took a moment to reflect on how blessed his life had become. The man sitting across from him winked.

"Who was he?" asked one of the blond women.

"He's a real estate man," said Semion. "A rich bastard. I love him."

It was seventy-nine days before Raymond Gaspar would be killed.

Semion Gurevich was thirty-five years old. He was born in Rostov-on-Don, Russia; when he was three, his family immigrated to Israel. They settled first in Kiryat Ono, and then in the Yud-Yud Gimmel section of Ashdod. It was a rough neighborhood, but Semion learned to blend in. Even as a troublemaker, he graduated high school with decent marks. He scored a high health report as well, and shortly after graduation he was conscripted into the Israeli Defense Forces. After seven months of dusty calisthenics, endless target practice, bland food, and crowded dorms, he found himself stationed near the Egyptian border. He spent his days caught between boredom and tension. He did things that still bothered him even now during that time: he broke an old Arab's nose with the butt of his gun; he tossed stun grenades at a group of children. But he survived.

Semion had grown up around drugs; there was plenty of heroin in Ashdod. He'd smoked it a few times in high school; he sniffed dirty cocaine at parties. He'd even sold a bit of ecstasy during his final year of high school. It was only natural that he fell in with the few soldiers in his unit who sold heroin. *We're doing God's work*, said one of them. *Selling drugs to Arabs.* At that point they were still just making beer money.

After finishing his service, he settled in Tel Aviv. A month later he began to think about selling drugs in earnest. With the contacts he'd made in the army, and the friends he'd made growing up in Ashdod, he was soon able to make good money importing heroin from Lebanon and selling it in the streets. His parents had raised him to be tolerant, and it served him well: he worked with Arabs, Africans, Bedouins, Jews, and Russians—and he insisted on mutual respect. He was a hustler, and he liked making money. It made him feel powerful.

After the first few years, Semion didn't even have to stand on the street anymore; he could sit back and manage the men. But one summer—a particularly hot one in his memory—Semion got into a conflict over territory with a Russian gangster named Abram Gorin. Semion's group had gone through a series of small expansions, adding a few men to their street crew along the way, and spread two blocks west to Sderot Har Tsiyon. This area turned out to be one that Gorin thought of as his own.

The Gorin gang operated on a different level: they were international. They had a reputation. One night, after Semion had drunk too many beers in a bar on Rosh Pina, a handsome-looking Russian man—bald, with bright blue eyes—stepped in front of him on the street and grabbed him by the shoulders. It was a friendly gesture, like an uncle measuring a nephew. Speaking Russian, the man said that Mr. Abram Gorin wanted Semion to know he was no longer allowed to sell heroin in Neve Sha'anan. He looked Semion in the eyes. "Do you hear me?" he asked. Semion didn't speak Russian perfectly, but he understood this, and, unable to do anything else, he nodded his head.

The next morning, when he woke, Semion felt equal measures of guilt and fear. *What had happened?* It was as if he'd been told he had cancer: one day he was healthy, the next he was not. Still, a depressed kind of disbelief kept him from telling his men to stop dealing. Six days later, his friend Schmuel Teper—a funny, chubby man—was pushed in front of a moving bus. Schmuel survived, but he would never walk again.

A week after that, the same Russian man approached Semion outside his home. It was early in the day, but the sun had already heated the dusty streets. The man wasn't rude to him; he simply smiled and scanned the area with his eyes, and then, having satisfied himself that they were alone, beckoned Semion toward him with two fingers. When Semion stepped closer he told him that he had to leave Israel. He made the visit feel like a favor. When Semion managed to nod the man slapped him on the back and walked away.

The next day, Semion called his group together. He invited them all to his apartment—a rare occurrence—and explained that they had to take some time off. Abram Gorin himself had insisted on it, he said. "We take a break," he said. "Lay low. See how it shakes out." He expected the men to resist, to call for war, but nobody did. Nobody argued. Three months later, Semion moved to Miami.

A few of his friends from the army—Russian Israelis, like himself—had been living there, and they helped him find an apartment in South Beach, in a tower overlooking Biscayne Bay. He didn't bring much—a bag filled with clothes, a computer, a razor, his toothbrush. He had a good amount of money saved.

One of his friends in Miami was Isaak Raskin. Isaak, a short man with the kind of strong jaw and dimpled chin normally associated with Hollywood actors, was preparing to open a nightclub called Ground Zero; Semion invested cash in it. The club did well, and over the next four years they opened three more. For a time it seemed like Semion might leave the drug trade behind. But eventually Isaak, who had connections in the shipping business, began talking to him about setting something up.

They would do things differently he insisted. No selling on corners to Arabs and Africans. No heroin. No rival gangs. They were going to be middlemen, and they would focus their attention on a benign corner of the market: ecstasy.

"Listen to me," Semion said to Isaak, arranging his words like a drunken professor. "If we're going to do this, we have to stay small. You get too big you attract the wrong type of attention. Trust me. I know this. We stay small; we make good money. But we stay small."

Isaak, for his part, simply frowned and nodded, as though he couldn't have agreed more.

A man named David Eban, another friend of Semion's from Israel, introduced him to a Flemish group that cooked drugs in a lab outside of Ghent. Eban agreed to sign on as a courier, and began to move the product across the Dutch border, to Rotterdam. Isaak had a cousin who worked as a second mate on an Israeli freighter that operated a line from Rotterdam to the Port of Virginia. He could walk right onto the ship with fifteen pounds of pure MDMA stashed in the false bottom of a duffel bag. Another Israeli, Mark Orlov, would meet the ship in Virginia. The cousin's cut—7.5 percent—was a ridiculously high price for a mule, but Semion and Isaak were not running a typical operation. There were less than ten men involved, no amateurs.

Semion kept the circle of dealers he sold to small. He never met them in person—Orlov took care of that—never communicated with them, and gave them a fair price. They always wanted more. After two years, Semion and Isaak were splitting almost a quarter million dollars every month.

All of this worked smoothly until, on a cold day in November, members of Belgium's federal police unit stormed the mobile trailer where Semion's Flemish chemist had set up shop. David Eban narrowly avoided arrest by fleeing Europe. They needed a new source.

It was Isaak who came up with the Southeast Asian connection. One of his oldest friends, Moisey Segal, lived in Bangkok. The picture Isaak painted of the man hinted at deep criminal connections. When Semion wondered if Moisey could be trusted, Isaak dropped his head, raised his hand like he was under oath, and swore that Moisey was their man.

"I know this guy," he said. "I've known him since we were schoolboys. You can trust Moisey Segal with your life."

Semion and Isaak flew together to Bangkok. Moisey—handsome, skinny, tattooed, with a shaved head—looked more like the drummer of a punk band than a member of a criminal gang. Semion was prepared to not like him. He expected Moisey to be a blowhard, but—almost against his will—he found himself charmed.

They stayed for nine days at a hotel near Sukhumvit. Moisey seemed genuinely curious about Semion; he asked question after question and listened to the answers like each one might offer a valuable lesson. Underneath this curiosity, Semion sensed a simmering core of discontent: it only made him like the man more. Every time Isaak would ask when the meeting with Moisey's connection would occur, his friend would first wave him off, as if the question was unreasonable, and then nod his head, as if it made perfect sense. After looking at his phone for missed messages—there never were any—he would wipe his nose, sniff, shrug, and say, "So, we wait."

They drank every day. Moisey took them to underground bars, rooftop bars, riverfront bars. On the fourth night, in Isaak's hotel room, he made them smoke *yaba*—little red amphetamine pills that tasted like chocolate. Moisey crushed one with his lighter, cooked the powder on chewing gum foil, and sucked the smoke in with a straw. When they'd all had enough, Moisey crumpled up the foil, threw the straw under the bed, and shouted at them: "No gear! It's fucking genius!"

That same night, he brought them to a dance club populated with Thai prostitutes. Before they entered the place, they sniffed bumps of crushed Viagra off one of Moisey's keys. Semion knew his hangover would be hell, but for some reason he couldn't say no. Isaak, for his part, didn't appear to be bothered by any of it. He kept talking and laughing as though he didn't have a care in the world.

They brought a group of Thai girls back to the hotel that night. Semion ended up alone with one of them; he had sex for what felt like far too long, and when they finally finished, he couldn't sleep. Gray light from outside leaked through the blinds. Semion sat in a chair and watched television and drank. The Thai woman slept on the bed.

They spent the next day recovering. The day after that, Moisey calmly told them that his connection was finally coming. In two days, they'd meet him at a restaurant in a small industrial city to the east: Chachoengsao.

"Burmese," Moisey said. "These motherfuckers don't play."

They took a taxi all the way and paid the driver to wait. The restaurant was a dirty open-air place, with chickens roasting on a spit and flies buzzing. It seemed impossible that anything of value could be found there, and for a moment Semion was sure they'd been set up. He was cursing Moisey in his head when a waitress pointed them toward a handsome man sitting alone at a table.

The first thing Semion noticed was that his hair was cut perfectly. He was in his forties, Semion guessed, and wore a light sweater over a collared shirt. The man looked rich. He smiled, stood, and shook hands with each of them.

"Nana," he said, nodding. "My name is Mr. Eugene Nana."

Semion had half expected to be met by a group of men, to be searched, maybe even blindfolded, and brought to another location. It was nothing like that. They made small talk in English for a while, noted the weather, ordered food—Nana swore that despite the place's atmosphere the restaurant had the best soup in the region—and generally enjoyed a quiet afternoon. When Isaak asked Nana if he was Burmese, the man winced, shook his head, and told them, "We are in Thailand. I am *Thai*." After tapping on the table as if he were transmitting a message in Morse code, he said, "No, sorry. You will never meet the Burmese."

Finally, he asked them what they were looking for. When Semion told him they were in the market for ecstasy, he looked disappointed.

"Not crystal meth?" he asked.

Semion shook his head. He noticed Nana glance at Moisey, noticed Moisey shrug. *They've been talking,* thought Semion. *Maybe Moisey led him on.*

Nana sat silent and blinking for a long moment. Then he said, "The price today is eight thousand American dollars for a kilo of crystalized MDMA. Good stuff—one hundred percent pure. Tell me," he said, pulling out a handkerchief and dabbing at his nose, "how much would you gentlemen be hoping for?"

Semion did the math in his head. They'd been paying nearly twice that price in Belgium. A kilo was more than two pounds, and they could sell a pound in the US for ten to fifteen thousand dollars. His face become warm.

"We would be looking for . . ."

He had to force himself not to stammer as he mentally doubled then tripled the amount he'd been planning on asking for.

"We'd be looking for something around sixty pounds. Something like thirty kilos a month."

"Not more?" asked Nana.

Semion glanced at Isaak. His partner nodded his head eagerly.

"No," Semion said. "That's it. Perhaps, if it's too small, you're not the group for us."

"No, no, we can do it, no problem," Nana said. "Don't worry. You get settled, make a lot of money, then you can decide if you need more. More money, more paradise, more vacation, more beautiful women. Everything in life will be perfect."

"Sure," said Semion, feeling proud of the way he'd handled the conversation.

"Why not take time now?" Nana said. "Take a few days, think."

"We need to figure a new shipping route," Semion said.

Nana shook his head. *Not my business.* "When you are ready, have your friend contact me." He pointed at Moisey. "He knows how to get in touch. We have a man in Miami, as well. He's called Mr. Hong. Very safe man, trustworthy. The best kind of man." He tapped his chest. "He will communicate with you there. He will accept all payment. He will tell you when order is ready. You pay him in cash. He will be the only one for you to talk to. As for us, gentlemen, we will never communicate again, unless you come back to Thailand, and we eat more soup." He pointed at Moisey again. "Also, once everything is underway, I advise you to cease communications with him. You need complete—what is English word? Complete compartmentalization."

On the drive back to Bangkok, when Semion expressed surprise that Nana hadn't wanted to perform any kind of background check, any kind of due diligence, Moisey explained that he already had.

"I had to tell them who you were," he said. "They wouldn't meet otherwise. They have people that'll make a whole file on you; they probably know the name of every man in your old unit. If you got a traffic ticket in New York, they know which cop wrote it. These fuckers are thorough, man."

Semion thought about this and felt a small wash of fear.

Two days after meeting Eugene Nana, Moisey introduced them to a Malaysian man named Fariq. Fariq owned a fish export company outside Bangkok, in Laem Chabang. He met them in his warehouse, during business hours. Workers in white jackets were busy unloading frozen squid—vacuum sealed in plastic—from a truck outside. Fariq led them upstairs into a cramped, fluorescent-lit office. Unlike Nana, Fariq looked like a criminal. He was a huge man, over three hundred pounds, and he had tattoos on his neck and hands. He wore a Hawaiian shirt and a gold chain, and he had dark circles under his eyes. His skin was gray from smoking too many cigarettes. As soon as he had them in his office, he closed the door, pointed at Moisey, and asked in heavily accented English if either of them had experienced the pleasure of having Moisey give them a massage. After that, he poured them plastic cups of cheap whiskey, and they drank.

Fariq, like Nana, expressed some surprise that the men wanted to move ecstasy rather than crystal. "More money in meth," he said.

"Yes, but with meth, more headaches," said Semion. "Hells Angels, Mexicans, fucking DEA, everything bad. Besides, we're simple club owners. You know, disco, house music."

"Fuck," said Fariq, nodding at Moisey. "Like this one, gay."

The price he proposed was disappointing. First, he asked what they were paying, and, in an unprofessional moment, Semion told him. Then, after making a pained face, Fariq said, "You'll pay me one thousand US, a kilo." They tried to talk him down, but he wouldn't budge.

"I," he said, pointing his huge finger at his chest, "I'm paying customs agents on both sides. I have to pay for the freighter, which stays fucking refrigerated. I pay the American Coast Guard. I pay everyone! I'll barely make anything by the time they're done. See that down there?" He pointed down the stairs. "You want a fish company? You want fish and freezers? Take it. Squid, and, and—let me explain to you: It's not hard to find shit here in Thailand. It's hard to move it. You know? Fucking Thai police? They throw me away. You know what they do when they catch you here? They give you a death sentence." He raised one eyebrow. "They weld the leg irons on your leg," he said. He nodded his head up and down, waited for a reaction, and when he didn't get one, continued. "On your leg!

You think this is fucking America? Fucking Israel? This is fucking Thailand!"

The sound of beeping forklifts filled the silence. Semion pulled out his phone and did the math: $9,000 a kilo was almost $4,090 a pound. That, times sixty pounds, worked out to around $246,000 a load. They could sell it to one buyer for more than twice that price: half a million a load. It was good. A lot more than they'd been making, even with the higher price for the freighter. He held his hand out to Fariq, and they shook.

That night, Moisey took them out to a fancy dinner at the top of a hotel in the Silom district. He insisted on paying. The food was excellent; they ate steaks and drank bottle after bottle of Bordeaux. Over dessert, they cemented their plans. Moisey was going to run everything for them on this end; they wouldn't be able to communicate with him except by intermediary, at least not for a while, and so it was important to talk everything through now.

"To Moisey," Isaak said, lifting his glass. "Our little angel in Bangkok. This may be our last meeting for a time, but our hearts will stay connected." Semion thought he saw his friend tearing up.

Moisey grinned. "To new friends and money," he said.

Semion wanted to say: "To staying small." But he didn't. Instead he raised his glass and said, *"L'chaim."*

Two days later, Semion and Isaak flew back to Miami.

They relocated David Eban, the man they'd been using in Belgium, to San Francisco. He'd be in charge of picking up the frozen squid. He was a good worker—quiet and sober. All he had to do was drive to a fish warehouse in Oakland, hand a slip of paper to a Chinese kid who worked for Fariq's organization, and throw the squid into his van. From there, he'd take it to a place he'd rented in Fremont, put it on the ground, and come back the next day, when it had thawed. Then he'd open it up and pull out the vacuum-sealed loaves of drugs. *I used to love squid*, he told them later. *I can't eat it anymore.*

In those early days, Eban drove across the country once a month. He'd pack the drugs into a false compartment in the trunk of his SUV, hang a cross from his mirror, set the cruise control to just below the speed limit, and leave some toys gift wrapped on the backseat. San Francisco to Miami—four days of driving. After a while, though, these trips bothered Semion and Isaak—they were clearly the most exposed element of their plan. What they needed was a buyer in California.

Eban suggested a man he knew in San Francisco, a Russian named Tyoma Chernov. Chernov had a history of moving drugs; he and Eban had met in Belgium, back when Eban lived there. As it turned out, he wasn't interested—he'd gone clean—but he knew someone who would be willing to work with them.

Chernov had served two years at DVI. He got a message to Arthur, and Arthur set Eban up with Gloria Ocampo. Eban and Gloria met face-to-face for the first time at a steak house on Van Ness Avenue. Afterward, he flew to Miami to speak with Semion and Isaak.

"She looked like a Filipino cleaning lady," he said. "But she's legit. I checked. She'll buy the whole thing. Chernov vouched for her."

"Can she be trusted?" Semion asked.

"Of course not. But she has money."

"Gloria Ocampo," said Semion. "How old is she?"

"She's older, fifty, sixty? She's normal, a normal old Filipino lady, not like a druggie. What do you want, someone with tattoos and blue hair? Rides a fucking Harley? She's good; she has money. She'll buy it, come back, buy it again. You'll never meet her. She'll never know your name."

"Ten a pound?"

David made a pained face, waved his hand. "No problem," he said.

That was how it began. When the Burmese group had a batch, they sent Mr. Hong an e-mail. Coded in the message would be the weight and location of the pickup. Mr. Hong would then go and find Semion at one of his clubs, where the noise made any kind of audio recording difficult. Semion would relay the information to Orlov, who would use a public Wi-Fi connection at a Starbucks to send a coded message to an intermediary in Israel. The intermediary would find a Wi-Fi–enabled cafe (never the same one twice) to relay a second coded message to Moisey, in Bangkok. Semion used a similar system to communicate with David Eban in San Francisco. Their messages bounced from earth to space, from phone to satellite, meaningless to everyone but them.

Every month, Mark Orlov delivered their payments to Mr. Hong's lawyer's office in Miami. Semion had no idea where their money went, but, if forced to guess, he would say he suspected it was laundered through several legitimate-seeming businesses or real estate purchases before being packaged and carried to Burma and China. Or maybe it was simply wired in nine-thousand-dollar increments by old Chinese women at different Western Unions all over the southern United States. Money, Semion knew, moves around like water. It fills open spaces and seeps through cracks.

On normal days, Semion would wake up hungover in his apartment. If he'd brought a girl home, she would make him breakfast or convince him to take her out. After that, he'd clear his hangover by going to the gym. He had a female trainer with a pierced belly button who made him do squats and planks and laughed at his jokes. Then he might call Isaak, and they'd go out on the bay. They didn't own boats themselves, but they had plenty of friends who did.

For dinner, they'd go somewhere like Nobu. They'd order bluefin toro tartare with caviar, sashimi, beef kushiyaki, bottles of Billecart-Salmon or Hokusetsu. They'd bring girls with them—the type who didn't act surprised at a four-thousand-dollar dinner. Then they'd get in Semion's car, a simple white Range Rover—why draw attention?—and head to one of the clubs they owned. They always entered as though going to a club was the same as walking down the red carpet at Cannes.

Their clubs, naturally, were outfitted with VIP rooms; there, out of sight, they'd snort cocaine, snort Molly, take pills. Women loved them. Men loved them. In the society pages of Miami magazines, they were called club owners or, even better, party promoters. They posed for pictures with DJs, basketball players, rappers, models, and the idle rich.

When an apartment above Isaak's opened up, Semion moved into the building. It was another tower, nicer, bigger, and still overlooking the bay. He bought the apartment with cash. Miami was the new Switzerland: Russians were buying property all over the city, and nobody looked at the money. Banks welcomed new customers with champagne. Luxury stores were sprouting up constantly, and Ferraris no longer stood out on the street. The city was turning into a money-laundering mecca.

Isaak had five siblings—two sisters, three brothers—and because he was born second to last, he developed a personality defined by a lack of neediness. He was the kind of person who would sit back, smile, and listen while others clamored for attention; as the Americans said, he was easygoing. Semion, on the other hand, was an only child; he was quiet, too, but he was arrogant. He was tall and wiry, with long arms and big hands, and he looked more Russian than Jewish. His face had already started to sag; he could picture a future where he looked like his saggy-faced uncles.

Because they'd both been stationed in the south—Semion at Nahal Oz, Isaak nearby, at the Re'im base—they had often met to drink in the intense way of young soldiers. When they finished their service, Isaak had gone to South America for a few years. It wasn't until Semion landed in Miami that they reconnected. They'd always liked each other, but they could just as easily have gone through life without ever seeing each other again. Semion was a child of immigrants, an immigrant himself. Isaak had been born in Israel, to an upper-middle-class family in Haifa. Semion had once summed it up by pointing out that Isaak, as a young teenage boy, had *had a fucking scooter.*

Differences aside, the two men got along, and their partnership worked well. Isaak tended to the clubs—he was better suited to handle payroll, insurance, licenses, the staff, and all the day-to-day paperwork that came with running multiple businesses—and Semion took care of the drugs. Isaak let him handle things exactly as he wanted, and the clubs provided the perfect way to launder the money. On occasion Semion felt resentful for having to share his drug profits, but in those moments he reminded himself that it was Isaak who had first come up with the shipping company, Isaak who had known Moisey, and Moisey who had introduced them to Nana and Fariq.

There were no bombs, no war, and half-naked women as far as the eye could see. They took trips to Jamaica, the Bahamas, Brazil. They were living the good life, a sunny Miami American dream, and yet Semion Gurevich wasn't exactly happy. He was lonely. He wanted a family.

And then he met Vanya Rodriguez.

He found her at Ground Zero, the first club they'd opened. Semion, feeling drunk and dull, had been sitting with Isaak and a man named Jimmy Congo and a few of their other friends. Jimmy was telling an endless story; Semion, his shoulders tense, was finding it hard to focus. His eyes drifted toward the bar.

She was wearing red heels and a white dress: *A sail filled with wind*, he thought. He'd sniffed some Molly and drunk vodka, and the combination had made him poetic. She held a clutch in her hand, and he instantly imagined what it contained: The lipstick—*to be that lipstick, and gloss those lips*. The credit cards, an ID card with her address—*she lived somewhere, owned a bed, towels that she dried her nakedness with, sheets that she slept on*. She had curly brown hair, tan skin, and could have been almost any ethnicity—Latina, Italian, Jewish, Arab. Semion felt a magnetic pull. He smiled.

She stood near a few other girls, but they were a blur to him now. He stared at her with his head dropped to the side. A strange feeling opened in his chest, something like fear mixed with happiness, mixed with the high from the drugs. After a moment he realized his mouth was open. He had to force himself to look away. This was a new feeling.

Eventually, the woman drifted closer to his table. He poured more vodka into his glass, dropped in a single ice cube, swirled it around, and drank. He noticed Isaak staring at him. The music was incessant; Semion wished that the DJ would make the song stop, that he could spend a moment in silence and appreciate this woman. He looked over and the DJ, meeting his gaze, pointed at him and grinned. *You're the man.*

What was it about her? He watched her laugh, watched her throw her head back. She was beautiful, of course, but that wasn't it—there was something more. The moment, there in the club, felt predetermined. It felt arranged somehow. In an effort to compose himself, he drank more.

The man sitting next to him, a loud Russian, was making a joke—something about a dog wanting meat. The other men laughed. Semion smiled at them, raised his glass. "Cheers," he said. *Cunts,* he thought.

He swallowed his drink and turned back to her. *Now,* he told himself. *Now.*

She turned toward him and met his gaze for what felt like an endless moment. He tried to smile, felt foolish, clamped it down, raised his eyebrows, fixed his mouth into its best shape, and—without even knowing what he was doing—gave her the same two-fingered *come here* gesture that the Russian man had used on him a few years earlier.

The effect was not the same. She simply looked away. He turned his head back toward his friends and wiped at his face. *Stupid, ugly face,* he thought. Then, recognizing the negativity of the thought, he willed himself to stay positive: *No, no, no, a king, a king, a Jewish king, a gentle Jewish king.* He licked his lips, looked at Isaak for help. *A tall king, a rich, tall king.* He tried to turn back to her, but he felt himself wilting, felt himself becoming depressed.

When he turned to look at the woman again she was walking straight at him. Time slowed; he took a deep breath and steadied himself to stand. He gave his nose a final wipe and saw that her shoulders were moving to the music. He looked at the white dress, studied the face, studied her walk, her collarbones, her hips. *Remember this*, he thought. She was a few steps from him now, within reach, and he knew he should smile, but instead he acted cool, shifting his eyes to the group of women she had just left. The beat from the speakers matched his heart.

"Hey, bitch!" she said, in accented English, walking right past him.

Isaak had been sending a text message, but Semion watched as he looked up, saw the woman, shook his head slightly, smiled, and said, "Oh, shit." He held his arms open to her, and she stepped into them. They exchanged kisses on both cheeks. Then, the greeting done, his arm still draped over her shoulder, Isaak turned her toward the group. Semion looked away. He forced a look of boredom on his face before turning back.

"E'rybody in the club gettin' *tipsy*," said Isaak. He let his arm fall from her shoulder. Semion stared. Suddenly the woman stepped toward him with a serious look on her face and held her hand out like an American businessman.

"Hello," he said, his face frozen. "I'm sorry, your name?"

"Vanya," she said. "Vanya Rodriguez."

Semion felt himself sway on his feet. He looked at Isaak for help, a sign, anything, but his friend was busy talking to the other men again.

"And your name?" she said.

"Semion Gurevich."

"Simon?"

"Semion," he said. He realized he'd missed his chance to kiss both of her beautiful cheeks. *Do I have dandruff?* he wondered. *Am I going bald?*

"How do you know him?" he asked, nodding toward Isaak. *Does my breath smell?*

"I met him here," Vanya said. "Two nights ago!"

Two nights ago? thought Semion. *They've fucked. I'll kill him.*

"You're Brazilian?" he guessed.

"I am. I'm from Rio."

"You guys dating?" he asked, cupping his hand over his mouth, yelling over the noise. He looked her in the eyes. A wave of depression had washed over him.

"No, stupid, you crazy?"

They were standing next to each other, and, in order to hear her he had to lean in. Their shoulders touched and stayed together for a moment. Isaak turned and motioned at Semion, pointing toward the back office and touching his nose. Semion waved him off. He asked if she wanted a drink, and she said, "Yes, a vodka Red Bull." Her accent made it sound like *hedge bull.*

Semion went to the bar and got two drinks. Normally, women didn't make him nervous, but now he found himself unable to come up with a line of conversation. She looked like a normal Miami girl, but he could tell she wasn't. He imagined her asking him what he was interested in, and he planned a vague speech about wanting to produce films, then cursed himself for stupidity. *Films, no, stupid, you want to help children. You want to produce films about helping children.*

When he returned to her she was applying lipstick, tilting her head back and using a small mirror. She turned, looked at him, and licked her lips.

"I have to go in five minutes," she said. "It's my girlfriend's birthday." She nodded vaguely toward the door.

"I'll come with you." He felt, suddenly, as if he was on firmer ground.

"It's not that kind of party," she said. She touched his arm, took a sip of her drink, stood on her toes, and looked around the club. "You guys own it?" she asked.

"Yeah," he said. "We own five clubs in Miami." *Stupid, don't brag.*

She shrugged her shoulders.

"Move the party here!" he said, licking his lips. His time with her was ending already. He could feel it.

She turned and looked him in the eyes. "Text me later," she said. "Maybe, I come back."

She gave him her number. He entered it into his phone and showed it to her when he was done. "Right?" he asked.

"Not I-A," she said. "Y-A: V-A-N-Y-A. Ciao." She leaned in and kissed him on the cheek. Then she walked away.

Semion found Isaak with their friends in the office upstairs. "Who is she?" he asked in English. Then, switching to Hebrew, he said, "Did you fuck her?"

Isaak had been bent over the desk sniffing Molly. He looked up, smiled, shrugged, and said, "No."

Semion took a moment to analyze his friend's body language. The shrug bothered him. He asked again, this time without words. He simply raised his eyebrows and stared.

Isaak smiled again. "No. No. No," he said. "Don't worry. She's yours and yours alone. She's probably a fucking virgin." The other men laughed. "Fuck," he said. "Have some." He motioned at the powder on the desk. "Have some!"

After cursing the men in his mind, Semion walked to the desk, took the rolled-up hundred-dollar bill from his friend, bent his head, and breathed one of the lines of powder into his nose. It hit the back of his throat, and he tasted it in his mouth.

"The last Brazilian virgin," said Isaak. The men laughed again.

The night felt transformed after that. Semion found himself loving all of the people in the club. He moved around, greeting everyone. Women flirted, and he flirted back, but that's all he did. His mind was on Vanya, and he kept checking the time on his cell phone; he had to give her at least an hour before he texted. But each time he looked, only a minute had passed.

After an hour, he sent her a short message: *You coming back?*

She didn't respond. And even though it took a heroic amount of self-control, he didn't text again. He was satisfied. He liked a challenge.

At five in the morning, after checking his phone for the hundredth time, he took two Xanax, drank a seltzer, and lay down on his bed. *This is my life,* he thought.

When he woke up—at noon—she was there in his mind already, the first thing he thought of: her face, her lips, her hair. He picked up his phone, convinced there would be no messages, and saw that there was one: *Sorry sleepy. Xo.* She had sent it at 6:14 a.m.

We have a doorman, he thought. *I could ask if Isaak had any visitors.*

* * *

Two days later he took her out to dinner. He'd spent the day at the gym, the tanning salon, the hairstylist. He'd gotten his eyebrows shaped, his back waxed. He'd bought a new shirt from Sartori Amici. A nervous dread filled his stomach, but he vowed to fight it. In his apartment, in front of the mirror, he stood for a few minutes turning and looking, squinting and pulling his face into different shapes. *I will smile*, he thought. *I will act excited.*

They met at his favorite sushi spot. *You like Japanese food?* he'd asked. *I love it*, she'd texted. He knew the chef and called ahead. *Nothing spared*, he'd said. *The best, the best, the best.* The chef had laughed. *Fins and scales?* he'd asked. *Yes, fins and scales*, Semion had said.

She arrived ten minutes late. He had waited for her out front, and seeing the way she held herself as she came walking around the corner made Semion feel stooped over. He fixed his posture and suffered through a sudden wave of pessimism: *This can only end in pain*, he thought. He felt dizzy as she approached.

She wore a yellow dress this time. They kissed on both cheeks; he lingered, maybe too obviously, and noticed the scent of gardenias. He looked at her face, saw a small scar on her forehead. *I love you*, he thought.

"You like Japanese?" he asked again, wincing at having repeated himself.

They sat at a table near the window, a small candle between them. The chef, a man who appeared on magazine covers, came over personally with their first dish. After setting it down he bowed to Semion, rubbed his shoulder, and said, "Welcome back, Mr. Gurevich."

Semion felt himself flush with pride. He hid it by rubbing at his face like a tired businessman. The chef gave a minute-long explanation of the dish to Vanya, who listened with shiny eyes.

They ate course after course of expertly prepared fish. When Vanya said she liked oysters—"I love the way they taste like the beach," she said—Semion had the chef bring her a dozen. She tilted the shells to her mouth and slurped them up.

The food kept coming, and she told endless stories in a singsong voice. Semion, unable to think of anything to say, felt thankful that she had decided to carry the burden of the conversation.

"I'm sorry," she said. "I talk so much." She mimicked a puppet with her hand. "Da-da-da-da-da."

One story, in retrospect, stood out. It was the only one she told him about her family.

"I'm not rich, you know," she said. "Most of us here, in Miami, Brazilians, are rich. Not me. When I was a child, we lived in a favela—you know—*Jacarezinho*," she said, sounding out each lovely syllable. "I had a sister, a little baby sister, who got in trouble with a group, and one of them tried to be in love with her, but she already loved a different boy. And the man—he's a scary man; he had the long fingernails—he yelled at her in public, and she cut him with a knife in the stomach." She laughed after that, and put a whole piece of sushi into her mouth. She shook her head while she ate it.

Semion stared at her while she chewed, trying to picture a smaller version of her—*a little baby sister*—stabbing a gangster in the stomach. *Why do I love you?* he wondered.

She asked him if he'd been to Brazil then, and he told her that he had, that both he and Isaak—instantly, he regretted mentioning Isaak—had gone to Rio last year.

"And you didn't call me?" she said—truly angry.

"I didn't know you."

She laughed again, and her phone buzzed: facedown on the table, it lit up and shook. Someone had texted her. She didn't check it, didn't turn it over, didn't acknowledge it, nothing. Semion watched her ignore it. The significance of this, he thought, could be revisited later.

Their date ended abruptly. When they finally stepped out of the restaurant, Semion, his mind working over the problem of what to do next, could only watch as Vanya turned and—in the strangest moment of the night—lifted her arm, sniffed her underarm, and, after making a face like she'd been confronted by a bad smell, closed her eyes and leaned forward for a kiss. He stared at her, and the street became quiet. Then he kissed her once, softly, on the lips.

"Thank you," she said. "It was the best dinner I've ever had in my life."

When he offered her a ride home, she refused, pointing vaguely at a few towers to the west. She had to meet someone, she said.

"Don't worry," she said. "It's a girl." She kissed at the air in front of his face, and then turned and walked away.

Who walks in Miami? he thought.

On their second date, after dinner at a French restaurant, she suggested they go back to his place and have a drink.

"Oh! Let me take a picture," she said, when they entered his apartment. She walked around the living room taking photos with her phone. She was looking at his furniture like she was shopping in an expensive store. "I wanna make a house like this," she said. He was thankful he'd hired a designer, proud of the place's white elegance, the view of the bay from the windows. He went to the kitchen to open a bottle of Krug Clos du Mesnil.

He popped the cork, poured the champagne, and put the bottle on the counter label side out. Then he returned to the living room, took her hand, and led her to the balcony overlooking the water. They toasted, sipped, and she asked where the bedroom was.

Startled, he pointed toward the hall. She led him that way, sat down on the bed, and then flung herself back. He kissed her; they pulled each other's clothes off. She wore plain underwear. *This is how I want to die*, he thought.

They had rollicking, brawling, sweaty sex. When they were done, tangled in sheets, her hair a mess, he looked at her and she pretended to pant like a dog. He laughed, and then they lay there while he wondered what he had gotten himself into.

Semion had, of course, slept with many women during his time in Miami. But since he'd left Israel, he hadn't had a serious relationship with anyone, and now he wondered if maybe this woman, this strange Brazilian shiksa who sniffed her own armpits and walked around Miami at night, this woman with a man's name, might end up being the girl he married.

She had fallen asleep and lay breathing next to him. She smelled spicy, he decided, like coriander mixed with mango. And then, just like that, in the midst of all this happiness, a gray cloud moved in: he pictured Isaak, saw his face, imagined him kissing her. He tried to push the thought from his mind, but the harder he pushed, the stronger it became. He stared at her for a moment, and then, quietly, he got out of the bed.

In the kitchen, after sipping champagne straight from the bottle, he noticed her bag sitting on the floor. *I'm a drug dealer*, he thought. *I have an obligation to protect myself.* He picked up the bag and brought it over to the marble counter that separated the kitchen from the dining room. *A man can't be too careful*, he thought.

It wasn't the little clutch she'd carried that first night; this was bigger, an expensive-looking black leather handbag. He wondered who had bought it for her. He sprung the latch and spread the bag open.

There was a clean pair of plain black underwear on top— the kind someone might wear to the gym. Next, a pair of socks, white and worn. He set them to the side and found her phone, a gold iPhone. He pressed the button on the top and the screen came to life, no passcode needed. He thumbed the photo icon first.

There were only three pictures: they showed his living room and bedroom. He didn't know she'd taken a picture of his bedroom; it gave him an odd feeling. He checked her call history next, and saw that it had been cleared. He moved to her contacts: hundreds of names and numbers, some just first names, some first and last, but nothing that jumped out. He didn't recognize anyone.

Finally, he checked her text messages. There were none. Zero. Maybe it was a new phone, he thought. But he could see paint missing from the corners, scratches on the back, a few scratches on the screen. He angled it under the light and saw that it was covered in oily smudges. An uneasy feeling spread through his chest.

She'd wiped her phone for some reason. Maybe she was recently divorced, or going through a breakup. Maybe she was married. Whatever it was, he didn't like it.

He went back to the bag. There were other womanly things: tampons, hair bands, makeup, some kind of face powder, eyeliner, red lipstick, lip balm, tropical-flavored gum. He found a condom, one lone gold-foiled Magnum. He pulled out her wallet, fingered every pocket. She had $387 in cash, a lot of money for a young lady. He found a California driver's license, and spent a moment looking at the large photo of her smiling face. Between it and the smaller ghost image on the right was her date of birth: 2/21/88. And, of course, her name: Candy Hall-Garcia. His breath caught.

What game was she playing? He looked back at the face on the license: it was her. The memory of her spelling her name for him on that first night played through his mind: V-A-N-Y-A. The license listed an address in San Francisco, on Oak Street. He found his phone, snapped a picture of the ID, and slipped it back into her wallet. She had one other card in there—a credit card, also bearing the name Candy. Nothing else.

He put everything back into the bag, set it on the floor, and walked to the window. *Candy Hall-Garcia.* He thought back to the dinner they'd had that evening. "I love Miami," she'd said. "It feels just like home, you know? Sun, beach, music, Brazilians—but not dangerous like home. No kids in the street, no gunfights—well, yes, gunfights, but not like Brazil, *ba-ba-ba-ba.*" She'd pantomimed firing a machine gun. He'd listened to her, smiling at the way she spoke with her hands, the way she shook her head while she talked, smiling at her accent.

"But here," she'd said, "in Miami, the only problem is everyone is fake. Nobody is who they say they are."

When he got back into bed, she scooted over to him. She didn't open her eyes, but she spoke.

"I had a crazy dream," she said. "I was at the airport and I'm taking all this stuff out of my suitcase, and there were all these lights and people everywhere. Like a stadium."

Semion stared at her face, trying to discern if she knew what he'd just done. *Taking stuff out of my suitcase.* She stopped talking. She had fallen back asleep already.

In the morning, when he woke, she was gone. There was a note on the counter: *Bye-Bye baby.*

Later, Semion went down to Isaak's apartment. He pressed the buzzer on the door and waited. Isaak, wide awake and not hungover at all, opened the door, smiled brightly, and waved Semion in.

"Where were you last night?" he asked. They tended to speak Hebrew when they were alone together.

"I need you to answer a question," Semion said, walking into the living room. It had the exact same layout as his own, and had been decorated by the same American woman; it made Semion feel like they were living in a luxury hotel. "Did you fuck her?"

"Who? The Brazilian?" asked Isaak. "Stupid, I told you: I'm not going to do this every time you meet someone. Look at you. You're acting crazy. No, no, no." He shook his head. Semion studied his friend's face. If he was lying, he wasn't showing it.

"*I never have known this woman*," Isaak said, switching to English. "Look at me—never. Never kissed her. I met her one time at the club, two nights before you did."

"I like this one," said Semion, wiping his hands together and flopping down onto Isaak's leather sofa. "I like her big-time."

"She's poor, you know?" said Isaak.

"What?"

"I can tell. I can tell when women grew up poor. I get a vibe from them. It's fine if you're into it. I like my girls to be rich. Better educated."

As soon as he was back upstairs Semion called their American lawyer friend, Jimmy Congo. The man was a criminal defense attorney. He had access to private investigators and was always willing to give out favors in return for a little VIP treatment at the clubs.

"Wait—wait a second," Jimmy Congo said. "You're saying you looked at her driver's license and she had a different name?"

"Yep."

"So what? This is Miami, she's probably a fucking illegal alien! You of all people should show a little sympathy on that issue."

Semion had already thought of that. "Can you look into it?" he said.

"It's dangerous to start looking into things—you know that, right? It's like an old house," Jimmy Congo said. "You never know what comes up when you start moving shit around."

"Yeah, yeah, yeah."

"Give me her name."

"Supposedly, Vanya Rodriguez. That's what she told me. The name on the license was Candy Hall-Garcia. There's a hyphen—you know, Hall-Garcia."

"And the DOB on the card?"

"February twenty-first, nineteen eighty-eight."

"Got it. What else?"

"That's it."

"Jesus, Gurevich, you know I charge four hundred an hour, right? You ever heard of Google?"

That night, Semion went to a bar owned by a friend of theirs. Isaak was there already, with two Russian girls. The Russians wore skirts and sleeveless shirts and dark red lipstick. They were absorbed in their iPhones when Semion joined them at the table and kissed each girl on the cheek. After having his first drink—vodka on the rocks—he proceeded via text message to get into his very first fight with Vanya.

She had texted him just after he arrived, asking what he was doing. *With Isaak*, he responded. She said she could meet him. He replied, using an American expression: *Boys' night.* She sent an emoji of a crying face. He smiled and thought the conversation was over. His phone remained silent for a few minutes, and then a flurry of texts came in: *I meet u later.* Then: *Boys' night how?* Then: *Misericordia.* Then: *Isaak and 2 sluts.*

The last message landed on target; he turned in his seat and looked at every person in the bar. It was a small place, and there were only about twenty people in it, counting the staff. The owner, a man named Carlos, was behind the bar making cocktails for a trio of soft-shouldered women. Semion looked toward the window facing the street. Had she passed by and seen them sitting there? It didn't seem likely. He looked at the two women seated across from him. Isaak was showing them some photos on his own phone, making them laugh. How had she known? Or had she guessed? Of course she'd assume that he and Isaak (two men) would be accompanied by two women (two sluts).

Semion excused himself from the table. In the bathroom he received another message: *If you busy with sluts I find my own fun.*

He put the phone in his pocket, washed his hands at the sink, fixed his hair in the mirror, and felt his paranoia collapse into depression. *Shit,* he thought. *She's crazy.* His phone buzzed again. He took it out and read the message: *Just kidding, ha ha. I'm playing.*

He felt so relieved that his hands shook. He punched in three hearts and sent them to her, watching the emojis pop up on the screen.

When he got back to the table, Isaak, his eyebrow raised—it was the kind of look that says, *I know exactly what you've been up to*—lifted his glass in a toast. Semion saw that his drink was empty and motioned to the bartender to come fill everyone up.

Two nights later, back at Ground Zero, he ran into Jimmy Congo. The lawyer—apparently still dressed for work in a black-and-white-striped button-up shirt with white cuffs and a white collar—approached Semion at his table and massaged his shoulders in a way that seemed meant to say: *This is my friend; this is how I can touch him.*

"Let's go to your office," he said, bending down close to Semion's ear.

Upstairs, Jimmy produced a brown glass vial, patted a small pile of cocaine on Isaak's desk, chopped out two fat lines, rolled up a hundred-dollar bill, and offered it to Semion. After they'd both sniffed a line, Jimmy wiped his nose and assumed the posture of an attorney in front of a jury—fingertips steepled in front of his chest, head cocked just so.

"I'll tell you, my guy—and my guy is good, ex-cop, the whole thing—he looked into your girl, and she came back clean," he said. "Candy Hall-Garcia, February twenty-first, nineteen eighty-eight, lives in San Francisco, just like the card says."

"San Francisco?" Vanya had never mentioned California. The card must be fake, Semion thought. *In Miami, the only problem is everyone is fake.* "And what about Vanya Rodriguez?"

"He said no obvious matches. Nobody her age with that name in Miami or San Fran. Blank walls, baby. Not much for Candy online, either. No Facebook, Twitter, Instagram, blah, blah, blah. There was one, I repeat, *one* news article from seven, eight years ago—Walnut Creek, California—regarding a high school track meet. Take my advice: a girl like that, no online nothing . . ." He shook his head.

"What?" asked Semion.

"These days, you gotta watch out for a person like that," Jimmy Congo said.

He saw her two nights after that. She'd told him she lived in Kendall, and he said he'd pick her up out there. He wanted to see her house, even if it was just from the outside. But at lunch, he got a text from her: *Get me instead in Calle Ocho mall. Shopping pretty clothes crazy.*

He picked her up at the mall. "Ave Maria!" she said, jumping in his Range Rover with two large shopping bags. "So much shopping! Look, look, look," she said, waving her painted nails. "I got my nails painted for you!" She leaned in for a kiss, received it on her cheek, leaned back, and looked at him. "What?" she said. "You looking at me like I'm crazy!"

"You are crazy," he said.

"Shh, no, he found out! Let me out of here!" She pretended to bang on the window. "And you? Oy! You crazy! Where we going, McDonald's?"

In fact, he did take her to a cheap place, El Palacio de Los Jugos. He wanted to see how she reacted to a regular restaurant. When he pulled into the parking lot she grabbed his arm and said, "No!" She stared at him with what seemed at first like horror, but was actually joy. "I love El Palacio," she said. "How you know about it? It's my favorite place!"

They ate fufu, salmon horneado, arroz con camarones, pollo a la milanesa. They drank guayaba juice and finished with flan. Vanya was in heaven. "Like Brazil!" she said. "How you know me so much?"

"I just do," he said.

"You do?" she asked, looking at him from across the table, her eyebrow raised. A car honked from the street, and a child cried from a nearby table, but all Semion could comprehend was her face. Her beautiful, perfect face. Something about it reminded him of his grandmother.

When they got in the car, she pointed at her stomach, round with food. "I'm pregnant!" she said.

He took her to one of their other clubs, a place called the Factory. It was early in the evening; a few groups of people dressed in work clothes sat at scattered tables. The bartenders stood at attention when he walked in.

He had chosen this club because he knew Isaak wouldn't be there. He ordered two drinks and took Vanya to a small windowless office in the back.

"Do you want to do something crazy?" he asked.

"I am crazy," she said, stepping right in front of him.

"You like to sniff Molly?" he asked.

"Oh, my—what?"

"Does that mean yes?" he asked. He pulled out a small glass vial just like the one Jimmy Congo had used two days earlier.

"Yes!" she said. She danced with her shoulders. "Then we dancing, we talking," she said. "All night, I love you, I love you, I love you."

He tapped a small pile of powder out onto a desk, then touched the pockets of his pants. "Do you have a card I could use?" he said.

A shadow passed over her face and vanished. "Yeah, yes," she said.

She opened her purse and pulled out her wallet. The same one she'd had in his apartment. Her face looked calm, but she was quiet. She handed him her driver's license.

"How cute," he said, then made himself pause. "Candy Hall-Garcia?"

She sniffed, breathed, thought. "My fake ID," she said finally, and seemed to blush. Then she looked him in the eyes.

"I need a green card," she said, her accent disappearing. "Need a green card," she said again, sounding like an American. A chill passed through him. She smiled big. "Ha ha, you like my American voice?" she said, switching back to her Brazilian accent. She brushed her chin, blinked like she was thinking, then sang: "I wear my stunna glasses at night" in accentless English. She looked at the drugs.

"I'm an actress," she said, reverting to the voice he knew. "I do voices. You like?"

He did like it. It thrilled him. He liked it so much that he forgot his doubts.

They sniffed the drugs. Drank their drinks. He hugged her. She put her mouth near his ear. "I'm going to fuck you tonight," she said.

He didn't want to wait. Normally, he didn't feel particularly sexual on Molly; tonight was different. He backed her against the desk. He could taste the guayaba juice in her mouth when they kissed, a hint of the drug underneath it. He kissed her neck, smelling her skin, her hair. She breathed loudly. He reached under her skirt and touched her thighs. But when he tried to pull her underwear down she pulled away, fanned her face, and said they needed another drink.

For Semion, it was a perfect evening. They went to different spots, places he'd never been, little bars with outdoor seating. Old men sat gathered in groups. They walked in together, his arm over her shoulder, her hip pressed to his. He listened to her talk, watched her eyes while she told stories. They sniffed more Molly, and even that felt new. It felt youthful.

He told jokes, and laughed at hers. He felt loose instead of rigid. The people around him all seemed lovely—perfectly lovely people in a lovely city. The weather matched his mood. The air, carried past them by a breeze, smelled like the sea. The only thing that seemed strange was the way Vanya kept checking the time.

If Semion's romantic history was to receive a grade, it would read: *incomplete*. He'd had only a handful of meaningful relationships. The most serious was with an Israeli named Bina. He'd lived with her after the army for two and a half years. The rest had lasted a night, a week, a month. *You're a coward*, Bina had said. Perhaps he was. He'd been beaten enough times—as a boy, a teen, a young man—for it to have had an effect on his psyche. His face, when he looked in the mirror, reminded him of this: the nose crushed by the older Russian boy who'd taken his first skateboard, the eyebrow scarred in a drunken brawl in high school, the pale line above his lip, earned in a fight with a fellow soldier.

So why, on that night with Vanya, was he feeling such optimism? There was something about her that made him want to do things he never did. He wanted to cook for her, drive her somewhere, take a trip. He wanted to confess everything he'd done and start over. All because of some combination of voice, look, smell, spirit. He couldn't make sense of it.

"Why you looking at me like that?" she asked.

"I don't know," he said. He leaned over and kissed her again. He couldn't help himself. He smiled, but she pulled back.

"You seem crazy!" she said. "Let's go, *bagacera*, come on." She banged on the table. "You said we go dancing."

She directed him to a Brazilian club. After pulling over a block away to sniff more Molly, they valeted the car. Inside, a small crowd was dancing to a battery of drummers onstage. She pulled him forward. Brazilian men pointed at him, smiled, gave him the thumbs up. He felt inspired. She was laughing and dancing; the drumming filled the room. Everything was perfect.

The last thing he remembered was her standing in the kitchen of his apartment—her hair tied back, her forehead slightly damp, her eyes dark. She'd said, "I make us one more drink."

* * *

Pain in his head. Sharp, like nothing Semion had ever felt before. It was worse than a hangover. He stayed still for a moment, his eyes closed, as a wave of nausea passed through him. Guilty feelings, shame. A vague memory of a dream, something about a crowded room. He moaned quietly, touched his face, and wondered what the hell had happened.

He tried to open his eyes, but even in the dark, even with the blackout curtains drawn, it felt too bright. *Fuck me.* He reached out to where the girl should have been, but she wasn't there. Empty space on the bed, and something wet. The bed was wet. He cracked his eyes open; the bed was covered in black paint. *Why is the bed covered in black paint?* He sat up a little more, then reached for the lamp and switched it on. The black became red. The paint became blood. The bed looked as though someone had butchered a lamb on it.

He cried out, fell to the floor, and dry heaved a few times. The pain in his head was unbearable. "Vanya!" he called out. *Shit, shit, shit.* He pushed himself up, the ground tipping and heaving, and stumbled out of the bedroom. The hallway, blindingly bright, stretched in front of him; he staggered to the bathroom, and in a slow movement, as though frightened of what might be on the other side, he pushed the door open.

The bathroom was empty and clean. He had expected to find her in there. Impossibly, he had convinced himself that the blood in his bedroom was somehow related to her period; now, the idea was absurd.

"Vanya!" he called out again.

He looked down at himself; he was wearing only his underwear. He realized now that there was blood on him, as well, blood on his right leg, his right arm. He lifted his right hand and twisted it. It looked like it had been dipped in blood.

He searched every room in the apartment and found nothing. Besides the blood on the bed, and the blood on him, there was no sign of violence anywhere. Vanya's bag was gone, along with her clothes. He checked the closets, pulled the couches away from the walls. She was nowhere.

He went to the front door, examining it for blood, and peeked out into the hallway. Nothing. He closed the door and locked the bolt and the chain. The pain in his head was unbearable. There was a bitter taste in his mouth he couldn't place. His stomach cramped.

Okay, he thought. *Okay, breathe.* He closed his eyes and forced himself to calm down. *Steps,* he told himself. *There are steps that need to be taken.*

He went back to his bedroom and turned the overhead light on. There was even more blood than he'd thought: It had pooled in the middle of the bed and dripped and smeared all over the floor. There were spatters on the wall above the headboard. Even the ceiling—fourteen feet up—had been specked with blood. He bent down near the bed and sniffed: it was real, unmistakable.

In the bathroom he found two Xanax and four Advil. He took them with a glass of water. He found his phone in his pants and took it with him to the kitchen. *Think now,* he told himself. *Before you do anything, think.* He pressed the button on top of his phone and entered his passcode. It was 11:14 a.m. Nobody had called or texted. He checked his call history and confirmed that no calls had been placed from his phone since he'd met Vanya last night.

He weighed the pros and cons of calling her. There would be an electronic trail, the call's time and location. He had called her last night, so he had already placed himself on that list. His hands sweated. He breathed in and out. *What are the scenarios?* An intruder could have broken in, killed her in the bed, and then taken her body away. It didn't make sense, but nothing did. He could have killed her in the bed himself, in a blackout state, then called someone to collect the body—but there had been no calls from his phone. She could have hurt herself, somehow, packed up her bag, and walked out. But there was too much blood in the bed, and not enough anywhere else. He closed his eyes and tried to remember.

There was something just out of reach. He could see her face, a knife. She was laughing. A knife, a ceramic knife.

He stepped to the counter and opened a drawer. Six slots, five knives. *Motherfucker.*

He thought back again. Before she'd jumped in his car, he had called her: she had a cell phone, he had a cell phone, they'd been together most of the night. The records would show them moving through Miami and returning to the apartment, both of their phones pinging cell phone towers as they went. He certainly wasn't going to call the police now, not with a bed covered in blood and a missing woman they could tie him to. *Fuck me*, he thought.

He'd clean the place, then. He'd say they had returned here, gotten into an argument, and she'd left. That was it. That was the last time he'd seen her. That was his story.

But first he would call her. *Why would a man who killed a woman try to call her?* He opened his phone, breathed in deep, and hit her number. It went straight to voice mail: *Hello, you have reached Vanya Rodriguez. Please leave me a message and I call you back soon, baby.* Her voice, the joy in it, shocked him. The phone beeped, and he left a message: "Hey Vanya, what's up, lady? Just making sure you made it home safe last night. Call me back, okay? Ciao!" He hung up.

The Xanax kicked in. He drank another glass of water, then walked to the bathroom, turned the shower on, and got in. He scrubbed his hands, his arms, his legs, watching the blood turn pink on the tile.

He dressed for the gym: sweatpants, a long-sleeve T-shirt, running shoes. He grabbed his phone from the kitchen—still no calls—walked to the door of the apartment, and realized two things at the same time: first, as soon as he stepped outside, he was going to appear on the hallway security camera, and second, the same camera would have recorded whatever happened out there last night.

He stepped out and walked to the elevator. When the doors opened, he stepped in and hit 28, Isaak's floor. The doors slid shut. A camera in the upper corner recorded him standing perfectly still. *Ding.* He stepped out and walked to Isaak's door, aware of the camera in the hallway. He pressed the black buzzer.

Almost instantly, the door swung open. Isaak—freshly rested, showered, shaven, and composed—started to speak and then stopped. Semion watched his face—his mouth, in particular—as it transformed from a friendly smile to something more concerned.

"What the fuck?" Isaak said in English. "You look like fucking hell."

Semion walked into the apartment and started crying. He couldn't help it. He went to the couch and sat down. A moment later Isaak was standing over him, one hand on his shoulder and asking what was wrong.

Semion gathered himself. "Shit is really bad. Really fucked up. I don't know what happened."

"Cousin, cousin," said Isaak. "Listen to me, from the beginning—tell me what the hell is going on."

"The girl," said Semion. "The Brazilian, Vanya. I saw her last night. I took her back to my place. We were fucked up. I passed out. When I woke up this morning, my bed . . ." He stopped talking for a moment, took a deep breath, and then continued. "My bed was covered in fucking blood. Everywhere, like a fucking—just blood, sheets, blanket, everything. And she was gone. Just gone. No sign of her."

"What did you do?" Isaak asked. The way he stressed the words made it sound like an accusation. Semion felt his heart speed up.

"Nothing. That's what I'm saying. I didn't fucking do anything. She's just gone, and my room—blood, like a fucking massacre."

"Where is she?"

"I don't fucking know!" said Semion. "Sorry, I don't know. She's gone. I didn't do anything. She's gone. That's it."

Isaak sat down on a chair next to the couch. He looked genuinely disturbed.

"Tell me everything you know about her," Semion said.

"Nothing. I told you. I met her at the club, one time. That's it."

Semion closed his eyes. *Why did I leave Israel?* he thought. "Fucking shit."

"The building has cameras," Isaak said, sitting up as though he'd hit on a solution.

"Trust me. I know."

"We need to see the video."

The manager's office was on the ground floor, behind the reception area. It was occupied during business hours by a self-important American who sat at his desk refreshing the Twitter feed on his phone. Before him, two monitors showed camera feeds from throughout the building. There were hundreds of cameras spread between the forty-six floors, the video overwritten every month. Both Semion and Isaak—careful men—had asked about the security when they purchased their units. They had been given a thorough tour, and a long explanation of the precautions building management put in place.

"You're right," Semion said, nodding his head. "But fuck."

"It can be done," Isaac said. "Fucking shit, when it rains it pours. Show me your place."

"You come in, you're on the video."

"Brother," said Isaak. "Brother, if you are in trouble, I'm with you. Fuck. Please. Come on."

They took the elevator up to the thirty-first floor. Neither of them spoke a word. Inside, Isaak looked around silently. He scanned the floor and the walls, then walked toward the bedroom. When he saw the bed, he flinched back.

"Fuck! What the fuck?"

Semion felt a wave of shame. *I didn't do anything*, he thought.

"It smells," Isaak said, putting his hand near his nose.

Semion pointed out the blood on the ceiling. The men walked through the apartment a few times; Semion decided not to tell his friend about the missing knife. He did mention that Vanya's clothes and bag were gone, and that he'd checked his phone and confirmed no calls had been made last night. When Isaak asked, he admitted he'd called her that morning and left a message. He assured his friend that he had sounded calm.

Isaak sat down on the sofa, stretched his legs out, and put his hands behind his head—the posture of a man lost in thought. He stayed silent for half a minute, and then, as though thinking aloud, he said, "No body. No blood leaving the apartment. If, and I say this not as an accusation, but simply in light of your lack of memory, *if* you didn't do anything to this girl—" he raised his hand to keep Semion from interrupting. "Then you're being set up. Someone will contact you. I hate to tell you, but I would guess the girl herself is involved."

Semion had been thinking the same thing. "That fucking bitch," he said.

They spent the rest of the morning cleaning up the mess. The blanket, the sheets, the pillow cases, and one stained pillow went into trash bags. The mattress itself, surprisingly, was spotless. They cleaned the walls and the floor after that. The ceiling would have to wait.

"It's two big men, black baseball caps. Can't say race, but they look white. They walk to the door, knock, wait. Door opens, they go in. Fifty minutes later—big fucking bag, both of them carrying it. They walk to the elevator, and that's it. They leave."

They were sitting in Isaak's living room. Isaak had gone downstairs and paid the manager to leave him alone in the office for half an hour. A thousand dollars can buy you anything, he'd said before he went. The manager, after taking out the operating manual for the Toshiba X400 Video Surveillance System and setting it on the desk, had left him alone.

"Even in the office, a camera," said Isaak. "I told him I want to see my own door."

"Two men?" said Semion.

"You can't erase it from there," said Isaak. "It's backed up. But in thirty days, overwritten. So, we wait."

Semion found himself doubting that Isaak had actually seen the video. He stared at his friend for a moment and tried to come up with a reason why he would lie about it. *You fucking bastard*, he thought.

Isaak, as though sensing Semion's doubts, pulled his phone out. He fussed with it for a moment and then handed it over. Their fingers touched; Isaak's hand was dry as a bone. *The man has ice in his veins*, Semion thought. He looked at the phone: it showed video Isaak had taken of the manager's computer monitor. Two men walking down a hallway. They stopped at a door, knocked, and were let in. Semion couldn't see their faces. The video was washed out, shaky. It ended after they went into Semion's apartment.

"That's it?" he asked.

"Next video," Isaak said.

Semion handed the phone back. Isaak found the next video and returned the phone to him.

"Forty-nine minutes later," Isaak said.

The door was closed, then open. The two men exited with a heavy bag between them. They walked to the elevator and disappeared.

"The body in the bag," Isaak said.

Semion took a deep breath. "So, we wait," he said.

The call came the next morning. Semion had been in a deep sleep; he woke to his phone vibrating. It took a moment to remember what was happening. The caller ID read: *Unknown Caller*.

"Hello?" said Semion.

"Listen, Jew," said a voice. Semion cursed himself for not being ready to record the call. "We know you killed her."

The voice sounded artificially deep, like it was being played through a filter. It went on: "We know where you buried her. We know you left a knife in the grave." It sounded like the man was reading from a script. "We know your fingerprints are on that knife. There are photographs of you in your own bed with the woman you murdered. The photos show the knife in your hand. The girl in this photo is fucking bloody and dead. Direct evidence. Do you hear me?"

Semion sat all the way up. "Yes," he said.

"You need to produce two hundred and fifty thousand dollars in cash."

For a moment, Semion almost smiled. The amount seemed so small. He had been prepared to be asked for ten million. "I can't come up with that," he said.

"You can. We will call you. No police. We're watching."

The phone went silent. Semion thought the man had hung up, but when he looked at his phone, he saw the line was still active.

"You may think you're smart, but you're not," said the voice. Then the call ended.

Semion sat there for a moment, forcing himself to be calm. He thought about sending Isaak a text message to memorialize the details, but decided it would be stupid to leave any digital tracks. He walked to his kitchen and found a pen and paper. Then he wrote: *Jew, knife, photo, bed, deep voice, 250.* He thought for a moment, then added: *fingerprint, grave, produce,* and *not smart.*

The puniness of the demand buoyed his spirits. He realized he had, up until that moment on the phone, suspected Isaak was involved. Hearing that figure all but crossed him off the list. It had been absurd to suspect his friend. His mind shifted to the girl.

He didn't want to believe she was dead. The video of the men leaving his apartment carrying that bag between them didn't prove anything. And as bloody as the bedroom had been, it didn't mean it was her blood. It could be the blood of a pig, a cow, or a dog.

His mind shifted back to Vanya. If she were alive, she was almost certainly on the side of the blackmailers. That was the worst part of it. The embarrassment flooded in then. *My life will become lonelier and lonelier, and then I'll die*, he thought. It felt like a brief panic attack.

He went down to Isaak's apartment and told him about the call. His friend shook his head and smiled. "They don't know what we do," he said.

"They think we're club owners," said Semion.

"A quarter million dollars!"

"Should we just pay?" Semion asked.

"We have more than that in the safe at the club," Isaak said.

They sat there thinking for a moment, and then Isaak hit his forehead with his palm. It was the gesture of a man remembering something, but to Semion it seemed practiced.

"Mr. Hong," Isaak said. "He came by last night."

Semion's blood pressure spiked. *Mr. Hong!* It hadn't even been two weeks since his last contact. A visit this soon wasn't just unusual; it was unprecedented. Not to mention the routine they'd established was that Semion—nobody else—talked to Mr. Hong directly. As far as Semion knew, Isaak had never spoken a word to the man. *But now they were speaking?*

"What'd he want?" asked Semion.

"He didn't say. He wouldn't tell me. Said he wanted to talk to you. I told him you'd come in tonight."

"Shit!" said Semion. "What could he want right now?"

"I can tell him you're sick," said Isaak.

Semion stared at his friend. What was going on here? It didn't make sense to forget to mention a visit from Mr. Hong. Isaak should have called him immediately. He could have been there in fifteen minutes. He felt nauseous.

Semion shrugged. "I'll see him tonight," he said.

Back upstairs, he showered, shaved, and put on a black Caraceni suit from Milan. He examined himself in the mirror, thinking for the thousandth time that his was a face even a bespoke suit couldn't fix. An ugly, sagging face, a face that appeared sad when he was happy, and wretched when he was sad. He pushed his hair back on his head. *Am I becoming my father?* he thought. Then he dotted his finger with cologne and pressed it to his neck. *At least smell good.*

In his kitchen he made himself a vodka and orange juice. It was his first drink since Vanya's disappearance; he was standing in the exact spot where she had been standing when she'd poured the one she'd made him. Loneliness spread through him. He sipped his screwdriver. His mind shuffled through a series of memories.

I make us one more drink, she'd said.

He remembered the awful taste in his mouth, the smell of her purse when he'd looked through it. Blood on the bed.

Hey, bitch, she'd said to Isaak that first night at the club. Semion closed his eyes and tried to recall what Isaak had said in response. He'd been looking at his phone. He'd looked up and said, *Oh, shit.*

Oh, shit, indeed.

Ground Zero. It was early; the crowd inside seemed younger than normal. People nodded and smiled at Semion as he passed under the red lights, but he felt like they were sizing him up. The DJ was playing cloying house music. *Let yourself be free-ee. Let yourself be free-ee. Let yourself be free-ee.* It seemed like a cruel joke.

He found Isaak in their normal spot, at a table in the far corner. Jimmy Congo sat next to him; next to the lawyer were a group of women talking with their hands cupped at their mouths. Semion didn't recognize them. Isaak smiled, stood, and held his arms open for a hug. Semion stepped forward, and they exchanged an awkward, back-patting embrace. *Humiliating*, thought Semion. He felt like he was being greeted in mourning.

"Look good," Isaak whispered in his ear; it was unclear if he meant it as a compliment or a directive. Jimmy Congo flashed a fake smile and held his fist out for a bump. The women smiled up at Semion with batting eyelashes. It was going to be a long night.

He turned his back to the wall and scanned the crowd. He realized he was looking for Vanya, and forced himself to stop. There were nearly two hundred people inside already. They stood clustered in groups and moved their shoulders to the music like apes; they surrounded the bar like ants. The lights made it all seem like a cheap nineties movie. Semion's forehead broke out in a sweat.

Isaak signaled to the bar for a drink, then leaned into Semion's ear again. "He already came," he said. "I told him to come back."

Isaak talking to Mr. Hong still didn't sit well with Semion. "Did he say what he wanted?" he asked in Hebrew.

Isaak shook his head. Then he shot his eyes downward, opened his palm, and revealed a tiny plastic bag of Molly. "Take it," he said, raising his eyebrows. "You look like a fucking Arab."

Semion took the bag. When his drink came he dumped it in, swirled the powder around with a cocktail straw, and drank it. They'd taken so much Molly in the past few years that it felt like drinking a cup of coffee—just a pick-me-up.

Semion welcomed the chance to take a break from his brooding. A night out of his head sounded good. If Isaak had pulled out a syringe filled with heroin, he would have unbuttoned his cuff and rolled up his sleeve.

After finishing his drink, he looked at the girls and felt a wave of shyness. He stood next to the group for a few songs, his shoulders tense, his face tight like a mask. The music improved. He told Isaak to get the table a bottle of vodka, and his friend, happy to oblige, walked toward the bar. Semion found himself nodding his head in time to the beat. *Boom-dat-boom-dat-boom-dat.* He felt himself loosening up. His hands were clammy.

"Don't worry, big brother," Isaak said when he came back. "Millions of fish in the sea." He placed a hot hand on Semion's shoulder and let it sit there.

And then the drugs started working. The shift came fast and hard: Semion closed his eyes for a second, took a deep breath, and opened them to a new world. Isaak was watching him. Semion turned his head and looked at the girls. They seemed, suddenly, like individuals, like women with their own stories, not just the generic female shapes that had been sitting there when he'd come in. He wanted to talk to them. Hear about how they'd ended up here. They were from somewhere else, like him. For a moment the idea of Vanya pushed into his mind, but then it drifted away. He glanced at Jimmy Congo: the man was smiling, moving his head to the music. The apes and ants had transformed into a sophisticated group of beautiful people. Miami was the center of the earth. Everything made sense.

The DJ had found the right beat. The music seemed perfect now: a tropical rhythm, the right thing for Miami, hand drums and bass. The man playing records was an artist; this was his art. You had to respect him for that. He'd crafted a life playing music, an honorable occupation. *I need to learn a craft*, he thought. He glanced back at the women. One of them smiled. She looked so serious, even smiling. A nice girl, but serious. He pushed his hair back on his head. It felt good. He danced a little, just moving to the music, not too fast, but the movements came easy; they felt natural. Isaak was bending over, talking to one of the seated women. A good man. *Why had I doubted him?* They'd been through so much. They were where they needed to be now. Miami, America, Ground Zero. Life was made for living.

"There's my boy," said Isaak, stepping toward Semion. "Stupid, you just needed a little *thiz-nation* up in your fucking dome, get your head off. Look at you now." Isaak talked like a black American when he was high. Semion smiled and sipped from his drink. Strong stuff. His legs felt firmly centered on the ground. He smiled at the serious-looking girl and she smiled back: two people recognizing the uniqueness of each other. He resisted a strange urge to press the back of his hand against the back of hers.

"Our club," Isaak said, motioning out at the room. "Our fucking house." Semion nodded. *Yes*, he thought. *We made this.* He felt hot, took his jacket off, folded it, and placed it on a chair. He closed his eyes, studied the beat. The image of the bed—blood on white sheets—popped into his mind for a moment, but he breathed it away. Isaak was tapping him on the arm. Feeling very high now, he opened his eyes, swung his head, and saw his friend pointing across the club at someone. Semion squinted: it was Mr. Hong.

"There," said Isaak. "Go talk to him."

A wave of caution passed through Semion. *Go talk to him.* He lifted his arm, a greeting, but Mr. Hong didn't see him. Isaak placed a hand on Semion's back and pushed him gently forward. Semion took one last glance at the girl with the serious face, raising his hand to let her know that he'd be back.

He moved through the crowd. He recognized faces now, nice people, good, kind people. He exchanged a gentle high-five with a man he knew. Then the dancers opened up in front of him, and he reached Mr. Hong.

Mr. Hong! He was wearing a white sweater, khaki pants, white shoes. He had a shy smile on his face, an apologetic smile, like he was sorry for something. Semion, using his sleeve, wiped the sweat from his forehead.

"Mr. Hong," he said, holding out his hand. Mr. Hong grasped it in both of his own—two dry, warm, friendly old hands.

"Where have you been?" Mr. Hong asked.

"I've been here," Semion said. "Do you need a drink?"

Mr. Hong squinted, shook his head. "Small problem," he said, raising his voice a little over the music.

Semion turned the words over in his head: *Small problem.* Yes, he was having a small problem, it was true, but how did Mr. Hong know about it? "I'm sorry?" he said.

"Can we talk?" said Mr. Hong.

Semion's ears popped. He felt something happening in his mouth, like a burp mixed with a yawn. "Talk?" Semion asked, guiding the man toward a table in the far corner, away from other people. He looked back to see whether Isaak was watching, but the crowd was still between them.

When they sat down, Mr. Hong's hands caught his attention. Gold rings, gold watch. The man was classy; you had to give him that. He looked up again to find Mr. Hong looking back with a flat expression.

"Small problem," the man said again. "Our associates have a problem. Maybe not a bad thing for you."

Semion didn't know what he meant. He tried to let the words settle into some kind of meaning, but they didn't. He was conscious of the fact that his face showed confusion.

"The Burmese need your help," Mr. Hong continued.

The Burmese need my help?

"Nothing so much," said Mr. Hong.

Semion's mind drifted for a moment. He hadn't felt this high in ages. How much had Isaak given him? He looked out at the crowd, everyone dancing to the same song.

"If I may tell you a story?" Mr. Hong asked. Semion nodded.

"When I was a boy in China, I had a friend who sold misplaced rice," the man said, leaning in. "He used a truck to take it to Shanghai. Commune business, you know, corrupt. But he did what he could to help his parents. You understand what I'm saying?"

Semion nodded again. He had no idea what the man was talking about.

"The boy got in trouble, because our commune boss wanted him to sell it for more than he was asking. I don't know if you understand me?"

Semion was utterly confused. *The Burmese want rice?* "No, I don't. I'm sorry."

"You Jewish," said Mr. Hong, pointing at Semion. "Me, I'm Chinese. Them—" he pointed with his thumb toward the wall behind him. "They are Burmese. You understand me now?"

Semion shook his head.

"We all work together. Each of us, connected. You know?" Mr. Hong motioned to suggest a rope connecting his chest to Semion's, a rope between their hearts.

Semion nodded. *Yes, connected!*

Mr. Hong leaned back in his seat. He regarded Semion like a teacher appraising a child's intellect. Then, carefully, he cleaned the corners of his mouth with his fingers and continued.

"My friend, the boy who sold the rice, very smart boy, he did the commune one better. He said, 'I sell my rice'"—here Mr. Hong smiled, a large, open smile—"'I sell my rice, but I will agree to sell your rice for you also.'" Mr. Hong nodded his head and leaned forward again. "He took their rice, sold it for them, everyone happy. He has money; they have money. Good for both."

"Mr. Hong, I'm sorry. What are you trying to tell me?" Semion said.

The man studied Semion's face. "The Burmese lost one of their routes." He wiped his hands together. "They ask if you would be willing to help."

"What happened?" asked Semion.

"Long story—market shifts. Ports closed. Now Burmese have shake-up in organization. They say we need to cut out all small-time partners. They need bigger partners. You understand me?"

Semion didn't understand. The drugs had overwhelmed him.

"They need you to buy more."

"How much more?"

Mr. Hong shook his head. "A significant amount."

"Maybe right now is not the best time to talk," Semion said.

"Listen to me," Mr. Hong said. "My associates, the ones I work for, they told me not to offer this to you. They said, 'We need a better partner.' I said, 'No, no, you don't know these men. They're good men, these Israelis. Give them a chance.' They said, 'Raise the price.' I said, 'No, he's loyal, same price, same market!' They said, 'They too small. They not buy enough.' I said, 'They buy more. Give them a chance.' I put my neck out for you."

The words washed over Semion. He couldn't find their meaning. "I don't know," he said.

"Yes," said Mr. Hong, shrugging his shoulders. "But?"

Semion looked at Mr. Hong. *How can you say no to this man?* He wiped his face, pulled himself together. "You're saying we have to buy more?"

"Exactly."

"How much more?"

"Not much. Only ten times. Same price. I get it for you special."

This was exactly what Isaak had been lobbying for, he realized. But Semion's drugged mind didn't quite allow him to feel anger. Instead he took in the lay of the land, and considered his next move.

"Same price?" he asked.

"That's it," said Mr. Hong.

"That's not how it's supposed to work."

"It is, in fact, exactly how it works."

"We buy more we should pay less," said Semion.

Mr. Hong simply shook his head.

"I'll need to think about it," Semion said. "You have no idea what kind of headaches I'm dealing with right now."

"Unfortunately, I've been told to offer you two days."

"And if we decide to say no?"

"Let me help you," said Mr. Hong. "Don't think: 'What problems will this bring?' Instead, think: 'What problems will this solve?'"

The night turned worse from there. When he found Isaak again, his friend seemed wildly high, inappropriately high. Semion wondered if he'd been smoking meth. Isaak's face was sweaty, his eyes distant. When Semion whispered Mr. Hong's proposal, Isaak, in response, simply held his hands up, a freak's smile on his face: *What can you do? Celebrate!* The music pounded on and on.

Semion, still very high himself, felt sober around his friend. He wanted to go back to their office and talk it through, but Isaak only wanted to dance. He kept pushing himself on Semion, grinding on him like a horny teenager.

When Semion tried to make him stop, Isaak changed strategies and pushed Semion toward the serious-faced girl. But the last thing Semion wanted was sex.

Jimmy Congo was high, too. He kept dancing in Semion's face, trying to lock eyes with him. Semion didn't understand their belligerence. Finally he gave up and snuck out of the club without saying good-bye.

He didn't want to go home. Instead he parked his car a few blocks away, lowered the driver's seat, opened his window, and sat staring at the sky. The quiet would do him good. He was still very high, but in a different way. His mind drifted: he remembered playing football in an alley in Ashdod. The boys he'd played with—Russian immigrants, like himself—had on occasion passed the ball so smoothly that they'd experienced moments of transcendence. Time had slowed down. The memory was interrupted by an image of Mr. Hong miming the rope between their bellies. Isaak appeared next: his sweaty face, that *what can you do* gesture.

It occurred to him again that this was exactly what Isaak had always wanted. Every six months or so, he would bring up the prospect of increasing their order. He'd even suggested they start selling to more distributors than just the Filipina woman in San Francisco. Semion, using the same story about his friend Schmuel Teper being thrown in front of the bus in Tel Aviv, had always succeeded in shutting him down. It wasn't a matter of superstition, either: he truly believed that with bigger orders came bigger problems. The key to survival was to stay small. You start making too much, people notice.

Shit, thought Semion. *He might get what he wants.*

* * *

When he woke the next morning, his depression—surely the product of depleted endorphins—didn't feel new; it felt old, native, inescapable. Finally, with effort, he raised his head and looked around the room. It was clean and white. Normal.

Don't think: "What problems will this bring?" Think: "What problems will this solve?" Semion's mind started pinging back and forth. His hands began to sweat. *Shit.*

He got dressed. *What problems of mine will it solve?* He brushed his teeth, went to his couch, stood, paced, all in an effort to delay what would happen when he went downstairs and presented the issue to Isaak. He didn't want it to be true. It couldn't be true.

I don't have any problems, Semion told himself.

He knocked on Isaak's door for two minutes before his friend—pale faced and bleary-eyed—finally opened it. Semion tried to step inside, but Isaak barred the way. "Someone's here," he said.

Semion stood there blinking, panic-stricken. *Mr. Hong? Vanya?* he thought.

"A girl," Isaak said, wiping at his face. "Hold on."

He closed the door. Semion, forced to wait, stood in the hall on aching feet. Finally, the door opened again, and the serious-faced woman from the night before stumbled out. She shot Semion a brutal look and staggered down the hallway.

"Sorry," Isaak said. "Come in."

Semion moved past him, wandered to the window, looked out at the bay, and then turned back to his friend. Isaak's face resembled that of a man who'd heard the same argument numerous times, and suspected he was about to hear it again.

"What is it?" he asked in Hebrew.

"Mr. Hong," Semion said. He stared at his friend, trying to gauge his reaction and seeing nothing. "The Burmese want us to buy ten times more," he continued.

Isaak looked down, and then looked back. "Yeah, you said, last night. So what? It's good. Ten times more, we can retire ten times sooner."

Semion wiped his sweaty palms on his pant leg. He felt his face become ugly. "What's good is if we ask for it," he said. "It's not so good if we're told we have no choice."

"It's still ten times the profit," said Isaak.

"We make good money right now," Semion said. "We have an easy situation. We buy from one, sell to another, and with this, we make enough money to live like fucking kings. But trust me, I've done this before, if we get greedy, people will notice. The gangs will notice. The police will notice. And then we will have nothing." He leaned toward Isaak. "This isn't fucking normal business. This isn't let's see how many clubs we can open. This isn't, you know, collect all the chips on the table. Trust me on this one."

"A thousand times you've made this speech," said Isaak. "And a thousand times I've said I agree with you. So, okay, I still agree with you, but if Hong needs us to take ten times more, well, what can you do?"

"He killed Vanya, Isaak. Maybe he hired her, too, but he's the one doing this."

"What?" said Isaak. His mouth fell open. "Have you lost your mind?"

"Last night, Mr. Hong said, 'What problems will this solve?' Get it? What problems? What problems do I have?"

"No," said Isaak. "You're being paranoid."

"No? Then who? Tell me, who would come into my home?" With a flat hand, Semion tapped his chest. He knew his face was red. He could feel it. He was short of breath.

Isaak shrugged.

Semion stared at his friend for a long moment. *You fucking spoiled little shit,* he thought. *This is exactly what you've been dreaming of.* He forced himself to calm down. "So I should tell them yes?" he asked. "Tell them: 'Yes, please come into my home, kill a girl in my bed, and blackmail me.' And then what? Back to business as usual? Sure, no problem." He shook his head. "It's not what you want, Isaak. We're not here to become drug lords. We're trying to make a little money, live comfortable."

Isaak looked embarrassed.

"So," said Semion. "I will tell him no. No deal."

"And then what?" Isaak said. "We lose our connection? Or worse? Brother, please, think about it. We don't even know he had anything to do with this."

"We'll find a new way," said Semion. "We'll get it from somewhere else. It's a big world. The lady will still buy from us."

Isaak looked away. "I don't know," he said. "I don't think we want to piss these guys off. This is not a group of hippies from Belgium, Semion. These Burmese, they're military, you know?"

"So are we."

Isaak winced. "Shit."

"Listen to me," Semion said, forcing himself to sound calm. "We need to know if he did this one way or another, right?"

Isaak raised both palms. "You have to be smarter than them, Semion. You know? The girl might not even be dead."

"So they carried her away in a bag. Okay? Fine. Tell me, in what world would you *not* want to know if Mr. Hong set that up?"

"I would not want to know—" Isaak paused, and took a breath. "If knowing meant we lose our connection, and start some kind of war with people we know nothing about, then no, I wouldn't want to know. Look." He pointed at another tower across the street from their own. "They could be in there, Semion. They could be anywhere. Right now, they could be watching us."

Semion stared at the building Isaak had indicated. Maybe it was time to quit.

"It's a shitty situation," Isaak said. "I'm sorry, brother. I'm sorry this is happening. Whatever you want to do, we'll do that, okay?"

"I want to know if Mr. Hong did it," Semion said.

Isaak said nothing.

That night Semion dreamed he had a loose tooth. He could feel a molar hanging in the back of his mouth from a thin piece of flesh. He found Isaak on the beach and asked for help. His friend tried to set it back in place, but it wouldn't fit. Semion couldn't close his mouth. Other teeth came loose. His mouth filled with chips of bone, with actual teeth, drool, blood. He woke up at dawn feeling panicked and trapped.

* * *

The next night, with Mr. Hong's deadline approaching, Semion spent four nervous hours in the office at Ground Zero, clicking through real estate listings, refreshing his Facebook feed, reading Israeli football news, and suffering from indigestion. He drank club sodas mixed with cranberry juice. He'd be sober when Mr. Hong came tonight.

Finally, a few minutes before 1:00 a.m., a tired-looking Isaak opened the door and whispered that the man had arrived. He glanced at the safe in the corner. They had put a quarter of a million dollars in cash in it that afternoon.

Semion walked out to the main floor and found Mr. Hong standing near the entrance. The place was full, and he looked strange there, under the lights, people dancing in groups all around him. He looked angry, Semion realized; it was an emotion he had never seen on the man's face before. The dread in his stomach doubled as he guided his visitor to a back table.

"Drink?" he said, when they'd sat down.

"No, thank you," said Mr. Hong. For a moment, the two men regarded each other without speaking. And then, skipping the formalities, Mr. Hong asked, "Did you have a chance to consider our offer?"

An interesting way to phrase it, thought Semion. "I did," he said. "And the answer is no."

The look on Mr. Hong's face surprised Semion. He looked sad, suddenly: his eyes dampened, and he looked around the club as though searching for help. It was not what Semion had expected.

Mr. Hong scratched his chin, looked back at Semion, and then, over the music, said, "We work together, me and you. Everything has been good?"

"Absolutely," said Semion.

"But now you have all these problems."

Semion leaned back in his seat. He felt anger well up in his chest. "What problems do I have?" he asked.

Mr. Hong pointed at Semion. His eyes became black and still. "You depressed," he said. "Always depressed. You have an ugly thing inside you. Need help."

The music pounded steadily. Semion felt sweat on his forehead; he was thankful the lights would disguise his face reddening. The air smelled stale.

"Anything else?" Semion finally asked.

"Maybe you not cut out for this business," Mr. Hong said.

"Fine," Semion said. "Maybe so. The answer is still no."

"Listen," said Mr. Hong, changing tack. "I like you. Now I'm pleading with you as a friend, all right? If—listen to me. If you tell me no, I can't promise you any—" He dropped his voice lower. "When my friends ask me to do something, I always try and make it happen. You understand? My friends need you. I'm asking you as a friend to do this." His face looked affronted.

Semion probed his teeth with his tongue. The music in the club boomed on and on, the same bass note.

"Let me guess what you're going to say," he said. "Something about how maybe I can beat the case, but do I really want to risk that? Something about American news media loving stories about club owners who kill girls? Is that it? Is that what you've come to me with? Show me the pictures, then. Call the police. Lock me up."

"I'm sorry?" said Mr. Hong. "I don't know what you're talking about."

Semion looked at him. "The girl?" he said.

Mr. Hong shook his head. He looked confused.

Semion's mouth became dry. He felt a new kind of fear sliding in.

"It's not you?" he asked. "You didn't do this?"

Mr. Hong reached over the table and grabbed Semion's hand. "Semion," he said. "It's not me." He squeezed the hand he held in his own. "Now tell me what is happening."

Semion had one short moment to decide whether to trust him. He took a deep breath. Then he told Mr. Hong what had happened with Vanya.

The Chinese man bent his head forward and listened. Semion, every few words, would glance at his eyes to reassure himself that the man had told him the truth. When he got to the part about the blood on the bed, Mr. Hong's eyes narrowed. At the end of the story he shook his head and said the whole thing was horrible.

"These kind of problems don't simply go away," Mr. Hong said. "They become worse and worse. If you pay, they will come back and demand more. If you don't pay, who knows what happens. I beg you, as friend, as partner—let us help you with this. We are equipped to deal with this kind of thing." He stared at Semion in such a sympathetic way that Semion was forced to nod his head. "But if we help you with this, you take the ten times more, right?" Mr. Hong asked.

Semion felt defeated. "Sure," he said. "Yes." He sighed.

Mr. Hong reached across the table again. The men shook hands.

Later, Semion found Isaak—looking sober and serious—in the corner of the club.

"And?" his friend asked.

"It wasn't him," said Semion.

"I told you!"

"I agreed to the ten times."

Isaak appeared to whistle, silently. "Whatever you want," he said.

Semion woke the next morning to the buzzing growl of his cell phone. He looked at the screen: *Unknown Caller.* The sun had only just risen.

"Hello?" he said, sitting up in his bed.

"Mr. Gurevich," said the deep voice on the other end.

"Yes?"

"I own you," said the voice.

"I'm sorry?"

"You murdered her."

"I don't—" said Semion.

"I won't talk to you on the phone."

"You called me," said Semion.

"Listen close. There is a fish stand located at 7900 Northwest Twenty-Seventh Avenue, in West Little River. Do you hear me? It's called Pike's. I need you to bring the money there in one hour. A quarter million, two fifty, all of it. There's a table near the corner. You sit there and wait for me to call. No jokes, Mr. Gurevich. Come alone. You don't want to make me mad. Now repeat the name of the place."

"Pike's," said Semion.

"Where?"

"West Little River."

"How much?"

"Two fifty."

"Good."

The line went dead.

Semion checked the time on his phone: 7:12 a.m. He walked to the kitchen and wrote: *Pike's, 7900 27 Ave, WLR.*

He called Isaak. No answer. Then he called Mr. Hong.

"They've contacted me," he said, when the man picked up.

"And what did they say?"

Semion told him everything.

"He gave you an hour?"

"Yes."

"Good. You have the money?"

"At the club."

"Hold please," said Mr. Hong. Semion heard typing. He pictured Mr. Hong peering at Google Maps.

"Wait to leave your apartment for half an hour," Mr. Hong said. "I'll need time to get my men."

Semion stayed silent.

"You hear me?" asked Mr. Hong. "You don't want to arrive early."

"Yeah, yeah," said Semion.

"After thirty minutes, leave your apartment, drive to the club, get the money, put it in a bag, and drive to the location. We'll be there. Don't look for us. You won't see us, but we'll be there."

"And then?" asked Semion.

"Give them the money. You'll get it back."

Mr. Hong said he would call back in twenty minutes to confirm everything. Semion sat down in his kitchen, fully awake now. *So, an end,* he thought. He took a quick shower, dressed in jeans and a T-shirt, and went down and banged on Isaak's door until it opened. Isaak listened and nodded as Semion filled him in. It had been twenty-two minutes since the first call.

A few minutes later, his phone rang again. It was Mr. Hong.

"Where are you?" the man asked.

"I'm in Isaak's apartment."

"Do you trust me?" asked Mr. Hong.

The question made Semion feel nervous. He looked at Isaak, who was staring back at him.

"Yes," he said.

Mr. Hong instructed Semion to take Isaak's phone with him.

"Use the Bluetooth," he said. "Call me from it when you get to West Little River." This way, he said, they could remain in contact throughout the exchange. Then he told Semion to make sure Isaak stayed away. "We will handle this," he said.

"A bump in the road," said Isaak, when Semion had hung up again. "That's all. Mr. Hong will fix it."

Mr. Hong will fix it. Mr. Hong will fix it. Mr. Hong will fix it. Semion couldn't help repeating the phrase in his head as he drove. It was bright and sunny outside—a perfect Miami day. He turned his radio on, and then switched it off.

Ground Zero was empty, dark, and stale smelling. After turning off the alarm and flipping on the lights, Semion hurried back to the office, unlocked the door, walked to the safe, and punched in the code. He took out the money they'd moved there the other day—twenty-five stacks, two hundred fifty thousand dollars. He counted it three times, to make sure. He'd had weekends that had cost more than this, he thought. So why get Mr. Hong involved? For the first time that morning, he felt genuine panic in his bones. Why hadn't he taken care of this on his own?

He rubbed his face with his hands and felt a keen desire to cry.

He took I-95 north toward the meeting place. It would take him eleven minutes according to his phone. He checked his speed, checked his rearview mirror. *Breathe*, he told himself. *Breathe and be centered. You're in control.*

The address ended up being a strip mall. At one end, in its own little island, was a McDonald's. Beside it was a horseshoe of unhealthy palm trees. A row of depressing stores stood on the other side of the lot. *Here?* Semion thought. A wave of distaste billowed in his core. He rolled slowly through the lot until he saw Pike's Fish Stand, a small restaurant at the southern end of the mall.

He'd forgotten to call Mr. Hong, he realized. Before he shut his car off, he dug Isaak's phone out of his pocket, synced up the Bluetooth, fit the piece in his ear, and dialed the man's number. Mr. Hong picked up and, without waiting for Semion to speak, said that his men were in place. Semion scanned the area as best he could with his eyes, keeping his head still.

"What will they want me to do?" he asked.

"I don't know," said Mr. Hong. "Just wait for their call. Leave me on. I'll listen to your end. Try to repeat what they say."

Semion shut the car off, grabbed the bag of money, and opened his door. It felt like an industrial heater was blowing at him from outside. He walked to the fish stand, carrying the bag in his right hand. There were four tables outside, all unoccupied. He figured that's where they wanted him to sit. He headed inside first, and ordered a soda from an acne-faced Latino teenager. Then he sat down at one of the outside tables, looked at the lot, and waited.

He wanted, suddenly, more than anything else, to sleep. He watched an SUV drive toward him, his heart beginning to pound in his chest. The SUV drove past and continued out of the lot.

"I don't see anything," he said, trying not to move his lips as he spoke.

"Just wait," said Mr. Hong. "They want to see that you're alone."

Semion waited. He watched a seagull fly over the parking lot, watched a man struggle to light a cigarette. The boy in the fish stand was staring at a television, his mouth hung slightly open. Semion's phone shook in his pocket. He pulled it out. *Unknown Caller.* Sweat pushed out from every pore.

"Yes?" said Semion.

"The money is in your hand?" asked the deep voice.

"Yes," said Semion. And then, for Mr. Hong's benefit, he added, "The money's in my hand."

"Good," said the voice.

Semion's mouth went dry. He sipped from his soda. He wasn't a gangster, he realized. This wasn't his role. He was a middleman. "Hello?" he said.

"Wait," said the deep voice.

"Okay," he said. "I'll wait."

The seconds ticked by. Semion watched an overweight woman emerge from one of the neighboring stores. He continued to watch as she made her way to her car, fastened her seat belt, and pulled away from her spot.

"When the truck comes, walk to the passenger window and hand over the money," said the deep voice.

Semion, confused, watched the woman's car as it exited the lot. He scanned the rest of the area. There was a truck rolling toward him now. It had been parked since he'd gotten there, he realized. It accelerated and pulled right in front of the fish stand, so that the passenger-side door was facing him. It was a new white pickup truck, raised up high in the American fashion. Semion rose from his seat and stared at it. The windows were tinted, but he could see the shape of two bodies inside.

"Give him the money," said the deep voice.

"Okay," said Semion. "No problem."

He walked toward the truck. The window slid down, and Semion ducked his head to look in. He was surprised to see two men wearing beige stockings over their faces. They looked like street robbers. They were big, fat, and appeared to be white. They wore faded T-shirts and had blurred tattoos on their arms. The one in the passenger seat raised his hand and pointed a gun at Semion's head.

"Thanks," he said, taking the bag with his other hand. Once he'd brought it inside the truck he lowered the gun, and

Semion stepped back. The truck moved forward, stopped for a moment, and then pulled away.

"I gave him the money," Semion said, staring after it.

"Good," said the deep voice. The line went dead. Semion lowered his phone, still watching the truck.

"They took it," he said, when it had pulled out of sight.

"Good," said Mr. Hong. "We'll call you." Then his line went dead, too.

Two hours later, back in his apartment, Semion felt his phone ring.

"We got them," said Mr. Hong, when he picked up.

"Who?"

"The people who set you up," said Mr. Hong. "Meet us at your club. I'll show you." He sounded almost jovial.

Semion found them at the back entrance. There was a large black Suburban parked near the door; he parked next to it, and got out. It was 11:42 a.m. Nobody was around.

The passenger door of the SUV opened, and Mr. Hong stepped out with a plastic smile on his face.

"I told you," he said to Semion.

Four other Chinese men emerged from the car. Semion had never seen them before. He felt a fresh wave of fear. They smiled at Semion, gave little nods. They were dressed casually, in button-up shirts and pants. Semion's eyes went back to Mr. Hong.

"So," the man said, pointing his thumb toward the back of the vehicle. "We have something for you."

He said something in Chinese. One of the men stepped toward the car's back door. It struck Semion then that he didn't know what he'd been expecting to see. Had he thought the bag of money would be sitting there? The two men from the pickup truck? The moment unfolded slowly. In the seconds that passed between Mr. Hong speaking and his partner opening the door, Semion managed a quick self-inventory: *body hot, back aching, armpits wet, mouth dry.* He breathed in, then exhaled. *Control,* he told himself.

The man opened the door. On the floor of the car, silver duct tape over her mouth, was Vanya. Next to her was the canvas bag, presumably with Semion's money in it.

Semion stared. Their eyes locked for a moment. Competing emotions fought in his chest.

"We got her for you," said Mr. Hong. "You can do whatever you'd like."

Semion felt a wave of revulsion. He looked at Mr. Hong. The man's smile faded. He raised his eyebrows and nodded toward the door of the club.

"What about the men in the truck?" asked Semion.

"They tried to put up a fight," said Mr. Hong.

Semion looked back at Vanya. She blinked her eyes three times, and instantly he understood what she was trying to express: *I love you.* She could explain, he knew. There had to be an explanation. He stepped forward and pulled the tape from her mouth.

"Fuck you," she said. "What, did you think you were going to save me?" She took a breath, prepared for more. "Did you think I loved you?" she asked, staring into his eyes. "Fucking worm." The bloody bed came into Semion's mind.

Her accent was gone; she spoke like an American. She was an American. There was nothing Brazilian about her. He understood, only then, that she hated him. The star-shaped scar on her forehead felt like a reminder of all the ugliness in the world.

"You can't hurt me," she said. "You're too much of a coward." The words were sharp, but there was a pleading quality to the way she spoke. "You don't exist," she said. "You're nothing."

Semion forced himself to smile. It was a fake smile, an ugly rictus. His stomach filled with shame. He badly wanted to be done with this business. He wanted to hide in his bed.

"Let her go," he said.

Mr. Hong put his hand on Semion's shoulder. "We can take care of her," he said. "Nobody will ever find her."

"No," said Semion. "Let her go." He felt like the parking lot was spinning.

"It's not the way we do things," Mr. Hong said. "Loose ends."

"I'm telling you to let her go," Semion said. "If you want us working with you, you'll do it."

Without waiting for Mr. Hong's reply, he leaned into the SUV to pull the tape from Vanya's arms. His head was near her hair. Involuntarily, he smelled her familiar scent.

"Turn around," he said. She shifted in her seat, and Semion dug his fingers beneath the silver tape. She scooted away from him when he'd removed it, and rubbed her wrists against each other. She looked like a different person. Her face looked transformed.

"Can I go?" she asked, looking at Mr. Hong.

Mr. Hong—looking tired—held his palm toward Semion.
"Go," said Semion.

She pushed herself out of the SUV and ran across the parking lot. She didn't look back.

Mr. Hong appeared to be embarrassed. Semion wanted to say something, but speaking seemed too difficult. He busied himself by scratching at his jaw like something was stuck on it, and squinting at the club like there was work waiting for him there.

"Take your money," Mr. Hong said.

Semion fell into a depression after that. His days and nights were filled with a panicked feeling. Two days after freeing Vanya, unable to face seeing him in person, he called Isaak on the phone.

"I've had a change of heart," he said. "The deal is off." He couldn't allow them to continue to do business with Mr. Hong and his men, he said.

Isaak didn't argue. All he said was, "Whatever you want."

Semion's eyes filled with tears. The gratitude he felt toward his friend was immeasurable. They would make it through this.

He drank screwdrivers and watched TV. He ordered takeout and ate it joylessly. In an effort to curb his anxiety, he masturbated. He considered committing suicide, imagined the gun in his hand, the grip, the weight. He stood on his balcony and looked at the sea. He thought about what he'd tell Mr. Hong. *I'm sorry. It's time to part ways. Business is business.*

At night he dreamed about a jungle. In the dream he watched a skinny Asian man trap a turtle. The man kept poking at the thing with a stick. After a minute, the turtle snapped at the stick, and the man trapped its head and cut it off. Then he hung the thing upside down from a tree and let it bleed out. Semion kept asking him what he was doing, but the man wouldn't answer. Semion watched as the man removed the shell, cutting off the bottom plate to reveal the pink insides. He cut off the legs and neck; he removed the skin and yellow fat. He put all the good meat into a pot and set it down on the ground. Semion woke up covered in sweat.

At one point, he drunkenly called Vanya's old number. A generic message declared that the person he was trying to reach was unavailable. What could he have said? *I'm sorry. I'm ugly inside. I'm depressed. I forgive you.* He didn't even know who she was.

The next day, as the sun was setting, Semion's doorbell rang. It took him a second, looking through the peephole, to realize that it wasn't Isaak—that the man standing there, who looked somewhat like a shaved-headed version of his friend, was in fact Moisey Segal, their man in Bangkok. *What the fuck is Moisey doing here?* Semion thought. He was never supposed to come Miami, never even supposed to communicate with them. He was meant to stay in Bangkok.

Moisey had a suitcase next to him. He smiled, warmly.

Semion opened the door.

At that moment, three thousand miles away, Raymond Gaspar was busy watching a handball game. Hundreds of men milled about in the prison yard.

"Come on, Tully," yelled the man standing next to him.

Raymond spat on the ground. He looked at his wrist for a moment, at the place where a watch would have been. In his mind, he calculated the days until his release: twenty-three. *Not gonna miss you guys*, he thought.

He thought about the women he'd chase when he got out. It had been a long time since he'd lain down with a soft body. There was a girl named Emily he'd like to talk to. *Get me some Mexican food, pizza, burgers, fuckin' Chinese.* He imagined driving a car. Looking at the ocean. Then he remembered he had to remind Arthur that his release date was coming up.

Seventy-two miles to the south, in San Francisco, Shadrack Pullman sat at the Bernal Heights public library. He liked to go there and surf the web. His bag, filled with gemstones, rested between his feet. He was reading a libertarian website, something about the United States Postal Service. There were a few different sites he liked to visit. He looked around to see if anybody was watching, then brushed his hair back with both hands and turned his attention back to the computer.

Shadrack's partner, John Holland, was stopping by a liquor store he owned on Third Street. The clerk saw him come in and asked if he'd seen the 49ers game.

"Yeah, I saw it," said John, shaking his head. "I saw it."

In Daly City, Gloria Ocampo was busy changing her grandson's diaper. She made cooing noises and sang a song into his little face: *You're my baby, my little baby.*

On the other side of the world, in Thailand, Fariq—the Malaysian man who made sure the drugs were placed in bags of squid, frozen, and packed into refrigerated shipping containers—was sleeping in his bed. He was dreaming about a boyhood friend of his chasing him through some tall grass. It was a happy dream.

In Bangkok, Eugene Nana, suffering from insomnia, sat in his living room and watched the financial news on television. His stocks were performing well, but he wanted them to do better. His wife was snoring quietly.

In Myanmar, a Chinese man named Zhou Qiang was just waking up. He was the chemist who cooked the drugs for the Burmese. He had a busy day ahead, and he liked to walk to the river and back before he started work.

In Cambodia, meanwhile, in Koh Kong City, a man named Sang Munny was trying to drink himself into oblivion. He'd been singing karaoke all night. He sang love songs. He had come to the bar alone, but he sang for his boss. He sang for his mother. He sang for his father and his brother. He sang for the turtles, the chickens, the pigs, and the ants.

Part 3

Part 3

Five days before he went to Miami, Moisey Segal found himself sitting alone in the living room of his Bangkok apartment, slumped over shirtless on his couch. He was feeling lonely and scanning through a grid of male faces on his iPhone. One face caught his attention: the man's name was Thong Kon. His picture made him look like a schoolboy. He wore a white button-up shirt with a loose blue plaid tie and a baseball cap. His face, lit by the sun, made it look like he was about to tell a joke. His profile header read: Lump of Gold. The app said he was within a kilometer. Moisey stared at the picture for a few moments, hoping the boy wasn't a prostitute, then hit the Chat icon.

Mo-Mo33: English?
Lump of Gold: Speak English. Ya!
Mo-Mo33: You 2 handsome for me.
Lump of Gold: Ha ha.
Mo-Mo33: Are you really 24?
Lump of Gold: Plus eight months!! Too old soon!! Ha ha.
Mo-Mo33: I like you just the way you are.
Lump of Gold: How pretty!

Mo-Mo33: Do you want to have a drink?

Lump of Gold: So happy to drink with you!

They decided to meet right then. Moisey lived in an apartment on Pan Road, in the Silom district; Thong Kon suggested they eat before drinking, and told Moisey to meet him at the chicken and rice stand outside Wat Khaek. *I wear a pink T-shirt,* he wrote.

It was a twenty-minute walk from Moisey's house. He decided not to take a motorcycle taxi, even though a cluster of orange-vested drivers stood gossiping on his corner. Sex addiction notwithstanding, Moisey was a romantic; he wanted to savor the moment. In his mind, he'd already upgraded Thong Kon from casual hookup to boyfriend.

The streets were overloaded with people, as always. The ground itself changed every few steps, from tile to broken concrete and back. Electrical wires crisscrossed above his head, and carts with food sizzling on flat metal grates lined his path. Every inch of every wall seemed covered in air-conditioning units, vents, pipes. He bought a pineapple juice from his favorite juice girl and paused to drink the whole thing before returning the bottle to her. She accepted it and stared over his shoulder without ever meeting his eyes. A homeless woman sitting on the ground held her hands cupped together like he might fill them with water. He smiled at her, and she smiled back.

When Moisey arrived at the chicken stand he saw Thong Kon waiting there already. The boy looked poor; he was skinny, almost malnourished. More than that, he seemed dirty. His shirt, though admittedly pink, appeared dusty and brown, as though he'd been working in front of a furnace.

He made a funny face when he saw Moisey, then walked to him and greeted him in the Thai way—palms pressed and head bowed.

"Mazzy?" he said.

"Moisey."

"Moi-zee," repeated Thong Kon. The men shook hands—his were clammy, Moisey's dry—and laughed. Thong Kon guided them to a plastic table.

"Are you hungry?" he asked.

"Little bit," said Moisey.

The younger man called something out in Thai to the cook, a skinny old woman with a grimace on her face. Moisey didn't speak much Thai, but he understood the words: *two chicken.*

They sat across from each other. Thong Kon scratched at the area under his Adam's apple. "Australian?" he said.

"Israel," said Moisey. "Israeli."

"Ahhh, I want to go there. Beautiful, historic land," said Thong Kon. "I know it."

Moisey asked him where he'd learned to speak English. Thong Kon's eyes shifted. "School," he said. "School, books, movie, television. And you? Do you speak Thai?" Moisey shook his head. "Not a little bit?"

"Ra ka tao rai?" said Moisey. How much is it?

Thong Kon laughed. "That's all?"

Moisey counted from zero to ten, raising a finger for each number.

"You speak very nice," said Thong Kon. "I teach you more. I teach you how to say everything beautiful in our country. Every word: sunset, moon, flower."

The food came. Chicken and rice. Thong Kon added spices, and Moisey did the same.

"How long have you been in Thailand?"

"Six years," said Moisey.

"No!" said Thong Kon. He covered his mouth. "And you don't speak Thai?"

"I do, though," said Moisey. *"Lot noi dai mai?"* Can you give a little discount? That he only knew how to speak about money embarrassed him. "Where are you from?" he asked, trying to change the subject.

"I'm from Bangkok. Ratchadamri? Near here!" Thong Kon pointed over his shoulder. "And you? Why you live in Thailand so long?"

The simple answer was that it was a better place to live than Israel. It had provided him with a tropical escape from his earlier life. But the more complicated answer had to do with the ease with which he could tamp out his inner blacknesses, thanks to the drugs, the sex, the sun. Also, of course, he had a job here. A very lucrative job, one he couldn't easily duplicate anywhere else.

"I like it here," he said.

They finished their food. Moisey paid, and they moved on to a bar chosen by Thong Kon. It wasn't a gay bar, which made Moisey thankful—just a normal Bangkok place, with seats that faced out to the street. They drank Leo beers and smoked cigarettes. Thong Kon asked what Moisey did for work. Without thinking, Moisey responded "bartender," and instantly regretted it. He saw Thong Kon study his face, and knew the man was measuring him in some way.

"Currently not working," Moisey added.

The touching began with a playful pat. They laughed at some joke, and Thong Kon pushed Moisey's shoulder. Even that felt weighted with sex. The dirtiness, Moisey noticed, didn't extend to the man's hands. He had clean fingernails, with large moons. *A healthy thyroid*, Moisey thought. He wanted to return the touch, but suddenly he felt shy. He hadn't taken drugs in over a month, and now he wondered if that was what was slowing him down.

Moisey had a hard time placing the Thai man economically. His English, refined and grammatical, seemed the product of university study, though Thong Kon denied that. His movements, his countenance, his posture, all seemed upper class to Moisey. But underneath, in the corners of his eyes, there was something thuggish, something criminal in the way he scanned the street while they drank.

It didn't matter to Moisey; he liked this Lump of Gold.

They drank beers and took shots of whiskey. Moisey grew drunk. He was having a hard time filling the silent moments between remarks, and his romantic feelings had mutated into a grumpy carnal desire. Thong Kon kept trying to teach him new words. The man's face shined with sweat. Moisey wondered whether taking him home was a bad idea; maybe he should rent a hotel. He thought about the crystal meth tucked away in his freezer, and suddenly he wanted to get high.

"Let's go," he said. Thong Kon raised his eyebrows and downed his drink.

They shared a taxi, kissing almost the entire way. By the time they arrived at the apartment, their breathing was heavy. Moisey noticed Thong Kon studying the address above the door when they got out. There was something determined in the way he stared at the numbers. When he noticed Moisey watching him, he smiled and said, "We live so close." He held his hand up for a high-five, and Moisey slapped it.

They continued kissing in the elevator. Thong Kon wrapped his arms around Moisey's shoulders and pulled him in. Inside, the Thai man stuck his head out like a turtle and moved it side to side.

"Nice," he said, drawing out the word.

Moisey's apartment was small, clean, modern, and open. He led his guest into the kitchen, opened the refrigerator, and pulled out two beers. He noticed himself breathing the way drunk men do, but he craved more. He needed more.

"Do you like ice?" he asked.

"In beer?"

"No, ice—sniff." He put his finger to his nose and sniffed.

"Ice! Me?" asked Thong Kon.

Moisey had been trying to wean himself off the stuff, but he'd held on to this last bag the way a person quitting cigarettes will sometimes hold on to a pack. As if having it close at hand would make him crave it less. Now he pulled the baggie out and held it cold in his palm. Something about the moment was off, he knew, but he couldn't stop. He held the bag up for Thong Kon to see.

"Me? No!" said Thong Kon. "I am sober," he added, pointing at his chest, although he was clearly drunk. Moisey shrugged his shoulders. He told himself the only way to salvage his mood was to sniff the drugs.

"You stupid, go, do it," said Thong Kon. He pushed Moisey's shoulder. "I don't care! Me, no. You do it. Sex, boom-boom, too much!"

Moisey opened the bag, and tapped a crystal out onto his kitchen counter. A small amount, the size of a large peanut. He pulled a spoon from the silverware drawer and began crushing the crystal into powder.

"I need use bathroom," said Thong Kon.

Moisey pointed. "That way."

He pulled out a card and pushed the powder into a line. Then he rolled up a thousand-baht note—the king's handsome face staring at him—and sniffed the burning drugs up his nose. *That's it*, he thought—meaning both that's all I'll do and that's exactly what I needed. He rubbed at his nose, drank from his beer, and became aware of the quiet all around him. He listened. What was taking the boy so long?

Finally, the toilet flushed, and his Lump of Gold walked back into the kitchen. His face looked sad. Moisey decided to pretend he hadn't done the drugs. "If you won't do it, I won't do it," he said.

"We need music," said Thong Kon.

They moved to the living room. The view showed the city stretching in all directions. Aware that Thong Kon would taste the drugs in his mouth when they kissed, Moisey sniffed and tried to clear his nose. He drank more beer, swayed, put his arm on his guest's shoulder, went to his laptop, and scrolled through his music. He found his favorite song, the one by Katreeya English, and played it. A love song. They began a slow dance. Moisey bent down and smelled Thong Kon's neck, kissed it, pulled the man into him. They danced like that for a long time. Moisey waited to kiss him again, drawing it out until he couldn't bear it.

The drugs had moved from his nose to his brain. Finally he felt a sense of peace. He rocked on his feet and pulled Thong Kon closer. With his eyes closed, he pictured what he was going to do to this Lump of Gold, and what was going to be done to him.

And then, almost predictably, the moment was interrupted by a loud banging on the door.

Thong Kon stepped away, a vacant look on his face. The knocking stopped for a moment—silence—and then picked up again, stronger. Moisey turned the music off. He was aware, instinctively, that only cops and gangsters knocked like that. He walked to the kitchen, opened the freezer, found the baggie, dumped the rest of the drugs down the drain, and turned the water on. The little button-sized baggie was stuffed into the bottom of his trash bin. His mind felt like a boiling kettle. The drugs were hitting home.

Thong Kon hadn't moved; he stood in the other room with the same downcast eyes, but now with both hands covering his mouth. Moisey took a moment to think. He'd dumped the only drugs in the house. There was nothing to connect him to his other business, nothing incriminating on his computer. He went to the door and looked through the peephole.

Four Thai men stood in the hall. Three were in Metropolitan Police uniforms, which made them look like soldiers. The fourth man wore a gray suit over a blue shirt and a maroon tie.

"One moment," Moisey said in English, through the closed door.

He stepped back to the living room. He wanted to warn Thong Kon not to say anything, but even as he turned toward him he knew the boy was responsible for his trouble. He balled his fist and pressed it against his visitor's jaw. "I'll fucking bury you," he said in Hebrew.

The knocking started up again, Moisey's heart racing to match it as he returned to the door. He wiped at the insides of his nostrils and cracked the door open.

"Yes?" he said.

The man in the suit stepped forward, put his hand on the door, and tried to push it open. For a moment, the two men stood there silently, leaning against opposite sides of the door.

"Yes?" Moisey said again.

"Open please," said the man. He said something in Thai, and one of the uniformed men, the biggest one, stepped toward them.

Moisey opened the door. He stood facing them, blocking their way with his body.

"What is it?" he asked. He tried to smile, but it felt fake.

"Big problem," said the man in the suit. "You speak Thai?"

"No."

"No Thai?" he asked again, in the same incredulous way that Thong Kon had. He pushed past Moisey, moving into the apartment. The other uniformed men followed. One of them went to Thong Kon, turned him around, and put him in handcuffs. It was for show, Moisey knew, but he watched as the cop sat Thong Kon down on the couch and the man in the suit proceeded to give him a long speech. Thong Kon listened with his eyes glued to the floor, nodding his head as though receiving a lecture from a parent.

Moisey only understood the curse words. But it was a setup, clearly.

He could see the whole thing in his head. Thong Kon worked with these men. Whether he did it voluntarily or not didn't concern Moisey. He found gay white tourists, waited until he saw drugs, and then made the call. They probably did it a few times a night. Earned fifty thousand baht on the side. The problem seemed manageable—regular corruption. No sign that it was part of a larger investigation.

"You live here? Or are you visiting?" said the man in the suit, sounding out each syllable like an English student. Moisey saw that he was older than he'd first appeared—over fifty, he thought. He had black eyes, bad skin, and a mole on his cheek.

"I live here, sir," Moisey said.

"And your business is?"

"I'm a bartender. But I'm between jobs at the moment."

The man in the suit swept the apartment with his eyes, the corners of his mouth dropping down. His face suggested that it was a nice place for an unemployed bartender to be living. Moisey could see the cost of the bribe rise.

"Your state of origin?"

"I'm sorry?"

"What country do you come from?"

"Israel."

"This man is a known drug dealer!" said the man in the suit, changing gears and pointing at Thong Kon. "We follow him here. You have a known drug dealer in your apartment. Very big problem!" He was speaking loudly now. "I ask you one question: Do you have drugs in this house?"

"Drugs?" asked Moisey. "No, of course not."

"Please, sit on the chair," the man said. "Don't rise again." He pointed at one of the chairs, and Moisey sat in it.

The man said something in Thai, then, and one of the uniformed cops walked into Moisey's kitchen. Moisey heard the sounds of drawers opening, dishes being moved. He steadied himself, picturing the baggie in the bottom of the bin. *Fine*, he thought. *Find it. Let's just get this over with.*

The man in the kitchen called out, and one of the other uniformed men went to join him. The man in the suit had moved to Moisey's desk, and was calmly looking through the things he'd left on top of it.

What, Moisey wondered, would happen if he stood and kicked Thong Kon in the head? He thought he could do it before the cops could stop him. The humiliation of having actually liked this dirty-shirted hustler stung him the most.

The man in the suit walked to one of the windows, took out a walkie-talkie, and began speaking into it. Again for show, thought Moisey. A performance meant to inspire fear that his troubles were becoming bigger by the moment. He pictured kicking the biggest cop in the knee, and breaking it.

The men came back from the kitchen. At first, Moisey thought they looked disappointed: their expressions were flat, slack, tired. But one of the men, the youngest, held up a plastic baggie pinched between his finger and thumb. For a moment, Moisey thought this was the empty bag, but then he noticed a small girth to it. It held something.

The suited man stepped that way. When he'd taken the bag, he bent his head, tapped something out onto his palm, and examined the substance like a jeweler.

"You have methamphetamine in your kitchen. Very bad," he said. The man shook his head. "Very bad for you."

"It's not mine," said Moisey. He sat up taller.

The suited man nodded to the biggest cop, who hand-cuffed Moisey roughly. A series of calculations ran through his mind as the man yanked at his arms: planting evidence put these cops on a different level, more dangerous, more criminal, but it also decreased the likelihood that they were looking for a bigger arrest. He allowed himself to relax a little bit. He'd be done with them by the time the sun rose.

"I have a daughter," said the suited man, holding his head back. "She is grown now. Twenty-three years old. She was in college, study to be an engineer, you know this? Then she meet a *farang,* look like you. Same shaved head. Same skinny, tattoos. He maybe is your brother?" The suited man looked at the larger cop, who nodded his head. "Maybe you know this man? He give my daughter this same kind of drug. Make her sick from it. You farangs bring it here, ruin our great country. You ruined my family."

Moisey couldn't help himself; the man's story was ridiculous. He smiled. In response, the suited man slapped him in the face. The sound, like a loud clap, shocked him. He kept his head down, and felt tears come to his eyes. Rage swelled in his stomach, but he decided it would be better to seem scared.

"I'm sorry," he said.

"You're sorry?" the man said. His anger seemed to expand. "You're sorry? My family ruined because of you."

"Those drugs aren't mine, and you know it," Moisey said. He couldn't help himself.

"What about if we take you to the station, test your blood for illegal narcotics? You see?" With his thumb and two fingers, the man imitated the squishing of a syringe. Moisey shook his head.

The man grabbed his ear and pulled up on it. Moisey was forced to stand, and then to rise to his toes. The man let go and pulled his hand back, ready to slap him again, but then turned toward the other Thai men instead, and began to yell at them. Moisey couldn't understand what he was saying. The large cop stood with his lower lip jutted out, shaking his head. Then he stepped toward Moisey, gazed into his eyes as if to make sure he was okay, and head butted him square in the face.

Moisey fell back onto the chair, and then off it onto the ground. Pain shot from his nose. He tasted blood on his lip.

When he opened his eyes he saw Thong Kon arguing with one of the policemen. The suited man lifted Moisey up and helped him back onto the chair.

"He said your attitude is ugly," the man said, nodding toward the man who'd head-butted him. "You haven't shown enough respect. He's too bossy. I can't control him. He's scared. All these drugs in your home, you're in such big problem now. He says he wants to arrest you. You go to Ratchada court. Next thing, you sleep in Bang Kwang, very bad place."

Moisey closed his eyes and breathed deeply. His nose didn't feel broken. "Maybe there's some other way?" he said.

The suited man shook his head. "Too big," he said. "No other way."

"Please," said Moisey. "Please, no trouble." He tried to insert the right tone of regret into his voice. "I can make it right. I promise." He decided to set an upper limit of three hundred and thirty thousand baht. Ten thousand US seemed like it would be more than enough to cover this stupid fucking night. He waited for the other man to begin.

The suited man walked back to Moisey's desk. He looked at his computer again.

"You have Bitcoins?" he said.

"I don't know what that is," Moisey lied. He scanned the faces of the other men in the room. It was a bad start, he realized.

"You have a computer. You live in Thailand. You use crystal meth. Surely, you are familiar with what Bitcoin is," the man said.

"I don't know it," Moisey said again.

The suited man turned toward the computer, bent down, grabbed the mouse, and brought the thing to life. Moisey felt relief at the sight of the lock screen.

"What can I give you?" he asked. There was nothing on his computer, but he still didn't like the man being near it.

"Open your computer," said the suited man. "Uncuff him. Open your computer and show us your bank account."

This had gone too far. "I don't have a bank," Moisey said. "I can call a friend, and have him bring you a hundred thousand baht. Tonight. Now."

The suited man's mouth twitched, but he said, "Not enough. You have too much trouble."

"Okay. The most I can do is two hundred thousand. Otherwise, you have to arrest me, because I can't get any more."

"Open the computer, log on to your bank, and show us your balance."

Moisey glanced at Thong Kon. The boy still had his eyes down, but his face carried a slight smile. It was the final straw. The planted drugs, the slap, the head butt—none of it angered Moisey as much as that quiet smile. The world tipped on its axis.

"Fuck you," he said.

The suited man's head snapped to attention. He looked genuinely concerned.

"Fuck you," repeated Moisey. "Fuck all of you. You don't know how easy it would be to have you all fired."

"Fired?" the suited man said.

"Listen to me," Moisey said, dropping any pretense of deference. "Call this number: 66-2-494-6601. He can pay you whatever you want. Okay? Or maybe he'll convince you that you've made a mistake."

"What? What is this?"

"Take your phone and call the number: 66-2—" He waited for the suited man to bring out his phone, which he finally decided to do, and then started over. "66-2-494-6601."

"Who is it? Whose number?" the suited man asked.

"Ask for Mr. Sukhontha," Moisey said. "He's someone who will listen to you." As he said this, he knew he was making a terrible mistake, but he couldn't stop himself. The new course he was setting lacked any kind of map.

"Call him," he said. "He'll either pay you what you want, or he'll convince you that you've made a mistake. Either way you win, right?"

The suited man's nostrils were flaring. The other men had shrunk back into themselves. Moisey wasn't sure whether they spoke English, but he suspected they recognized something in his tone. He turned and stared at Thong Kon, working to memorize his face. After what was about to happen, the boy would probably want to delete his Grindr account.

The suited man made the call. He stood with the phone pressed to his ear, his sad eyes watching Moisey. The sound of the air conditioner filled the room. Moisey thought he could almost hear the ringing on the other end of the line. But then the suited man shook his head slightly, looked at his phone, and ended the call.

"No answer," he said.

A new wave of fear rose in Moisey. The confidence he'd felt disappeared; his hunger for revenge vanished. Everything was about to change. His mind raced through ways to turn back. He'd pay the cop anything, he realized, if, in a few moments when his phone lit up, he would just tell Sukhontha that he'd dialed the wrong number.

But it was impossible. He couldn't even begin to explain it to the man.

Before anyone in the room could speak, the suited man's cell phone vibrated. Moisey's stomach rolled under his heart. The cop answered the call, bending his head down and plugging his left ear with his finger. He murmured something in Thai, then looked at Moisey and asked, "Name?"

"Segal," Moisey said.

"Segal," the man repeated, pronouncing the word *Say-go*.

Moisey watched the man's eyes move as he listened. He watched him look at the other cops in the room and wet his lip with his tongue. The man said something he couldn't understand, then inserted the English word *ice*, followed by more murmured Thai.

Then Moisey heard him apologize.

The man in the suit repeated the apology a few times, then hung up. With a softened face, he turned his attention to Moisey.

"I am sorry," he said in English. "I made a mistake in coming here." He put his hands together at his forehead and bowed. "We all made mistake. Wrong house. I am deeply sorry."

He said something to the large cop, who moved to uncuff Moisey. Then the suited man began cursing at Thong Kon, stepped toward him, and slapped him hard in the back of the head.

"This one," he said, pointing at Thong Kon. "This man's fault." He slapped him again. Then the men, all five of them—Thong Kon still cuffed—left the apartment.

Moisey didn't move from his seat. He stared out the window. Somewhere out there, among the lights of Bangkok, Sukhontha was making more phone calls.

Moisey wasn't able to sleep until the next afternoon. Instead, he paced his apartment and thought about what he'd done.

Aawut Sukhontha was an attorney in Bangkok. Moisey had never met the man; he'd been given his number by Eugene Nana, his connection to the Burmese outfit. Nana had told him to memorize it. Sukhontha, he'd said, had connections within both the Phak Phuea Thai and the Phak Prachathipat, the two rival parties in power. He also had men inside the Royal Thai Police Special Branch. He could get rid of any kind of trouble with a single phone call. Moisey, though, was supposed to use the number only in the event of a great emergency: specifically, if he were to be stopped while transporting the Burmese merchandise. This had not been one of those situations.

The fucking police had been digging around. If they'd kept digging, who knows what they would have found. But he knew this argument wouldn't hold up; they wouldn't have found anything, not in his apartment. Why hadn't he just paid the men? Why hadn't he shown them his bank account? He had nineteen thousand US sitting in his Bangkok bank; the rest—just as the cop suspected—was in Bitcoin. Why hadn't he shown them that, and then emptied it for them? Why had he chosen that fucking Lump of Gold in the first place?

When he woke, his cell phone showed no missed calls. No texts. No e-mails. A dull hangover settled in on him. He thought about getting in touch with Eugene Nana, but felt overwhelmed by it all. He could reach out to Isaak Raskin in Miami, but that felt too dramatic. What could he say to him?

Around nine thirty that evening, just as he was starting to think maybe it would all pass unnoticed, his phone buzzed in his hand. A Bangkok number he didn't recognize.

"Hello?" he said, answering in English.

"Mr. Segal?" asked an accented female voice.

"Yes."

"Your friend would like to see you."

"Which friend?"

"Mister from up north, please."

Moisey understood this to mean Eugene Nana.

"Where?" he said.

"There is a ride waiting outside your door."

When Moisey stepped outside, the car he'd expected was nowhere to be seen. An orange-vested motorcycle taxi driver got his attention by waving his hand like an English queen. Moisey shuffled toward him.

"Yes, yes, Segal, this way," said the man, lifting the visor of his helmet to speak. Moisey climbed on the back of the bike, touching what felt like a holstered gun underneath the man's orange vest.

The man sped out into traffic. Moisey turned and saw two other men in identical orange vests following close behind.

"Two men are following," shouted Moisey over the wind.

The driver, accelerating, looked at his side mirror, raised his visor again, and shouted, "With us."

My God, thought Moisey. *A rather large production.* He tucked his knees in and held on as the driver cut between a bus and a truck. They skirted north through small side streets, toward Ratchathewi. Everywhere the madness of the close-packed city pressed in on them. The sun had set over an hour ago, but the heat remained. Every few seconds, the driver slid through some new obstacle without slowing down. Moisey, more than once, felt compelled to close his eyes.

Finally, somewhere near Chatuchak, in a neighborhood he had never been to, they entered a parking garage beneath a mall. The two other bikes had stopped outside; Moisey's driver sped through a few turns and then shot out the other side of the building, back out onto the street. They traveled down two more back alleys before entering another garage, this one below a nondescript glass-covered tower. The man at the entry booth waved them forward.

A heavyset man in a navy suit at the far end of the garage rose from a metal folding chair as they approached. He spoke to the driver when the bike had stopped, touching him like they knew each other. Then he ushered Moisey through a door and into a brightly lit hallway. At the elevator, his new guardian pressed the button for 12.

They rode in silence. The man kept nodding his head slightly, as though in some kind of commiseration. When the doors opened, he led him into an unfussy office, where a receptionist speaking on a headset looked at them and then looked away. The man opened the door of a conference room, gestured for Moisey to enter, asked him if he wanted water—which Moisey accepted—and then left him alone.

Moisey, his feet itching inside his shoes, sat looking at his iPhone. He didn't want to be caught doing something that would make him seem guilty. He looked at pictures of his friends on Instagram and felt contempt for everyone in the world.

Ten minutes later Eugene Nana came into the room. His clothes, as always, seemed to suggest that he was a man of leisure: a black polo shirt, a Windbreaker over his arm, pressed khaki pants, loafers. He looked like a movie star. Even now, under these circumstances, Moisey felt attracted to him. *Can't we just work this out,* he imagined himself saying. *Can't we just fuck and call it a day?*

Nana shook his head, frowned, and sat down on the opposite side of the table. His face—his eyes in particular—looked uneasy. He peered around the room as though it were his first time in it, then turned his attention to Moisey.

"Do you know how the substance we sell you is made?" he asked in English.

"The ecstasy?" said Moisey.

"How do they make it?"

"The Burmese?"

"Yes."

"From safrole oil?"

"Yes. But where does safrole oil come from?"

Moisey shook his head. "China?"

"Yes. But before that, where?"

Moisey didn't know.

"We get it next door. Cambodia. A tree grows in the mountains: they call it *Mreah Prew Phnom.* A beautiful tree. Big   you see a statue of the Buddha made of it in the market. Have you seen it? Hold it, smell the statue." He mimed the act of smelling a small thing in his hands. "Smell like black licorice. Same smell. It's the smell of safrole. You cut the tree down, distill the oil, right there in the jungle. Take oil, easy chemistry, make drug." He paused. "Moisey, my friend, you know what happened to me this week? I had a man go to the jungle—he's from Phnom Penh; he's Vietnamese—but he always live in Phnom Penh. He went to the jungle, took a group of villagers, laborers, find the tree, cut it down, boil wood, distill oil. This man, he brought his driver with him, assistant, a Khmer boy from Phnom Penh called by the name Sang Munny. He is a young boy, twenty-two year old. They went into the jungle with the five laborers from Osaum Village, and you know what the young driver did?"

Moisey shook his head. He had no idea what this speech was about.

"He killed his boss. Shot him in the head. They call me, I have to go to Koh Kong Province, talk to the villagers, fix everything, talk to family. You know what they said? Villagers and driver—all Cambodian—they say the boss start acting crazy in the jungle. He start being—"

Nana waved his hand in front of his face, opened his mouth, let his tongue hang, made his eyes wide like a zombie.

"He act like a, like a, what's the word in English? In Khmer, they say he got taken by a *neak ta,* you know, a tree spirit, a ghost. They say he became possessed, start hitting all the villagers, hitting the driver, he spit at them. He bit villager on the hand, break the skin. You know what the villagers said? The driver, all of them, they say his teeth turn bright black. Black teeth. Violent. He hit everyone. The villagers said he make a bonfire burn up into the sky, like a building, and the man, his name is Phan Van Duong, he went crazy. Hitting everyone, arguing. At night—before it happened—at night before his teeth go black, he sleep, yelling, talk in sleep, speak what sounds like Chinese to the villagers. Next day, he's attacking everyone. The driver, the boy, Munny, got his gun and shot Phan Van Duong in the head. Killed him. All the villagers say the same thing. They say, 'The boy saved us. The boy saved us.'"

Nana pursed his lips, looked at Moisey to confirm that he was listening.

"The problem for me is that Phan Van Duong comes from a big family. They control port in Haiphong, very important. You know that?" He dropped his voice to a whisper, "Very important seaport. Important place. And their son get killed in jungle. Killed by Cambodians. You know what kind of problem this is for me? I have to talk to everyone like a peace-keeper. Smooth everything. Very diplomatic. Vietnamese mad, Cambodians scared, Burmese become nervous. You know? Same week."

Nana cast his eyes down at his hands. He seemed to be thinking about what he was going to say next.

"The same week, now I get a call from Sukhontha that he has a telephone conversation with a detective from Royal Thai Police. Moisey, I tell you all of this about the jungle to show you a complicated thing: They have ghosts out there, bring bad luck, get cursed. They have spirits make a man become crazy, teeth turn black. But for you—you don't have those kind of ghosts in Bangkok. You're a farang. Only ghosts you have are the drugs you use, the ice you smoke, make you go crazy. I am honest with you. I think maybe the same ghost attack Phan Van Duong in the jungle. Maybe he smoke too much ice, too. But this little problem you have brings a much bigger problem for me. It makes Sukhontha and his Burmese clients very upset. That detective you had in your house has ties to American DEA officers. When they hear that a farang is able to call Mr. Sukhontha, have him wipe up the problem for you, maybe they become interested in you, maybe they start to wonder, 'Who is this farang who can place a call and get himself out of so much trouble?' Maybe they start to think, 'We should begin to watch this Jewish one, see who he is friends with.'"

Moisey, depressed and petrified, stared at Eugene Nana.

"I told you a long time ago, you must only call Sukhontha in an emergency. Only if you are stopped during a delivery, right? Not if you get in trouble with a Thai boy, not with police detective looking for bribes. How much could they have wanted from you? Why not pay them little bit money?"

The memory of Thong Kon's smile passed through Moisey's mind. "They wanted to look at my computer," he said.

"So? What could they see there? What would you have on your computer? Pornography?" His eyes narrowed; his voice dropped. "You're not saying you have any of our business on your computer, are you?"

"No."

"Then what? So what if they look at your computer? They see that you what? Watch a movie? Maybe pirate a movie? How much trouble would that have made for the group?"

Moisey's mind spun. Why hadn't he planned what he was going to say?

"I didn't like them nosing around," he said. "I wanted them to stop. I thought it would be bad for all of us."

Nana, the two fingers of his right hand supporting his head at the temple, stared at him, blinked. Seconds passed.

"We all have pressures, my friend," he said. "But we put ourselves where we are with the strict understanding that we will not tumble over with the first sign of wind. You know this? You have background in military. You are supposed to be trained to handle stressful situations. If you get stressed, you have to breathe into your diaphragm. You know this?" He took a deep breath to illustrate. "Breathe in deep to calm your nervous system."

"I'm sorry," Moisey said. He bowed his head. "I made a mistake. It won't happen again." He took a deep breath, to show he was learning.

"Sorry is good, but Mr. Sukhontha has decided that you—you personally—cannot continue moving the stuff here. Too dangerous. I tell you in secret: some of the Burmese said you should be killed. I said, 'No, not Segal, he is a good man who made a certain mistake.' I told them, 'He has been working for us for a few years now, never a problem.' They say your association too small. They say these Jewish in Miami take too small of an order. They decide it's not worth it to continue with your group. They said doing work with your group is like throwing peanuts to a lion."

Moisey's forehead began to sweat.

"Picture a shoe factory," said Nana. "Lots of shoes being made, Nike, Adidas, all models. Now picture the factory make shoelaces, and they only sell a few to a certain person. Should they continue? What if person decide to buy more than a few, say thousands of shoelaces? Maybe that start to make sense to the factory. You understand what I'm saying?"

"You'd like us to buy more?"

"They want you to buy more. Not me. I don't care what you do. But the Burmese say maybe it is the way to fix the problem. Your problem."

"I'm not the one who—who . . ."

"You introduced us to them. You are great friends with the one, Mr. Isaak Raskin."

Moisey stayed silent.

"Perhaps he would be willing to make more money to help his friend? Everyone happy. Everyone win."

"How much more?"

"Ten. Ten times more. Same price per unit."

Moisey felt his face turn sour. Nana shrugged.

"I wouldn't know where to begin," Moisey said.

"If I were you, I would begin in Miami."

Three days later, Moisey flew to Miami. A gray depression filled his head and chest during the flight. His mind danced between memories and fantasies of the future. What, he wondered, would happen if he failed? His life in Thailand would be over. Miami felt too close to all of his problems. Maybe he'd resettle in Mexico, or Argentina.

If it were only Isaak he had to convince, it would be one thing. But Semion, little more than a stranger to Moisey, presented more of an issue. They'd had their fun in Bangkok, but even then he could sense a certain kind of arrogance in the man, a stiffness. Perhaps he'd get better results if he told him: *Under no circumstances should you consider increasing the order.*

He'd met Isaak in Haifa when they were both eleven years old. Moisey had been sulking in the shade of a palm tree in the middle of a roundabout, near the Kiryat Yam beach. He lived with his mother, father, and two older brothers in a small beige apartment down the block. Isaak, with two of his sisters in tow, had seen Moisey sitting there and called out, "Beggar, which way to the beach?"

Moisey chased him down the block, but when he caught the boy, Isaak broke out in such carefree laughter that Moisey was forced to forgive him. They all went to the beach together that day. The sisters, rich girls, tan and long, seemed like movie stars, and Isaak, joking constantly, made it easy to be friendly. They hung out together for the rest of the summer.

A year later, their relationship briefly turned romantic—in a teenaged, dry-humping way—but that soon petered out. They remained close through graduation. Moisey often slept at the Raskin house; it seemed like a palace then. Isaak's mother grew Jaffa oranges in the backyard.

Moisey began sniffing glue the summer after they met. A Russian boy, not even Jewish, had shown him how. He and Isaak took ecstasy for the first time the summer after that. He could see the pills in his memory: circles stamped with a Nike swoosh, eggshell white flecked with brown. The pills were speedy, and inspired endless proclamations of undying love. They'd been in Isaak's bedroom; he had set up red lights to make it look like a disco. They had their own private rave in there, the stereo pumping out techno. *I love you, I love you, I love you,* Isaak had said, dancing like a girl.

After graduation, the two men did their military service on different sides of the country. Moisey moved to Bangkok after that. It wasn't until Isaak contacted him about a connection that the two men saw each other again.

By then, sometime around his fifth year in Thailand, he had begun working as a low-level go-between for a group of Israelis and Russians in Trat. They were moving Burmese meth to Australia. When a shipment was ready, he would drive a tour van complete with bikes on top of bike racks up north to a rice plantation in Lampang Province. There he would be given large sacks of rice, which contained smaller sacks of crystal meth. He usually moved around fifty pounds a trip. It was on one of those runs that he first met Eugene Nana.

* * *

Moisey didn't tell Isaak he was coming to Miami. Better to do it in person, he thought. He rented a car and checked into a cheap motel just north of the airport, far away from the beach, the sand, the sun. It wasn't what he was there for. He spent the first two days in his room, watching American television and drinking beer. He told himself he wanted to be well rested when he first saw his friend, but in reality he was simply procrastinating.

He finally called him on the third morning. Isaak didn't pick up, but he called back within minutes.

"Surprise," Moisey said. "I'm in Miami." He told Isaak he had to speak with him. "No, not an emergency," he said, "but issues, yes." Nobody else needed to know he was there, he said.

Isaak knocked on his door forty-five minutes later. Moisey arranged his face into a pained smile and opened his arms to hug him.

"Brother," he said.

"What the fuck?" Isaak said. "What is this?"

Moisey sat him down and told him the whole story. He told him about the boy, the drugs, the cops, all of it. Calling Sukhontha, he said, was one of the stupidest things he'd ever done. Isaak waved that off, but his expression suggested that he knew there was more coming.

"So? So what? So what does it mean?" he asked, sounding calm, almost bored.

Moisey told him about the meeting with Eugene Nana. He explained that the man had demanded they increase their order by ten times.

"My fault, I know," he said. "I am prepared to disappear if that's what you say. I can move away, but I didn't want to make anything worse."

Isaak, apparently thinking the problem through, stayed silent for a long moment. Moisey waited for him to suggest getting a new partner. It would be easy; they could go to China. "Did they threaten you?" he finally asked.

"Nana said members of the group thought I should be, you know, taken out of play."

"Killed?"

"Yes, but—" Moisey waved his hand like the topic was distasteful. "But it's just talk, you know. Stupid tough-guy talk."

"Shit."

"Yes, shit."

"Ten times?" asked Isaak.

"Ten times." He sniffed, breathed, waited. "Ten times, same price per unit." He felt like he'd snuck the last bit in.

Isaak winced. "Semion will never go for that," he said, his voice rising. "We should get a lower price. Simple market rules. It's bullshit. They're pushing us into a corner."

"I know."

"How did you leave it with Nana?"

"I told him I was going to come here and try to sell it to you. He said I should be in touch with Mr. Hong." Moisey tried to read his friend's reaction. "He said Mr. Hong will help with whatever we need."

Isaak rubbed his hands in front of his face like a man blowing on dice. "That's how you do it," he said, pointing. "He'll never say yes to me, or you—but Mr. Hong, maybe." He stared at Moisey.

"You fucked up everything this time," he said, a cold smile on his face. "I hope that Thai boy was fucking worth it."

The next day, following Nana's instructions, Moisey dialed a Miami phone number. An American woman answered the phone by saying, "Lannan, Evans, and Loftus." Moisey asked for Mr. Hong, and was told he could leave a message.

Six minutes later, his cell phone lit up. The same receptionist asked Moisey if he would please meet Mr. Hong outside the Four Seasons Hotel on Brickell Avenue, tomorrow at three in the afternoon. Moisey said he would. She told him a car would be there to pick him up. Moisey said that Isaak Raskin would be accompanying him.

"I will inform Mr. Hong," said the woman.

The following afternoon, Moisey and Isaak stood sweating under the porte cochere of the Four Seasons in downtown Miami. Both men wore sunglasses and rocked back and forth on their feet. At five minutes past three, a shiny black SUV pulled up. The window lowered, and Mr. Hong nodded to the men. It was the first time Moisey had ever seen him. He looked older and gentler than he'd imagined—more an uncle than a fixer. His hair shined as though he'd put Vaseline in it.

The interior of the vehicle was cool and smelled minty. Mr. Hong rode in the front, next to the Chinese driver. He seemed to be in a pleasant mood. They headed north, past palm trees and empty sidewalks.

Moisey introduced himself first, and then, not sure of the exact state of their relationship, asked if Mr. Hong knew Isaak. Mr. Hong turned in his seat, smiled, and said, "Yes,

yes, of course I know Isaak Raskin. Longtime friend. I know everything about him, actually." His eyes turned up for a moment, as though accessing a memory. "Born in Haifa, May twenty-ninth, nineteen eighty-seven. Son of Benny and Daphna. Brother of Nina, Esti, Avraham—and, and, and—David. Oldest brother is Sergey."

Isaak and Moisey remained silent.

"My memory is too strong," said Mr. Hong. He tapped his temple, smiled again. "I have photographic memory. You tell me something, I never forget, remember forever. Too much memory."

Moisey felt sick. The vehicle's interior seemed to shrink.

"I hate my family," Isaak said, his voice perfectly mild. "Do me a favor, don't mention them again unless you plan on killing the entire lot. After you do that, we can go out and drink vodka together, okay?"

"I'm sorry," said Mr. Hong. He dropped his eyes in such a sincere way that Moisey felt genuinely confused. But he needed to push forward.

"Okay, okay," he said. "Enough. We have a problem. I'm sure Nana has explained to you."

Mr. Hong shook his head.

Bullshit, thought Moisey. "I've been sent here," he said, "to try and convince this gentleman and his partner to increase the size of their order."

Mr. Hong shook his head again, as though he didn't know what Moisey was talking about. His face looked curious. *Tell me more,* it seemed to say.

"He feels it's fine to increase the order. Right?" Moisey felt like he was rushing things, but he couldn't slow down. He looked at Isaak, who nodded his head. "Our problem is we don't think Semion will go for it. He's stubborn, you know?"

"I've only had good experiences dealing with him," said Mr. Hong.

"Fine. Look, he's a good man, sure, but set in his ways. What I'm saying—" A cop car with sirens blaring sped toward them from the opposite direction. Moisey watched it go for a moment, then continued. "What I'm saying is that we believe he might be more open to *you* suggesting the increase, rather than us."

"Me?" said Mr. Hong. He looked dubious.

Moisey felt impatient, irritated. He was tired of this man's games. "Do you answer to Eugene Nana?" he asked.

"He's an associate of mine," Mr. Hong said.

"Do you answer to him?"

"Yes."

"Well, this is what he wants."

Mr. Hong thought about it for a moment. "Do you agree with this reading of Mr. Semion's state of mind?" he asked, shifting his focus to Isaak. "Better for me to ask him, than you?"

"Yes," Isaak said.

"Then fine, no problem," said Mr. Hong in a happy voice, as though they'd reached the end of some kind of negotiation. He turned and faced forward again.

"Good," said Moisey. His mouth had gone dry. One piece had fallen into place; the rest could follow. He felt exhaustion weighing him down.

They rode in silence for a minute. Moisey noticed when the driver glanced at him in the rearview mirror. What could he want to see? The face of the man who speaks so freely to his boss? Or the face of a man not long for this earth?

"We have an expression in the business world," said Mr. Hong, turning back to them. "In chaos comes great opportunity." He handed a business card to Isaak. "When you need to contact me, call him," he said, nodding toward his driver.

The next afternoon, Moisey woke from a dreamless nap to loud banging on his door. He was covered in sweat. For the first few seconds, he had no idea where he was: Bangkok? Pattaya? Trat? Then it became clear. The knocking continued. The thought that it might be Semion filled his belly with dread.

"Who is it?" he asked.

It was Isaak. When Moisey opened the door, his friend pushed his way into the room, then pushed Moisey back until he had to sit on the end of the bed. Isaak stood over him staring. Moisey's fear bordered on outright panic.

"Tell me once," said Isaak, holding his finger right in Moisey's face. "Tell me you didn't have anything to do with this."

"With what?"

"With this shit in Semion's room."

"What shit? What?"

"The blood, the girl."

"I have no idea what you're talking about," said Moisey.

Isaak slapped him. It was the second time he'd been slapped that week. He watched, shocked, as Isaak pulled his belt off. He held it up like he was about to whip him with it.

"The girl, the Brazilian girl. Tell me right now, or I will choke you out. I'll fucking kill you."

"I swear," Moisey said. "I have no idea what you're talking about. I don't know anything."

Isaak raised the belt up. "Fuck you," he said. "Tell me what you're doing."

"Nothing. Nothing."

"It's not you?"

"Not me."

"You don't know anything about this?"

"No idea." Moisey was afraid he might start sobbing.

Isaak shook his head, put his belt back on, smoothed his hair. The only light in the room came from beneath the drawn blinds.

"What is it?" asked Moisey. "What happened?"

Isaak told him what he knew. Semion had brought a woman home and woken up with his room covered in blood. He told him about the video from their hallway: the two men, the heavy bag.

"Fucking shit, man," he said when he'd finished explaining. "We've been cursed."

"Mr. Hong?" asked Moisey.

"My first thought. But no, I don't think so. Not their style."

Moisey's exoneration had left him feeling strangely elated. He sat there blinking, imagined unzipping his friend's fly, taking him in his mouth. Isaak had a big dick, he remembered. Everything could be solved if they could just do that. They could quit everything, run away. Sleep, dream.

They spoke with their eyes for a second, but then Isaak seemed to lose faith. "Semion has lost his shit," he said.

Semion, thought Moisey. *Fuck Semion.* He stared up at Isaak, wondered for a moment whether he was capable of orchestrating this whole thing. Anything was possible. "How long has he been with this girl?" he asked.

"Not long. Less than a month."

"So, if not us—" He studied Isaak's face for signs, didn't see any. "If not us, if not Hong, then . . ."

"An opportunist."

"A well-timed opportunist."

"Shit," said Isaak.

"A typhoon and an earthquake in the same week," said Moisey. Nana's story about Cambodian tree spirits passed through his mind. Maybe they really had been cursed. "Shit in hell," he said.

They called Mr. Hong's driver and told them they had to see the man—that an emergency had come up. Mr. Hong arrived at Moisey's motel an hour later.

He came in alone. The scent of expensive cologne followed him in. Isaak told him what they knew, and Mr. Hong, looking either furious or scared, sat on a chair shaking his head. Neither of them asked whether he had anything to do with it. What was he going to say, after all?

It was Mr. Hong who broke the silence. "Women here in Miami, they can be very manipulative," he said.

"So what do we do?" Isaak asked.

Mr. Hong dropped his voice to a whisper. "Friends, you don't want the Burmese to know how vulnerable you are. Please help me do my job. Get this new deal done, and we help you with everything else."

He was pleading with them, Moisey realized.

"Find your friend," Mr. Hong went on. "Mr. Semion. Tell him I'm looking for him. Tell him to come to the club tomorrow night. I will make him an offer. I'll tell him the Burmese insist. I tell him we help him with all this bad stuff. Maybe all this trouble ends up being good thing for us." He pointed at Moisey. "Maybe it makes Semion become more gentle."

He rose from his chair, brushing imaginary crumbs from the front of his pants, and shook hands with both of them. "We get through all this bad time together," he said. "Ten times more, you make ten time more profit. Not so horrible. Money make all the problems go away. It make us smile." Then he left.

"You know what would make Semion smile?" Isaak asked, when they were alone again.

Moisey shook his head.

"Molly," he said. "Molly, Molly, Molly." He motioned like a man sipping tea. "That would turn him into a regular fucking puppy dog. Him and Mr. Hong will be giving each other massages. Fucking hugging. Saying, *I love you. I love you.*"

Moisey spent his time alone after that. The only occasion for leaving the motel was when he went to eat twice a day, and then he'd just drive down the road to a restaurant near the airport. Semion would never think of going to a place like that.

American waitresses served him french fries and hamburgers. He drank Diet Coke out of large red plastic cups. He watched sports on the television. He daydreamed about fucking the Latino busboys.

One waitress, a plump woman in her fifties, asked him if he was Italian.

"I'm from Israel," he said.

"I'm Jewish!" she replied, smiling.

"I know. I can tell, because your name is Hannah," he said, pointing at her nametag. *Do you want to fuck?* he wanted to ask, but he didn't. Instead, he leaned out of his seat and stared at her backside when she went to get him more Coke.

He felt like a refugee. At least in Thailand he knew where he stood. Here, what was he? A man who waited in a room. A fearful, quiet, tired man.

Late that night, after he'd spoken to the waitress, he got a call from Isaak.

"It happened."

"What?"

"They met."

The muffled sound of dance music came through the phone.

"And?"

"Semion left."

"What'd he say?"

"Didn't. Come here, Misha." Isaak, for no known reason, used to call him that.

"Where?"

"To the club."

"Have you lost your fucking mind?"

"I'll tell you something," said Isaak. "No bullshit, everything's going to turn out fine. I know this because—well, because I know it." *Questionable logic*, thought Moisey.

"Don't argue with me," Isaak went on. "I'm smarter than Semion. Smarter than Mr. Hong. Smarter than these Burmese bastards. You know it, right?"

"Sure," said Moisey, but he didn't feel at all reassured. "Call me tomorrow."

"I love you," said Isaak. "Love you, love you, love you."

The next day, unable to spend another moment in the motel, Moisey got in his rental car and headed north, toward Fort Lauderdale. Halfway there, his phone lit up. Isaak, sober now, sounding depressed, told him that Semion had become convinced Mr. Hong was behind everything.

"Maybe he is," said Moisey.

"No, no, no. Not Hong. Trust me, this is amateur shit. They called him—didn't I tell you that? They called Semion and asked for two hundred fifty thousand dollars. They think we're fucking club owners. I told Semion, 'I'll fucking pawn a watch for you, man.' It's bullshit. I said, 'We'll pay, no problem. Fix it; it's done.' I could fucking kill him."

"I have to call you back," Moisey said. He didn't want to listen anymore.

He drove past a harbor filled with white sailboats, surrounded by green trees and black water. *The reality I know is the one I see*, he thought. *I'm in a car, on a freeway. I can see blue sky. I can feel the steering wheel in my hand. The only thing I can control is the present moment, and right now, in this present moment, I am not in trouble. Fucking hell. Breathe.*

A memory from when they were fifteen, or sixteen: Isaak, standing in the doorway of his house, berating him. *None*

of my friends like you. They all say you don't know how to have
fun. You never have anything nice to say. You're not helpful.
You piss everyone off, and nobody wants to hang out with you.
Moisey had walked all the way home, thinking: *I'm fucked.*
My parents are fucked. The world is fucked.

He didn't hear anything over the next few days. Apparently,
he'd been taken out of the loop. He continued his television
watching, his morning calisthenics, his beer drinking, his
drives around Miami. Occasionally a foreign kind of optimism made advances on his mood. Maybe Semion would
come around. They could deal with his little bribery problem. They'd get through it. And then, when it was done, he
could make an exit plan. Start a new life. Move back to Israel,
turn himself into an actor. His face—rough with years of
hard living—looked authentically criminal. He could get the
parts. He could write a memoir. Write a thriller. Screenplays.
He could bartend. A simple life. A chef, if not an actor. Thai
food. A falafel house in Vancouver.

His phone rang.

"I need you to come to my apartment," Isaak said.

"I can't do that," Moisey said. "What if I run into Semion?"

"You won't. Take a taxi. Come now. The doorman knows
you're coming."

Numbly, he took a taxi to Isaak's. He imagined meeting
Semion in the lobby. *Hello, friend! Just passing through town.*
The driver listened to talk radio, but Moisey caught only
every third word: *Agenda . . . spending . . . downward spiral.*
The muscles in his shoulders felt like steel ribbons.

They pulled into a roundabout in front of a large white tower. Moisey had never seen the building before; he sat staring up at it for a moment, and then paid the driver with cash. Inside, a tired-looking young Cuban man in a khaki suit sat behind the front desk. He called up to Isaak's apartment and announced his guest.

"Take the elevator to twenty-eight," the man said, when he'd hung up the phone. "Mr. Raskin is number twenty-eight fourteen."

The fear in Moisey's stomach increased with each passing floor. He had no idea what was waiting for him. Perhaps his partners would greet him with champagne. *We did it! We're done! Ten times more money! Ten times more fun!* Maybe they'd go out to one of their clubs and celebrate.

The building was silent. He walked down a clean, carpeted hallway and rang the bell on Isaak's door.

Isaak's clothes, when the door swung open, registered in Moisey's mind as an expensive beige and pastel blur. He tried to read his friend's face, but it was blank—weary around the eyes, maybe, but free of any other emotions. Moisey stepped into the living room—brightly lit by the sun—and felt immediate disappointment upon seeing Mr. Hong and three other Chinese men sitting there.

"Misha," whispered Isaak. "Sit down. Would you like a drink?"

He did want a drink, but he shook his head. He noticed himself sniffing repeatedly—something he did when he was nervous—and tried to stop. He looked at the four Chinese men, one by one, and then at his friend.

"Over the years," began Isaak, "Semion has proven to be a difficult partner. You know this. He's become stubborn. Intractable. His Russianness—it's real, you know, he's thoroughly fucking Russian. He's really fucked everything up for us."

"Did you pay them?" asked Moisey, trying to steer the conversation in another direction.

A look of annoyance flashed across his friend's face. He waved his hand—a stupid question. "Yes, they've been dealt with," he said. "But we have other problems now. I mean, fuck, Misha, you've brought bad luck with you like a fucking bedouin. Semion has decided he's going to discontinue our relationship with—" He gestured at Mr. Hong. "With them. He's done, he says. He's all decided. It's over."

Moisey felt his eyes squint. He didn't understand why they were having this conversation in front of Mr. Hong.

"Listen to me, Misha," said Isaak, speaking gently. "There are certain things you can't do. We had a deal. Semion made a deal. He promised, if Mr. Hong helped him with his little fucking problem—a problem, I remind you, he brought on himself. And Mr. Hong helped, all right? He took care of it." He dropped his voice and switched to Hebrew: "They fucking killed them, you know that?" He went on in English: "You can't promise things in this world and then change your mind on some whim. You know? Bad for business. It puts us all in danger. Throws the world into chaos."

Moisey felt lightheaded. "So give him time," he said in Hebrew.

"We've run out of time."

"What are you talking about?" Moisey asked, switching back to English.

"Certain lines cannot be crossed," said Isaak.

"So we'll convince him," Moisey said, aware of the desperation coloring his voice. He sniffed again. "You'll go and convince him. We'll go together."

"Not the issue."

"Then what?"

"Semion needs to go," Isaak said.

"Killed?" Moisey asked, in Hebrew again.

Isaak nodded. The Chinese men were staring at them. One of them, the driver from the other day, chewed on his gum as though milking it for lost flavor.

"You can't let them do this," Moisey said in Hebrew. "You're talking like a fucking monster."

"No more Hebrew, man," Isaak said. "Please, it's rude."

"So what? You're going to let them go and kill him?"

"Not them."

"You?" Moisey asked.

"No." Isaak shook his head.

Moisey imagined locking himself in the bathroom, sending a text message to Semion: *Run, right now. Run for your life. These men have lost their fucking minds.* But he didn't even have the man's phone number. And then reality clicked together.

"Me?" he asked.

"It's the only way," said Isaak.

"What the fuck are you talking about?"

"If you don't do it, Mr. Hong has to clean up everything. You understand me? Everything."

Moisey wanted to slap his friend's face. Choke him. Beat him senseless. The man's flat affect was unbearable. He looked at Mr. Hong, who stared back at him. He could feel the other men staring, too. He could feel everyone in the room breathing in and out.

"No, no, no, fucking no, no, no, no," he said.

"We're not asking."

"You've lost your fucking mind," said Moisey, switching back to Hebrew. "You need to tell these men to leave, and we need to find new partners. You need to do it right now. This has become fucking crazy. You understand? It doesn't matter. None of it matters. It's business. Mistakes happen every day, but these men are going to wait. Every time we screw up one little tiny thing, they are going to move in and take another fucking piece. You understand?"

"No, Misha," Isaak said. "If you don't take care of this— today, right now—these men are going to kill me. Okay?" Isaak's eyes filled with tears, but Moisey knew from past experience that his friend could do this at will.

"What do you think we're sitting in here for?" he went on. "You think I invited them up so we could all have a nice little meeting together? Misha, stupid, they have guns. They are going to use them."

"You lying piece of shit," said Moisey in English. He turned to Mr. Hong. "Why me? Why don't you go and fucking kill him?"

Mr. Hong regarded him with apparent sympathy.

"We have two options," said Isaak, gesturing for Moisey's attention. "We can say no to these men and get killed right now. Have our bodies dumped in the middle of the fucking ocean. Or you can do this, take care of our problem, help me show them that you are loyal, that I am loyal, that we can both be trusted. That we can all continue doing work together. I'm fucking begging you, man. You want me to get on my knees? You do it and we move you here; you take Semion's place. My second in command. We reorganize, send someone out to replace you. Continue living, breathing. You fucked up, all right? Not that bad, but you fucked up. Semion, on the other hand, has declared war."

"Is what he's saying true?" asked Moisey, directing his question to Mr. Hong.

"Everything he says is true," Mr. Hong said.

You're both lying, thought Moisey. *It's ludicrous. That phone call I made doesn't matter. Semion changing his mind doesn't matter. None of it matters.* He looked at Isaak. *It's you,* he thought. *It's all you.* Mr. Hong's posture, the way he held himself, none of it looked like a man making commands. No, this was clearly Isaak's plan.

Moisey put his head down. He almost had to laugh. There could have never been any other outcome, ever since Isaak had called out to him as a boy. *Beggar, which way to the beach?* All the way here, to this fucking apartment. *Fine,* he thought. *Fuck it.*

"Give me the gun," he said. "And give me a drink. Whiskey, ice. Give me the gun and let's get this fucking thing over with."

Mr. Hong said something to one of his men, who leaned forward and opened a small gym bag that sat at his feet. Moisey hadn't even noticed it. The man dug something out and brought it to Moisey: a neatly tied bundle, like something from a damn picnic. It was heavier than it looked. Moisey set it on his lap and unwrapped it. Inside was a Glock 23 and a suppressor. He lifted the gun, pulled the slide, found a bullet chambered, popped the clip, and confirmed that it was fully loaded. His heart punched away in his chest like a scared rabbit. Fourteen bullets. He could kill them all right now.

His mind pushed the idea out like bitter poison. He was a coward. No, instead, he would go up there, knock on Semion's door, and tell him he had to leave, right then, that Isaak and Mr. Hong had ordered it. No time to pack, go right now, run for your fucking life. And then he'd leave, too.

Isaak brought him the whiskey. The tumbler—heavy, wet on the outside—was filled nearly to the top with ice and gold liquor. It spilled onto Moisey's hand when he took it. He looked at Isaak, nodded, then held the glass up to the other men and drank. Two of the Chinese men began speaking quietly to each other. *Each of us in our own private hell*, thought Moisey. Isaak and Mr. Hong looked equally wan.

He looked up from his drink and realized that everyone was waiting for him. The glass was half empty now. He sipped again. Mr. Hong took his phone out and began checking messages. Three-quarters gone. He wished he had more. *I'll tell him to run.*

"There are cameras in the hallway," said Isaak. "You have to get into his place before you pull the thing. After that, we'll come up. Get his body out. In five days I'll buy him a plane ticket from his computer, on his credit card. I have a man who will fly under his name, using his passport. They look like fucking brothers. He'll go to Brazil. He'll send e-mails to me from Semion's account, say, *Man, fuck you're missing a great time here. Come meet me.* He'll use his credit cards, and then he'll disappear. I'll report him missing after that. A simple missing-person report. They won't even begin to look. Nobody will miss him."

You planned everything out, you sick fucking bastard, thought Moisey. He sipped the last of his drink, swirled the ice in hopes of making more liquid appear, and then set the glass down on the table. *I'll tell him he has thirty seconds to leave.* He screwed the suppressor on to the gun. His stomach was warm from the whiskey.

"After some amount of time," continued Isaak, "as his business partner, I'll be able to collect some of his assets. The house, the car, I don't know. It's all probate shit. I'll have to check with my lawyer. We'll split it, of course, you and me."

Moisey nodded.

"Hold on," his friend said. He left the room and returned a minute later with two large suitcases. "Carry these. It will make you appear more appropriate."

Moisey stared at the bags. *Absurd, absolutely absurd.* He stood on rubbery knees, sniffed, and walked toward Isaak. They were fancy roller cases, the kind that could move on four wheels in any direction.

"Maybe two is too many?" he said. "I need a free hand, you know?"

"Yeah, right, sure," said Isaak. "Take one, roll it, let him see it. We'll bring the other up. We need something to carry him out."

They were going to cut Semion into pieces, Moisey realized. The final absurdity.

"Good," he said. He considered shaking his friend's hand, but he patted his shoulder instead. He checked the safety on the gun, then slid it into the waistband of his pants. He stepped to a mirror by the door and practiced pulling it out. The suppressor made it ungainly. His reflection showed him as a ghastly man, skinny, pale, dark circles under his eyes. His head looked like a skull.

I'll tell him to run. I'll tell him he has to go, that's it, game over.

He grabbed the suitcase. Mr. Hong rose to his feet. Moisey nodded to him and walked with Isaak to the door.

"I'm sorry," Isaak whispered.

Moisey stared at his pouty bottom lip and marveled at how long it had taken him to discover that his friend was a complete sociopath.

"It's floor thirty-one. He's in thirty-one twenty. We'll come behind you."

Moisey stood alone in the corridor. There was an emergency exit at the end of the hall. He looked behind him and saw one at the far end, also. They could take opposite stairs. He walked toward the lift feeling like he was somehow outside himself. In a daze, he pressed the button to call the elevator. *Thirty-one twenty*, he repeated Semion's room number in his mind.

His mouth was dry. As the doors opened he realized that he had to urinate; the feeling was so strong that for a moment he thought about going back to Isaak's apartment. But instead he pulled the suitcase in behind him and pressed 31. The doors closed and he felt the pull of the rising elevator.

The elevator door opened and he began walking toward the apartment. The fear inside his chest was unlike any he'd felt before. A perfect and complete fear. He stopped in front of Semion's door, staring at the rug in front of it. Someone had placed a rug so that people could wipe their feet. Had Semion done it? The gun pressed the skin under his belly. His ears picked up the low drone of the elevator kicking back to life. *Let it go down to the ground floor*, he thought. But it stopped too soon.

He pressed Semion's doorbell. In his mind, strange fragmented memories: *his mother, a dinner he'd eaten in Thailand, a ferry he'd once taken*. After a moment, the peephole darkened. Moisey forced a smile.

The door opened. Confusion filled Semion's eyes. A white room stood behind him. High ceilings. Blue sky. Clean floors. Semion was backing away, his hands up near his chest. The gun kicked, making a hissing noise. Smoke in the air. Blood pouring through Semion's hands from his throat. Blood coming out like water.

Two more shots. One in the chest, one in the head. The room became quiet. He was already dead.

Part 4

Part 4

Vanya Rodriguez, also known as Anna Monticello, also known as Candy Hall-Garcia, Candy Thompson, and Candy Valentino, was born with the name Jacqueline Rose Infante. In her mind she thought of herself as Jackie Santos. She was born in Brazil but grew up in Newark. She had dropped out of Rutgers after her sophomore year, and not too long after that she had gone to prison: two years at the Bedford Hills Correctional Facility in Westchester County. She had been arrested in Queens holding an ounce of cocaine and nearly a hundred thousand dollars in fake gift cards for Fifth Avenue stores. She was twenty-three years old when she got locked up.

After she got out, she linked up with a group of credit card forgers operating in Dallas and San Francisco. Over the next few years, Jackie Santos developed a small reputation, among certain types, as a woman who could talk a sober man into doing just about anything. She liked running with thieves. The normal world bored her.

The idea to go after Semion Gurevich was brought to her by a man named Tom Roberts. Roberts was an ex-cop, a felon, working as an unlicensed private investigator in San Jose. He could get things done that other PIs couldn't. He was what the Jewish Mafia referred to as a *handy man*. He was good with wires, crowbars, lock picks, GPS devices, guns, baseball bats, all of it.

"All you gotta do is just meet this guy," said Roberts, when they first spoke about it. They were sitting at a back table in a hotel bar just south of the San Francisco airport. The place smelled like a fast-food restaurant. Roberts drank coffee; Jackie sipped a wine spritzer.

"You get to go to Miami for two weeks, all expenses paid. Just get me into his apartment."

"And?"

"A thousand a day," said Roberts. He was a big bald Caucasian. His neck went straight down from his head. He had hairy knuckles and hair coming out of his ears. He looked like a cop. Jackie had a soft spot for him because he'd never tried to sleep with her.

"What do you need me for?" she asked.

"This guy lives in a fancy high-rise," said Roberts. "I'm not gonna be able to just break in. I need a pretty girl like you to help me get in there first."

"Sweetheart, I'm kinda busy right now," she said, opening the negotiation. She was dressed in a white romper and a black satin jacket. She'd shown up with wet hair and red lipstick.

"Harvey said he'd forget that little business if you did me this one."

It would be nice not to owe Harvey anything. He had a claim on eighteen thousand dollars from her after a complicated deal that involved real estate fees in Redwood City. Roberts had her attention.

"Two thousand a day," said Jackie.

"One-five," said Roberts. "I'm only getting three."

"Let me think about it," Jackie said.

They had worked together in the past. Roberts ran a scam for a divorce attorney in San Jose. He would send Jackie into bars to accidentally meet the poor guys who'd become their targets. She'd flirt with the men, get them drunk, and then ask them to drive her to her hotel. On the way, they'd be stopped by one of Roberts's cop friends; the men would be arrested for driving under the influence. The attorney would then use that DUI charge against them in divorce court. It was all about leverage. It paid well.

The Miami job didn't sound that complicated. After calling Harvey Bloom and confirming that he'd clear the debt, Jackie agreed to go. Roberts told her that his client had hired him to set up a wire in the man's house; that was all. She'd meet the guy, seduce him, knock him out with GHB, and open the door.

No matter how hard she pressed, he wouldn't tell her anything about who had hired him, or why this client wanted to listen to Semion Gurevich's private conversations.

They went to Ground Zero on their first night in Miami. Semion wasn't hard to spot; there were photos of him all over the Internet. The man hovered in the VIP section like a Russian oligarch. They identified his partner, too. She even managed a brief flirtatious conversation with him.

"I know how we do this," she said afterward. "You know how a magician will say keep your eyes on the prize—look over here—then, whoopsie, sorry baby, you lost all your money?"

Roberts shook his head. They were sitting in his rental car outside their motel. The windows were down. Jackie's seat was leaned back like a lounge chair.

"Listen," she said. "We come out here so you can put your little microphones in his room, right?" Roberts nodded. "So, it's easy you make him pay some money, too. You understand me?"

Roberts shook his head again.

She explained how she would do it. She'd done it before, she said. You knock a man out, pour blood all over his bed, and then you blackmail him. It's easy. Usually, she did it to married men, but the same principles applied. She said you called it Red Bedding.

Roberts didn't like it. They had a job to do, he said. They couldn't get sidetracked.

She felt like she was talking to a child. She sighed and started over. "Wait, wait, I'm saying—if we scare him, if he's trying to figure out what happened, he doesn't even stop to think if you put a little microphone in his room. See? It makes it even better for you."

Roberts, softening right before her eyes, looked at her.

"He pays us a little something," she continued. "Your boss pays you a little something nice. Two for one. You make the rules about how you do the job, right? You decide what's the best way."

"You want to paint the room with blood?" Roberts said.

"It's easy."

"Human blood?"

"Pig blood, stupid! Look, you knock him out. You take pictures—" With her hand, she mimed taking a photo. "Take a picture of him lying with me. I'm covered in blood. My chest is out, my tits, you know, bloody, cut up and killed. You put the knife in his hand. You put your little microphone in his room. We take the knife. We leave. Then you call him, tell him my body's buried somewhere and unless he wants the police to start asking questions, he pays us our money. He's rich—you could take him for a million, five million. Maybe we just say pay us a quarter million, keep it simple. We split it up. And at the end of the day, you got your little tape player tucked away in his wherever."

"And my client?" Roberts said. "What's he going to think when his recording comes back full of talk about all this shit?"

"What, you don't know how to edit tape? Just snip, snip, cut it out. We split two fifty large. Think about it. That's like a month of good living for me, a year, maybe two years for you!"

Roberts bent his head, scratched his neck. She watched him think it through. When he looked up, his face wore a boyish expression.

"You are the craziest woman in this world," he said.

"That's why you call me," she replied. "You love me."

The only thing he insisted on was that someone else had to pick up the money. "Otherwise it's too risky," he said. "You want word to get back to San Francisco that someone looking like me was in on this? These people know each other." He would bring in two of his partners from California, he said. Two ex-cons from Stockton.

The men were named Danzig and Denver Mike. Roberts had met them at the California Men's Colony, in San Luis Obispo. He'd served thirty months there on a drug case; because of his law enforcement history, he was placed in protective custody. He never told Jackie what the other two men were doing on the protected yard, but she assumed they were either snitches or pedophiles.

They arrived in Miami—already sunburnt—just after Jackie met Semion Gurevich for the first time. The two men spent their days drinking cans of Coors beer and smoking cheap cigarettes outside their motel room, kissing all the time and holding hands. Jackie didn't have a problem with that, but she still thought there was something vulgar about them. They were big and ugly, like Roberts. The three of them looked like unemployed construction workers. When they got drunk, their eyes turned red. Roberts acted differently around them. Jackie wondered if he'd slept with them in prison.

Danzig and Denver Mike rented a white pickup truck. On the day everything went down, they were supposed to meet Jackie, drop the money, take their cut—twenty-five thousand, 10 percent—drive to Fort Lauderdale, and fly back to California. Easy breezy. All Roberts had to do was call Semion Gurevich and monitor the exchange.

Jackie waited for it all to happen in a motel she'd moved to that morning. At ten twenty-five, Danzig and Denver Mike arrived with the money. They were amped up. Denver Mike was yelling the second he came in.

"You should have seen the look on his face!" he shouted. " 'This ain't shit to me.' Like he's Jay-Z rich. 'I'm God and you're shit.' "

"Give me the money!" shouted Danzig, apparently reenacting the moment. "We should've taken his ass for more than that. We could've, too."

The men smelled strongly of beer, cigarettes, chemicals. They were drunk. The energy coming off both of them made Jackie's skin crawl. She stood up straight and tried to make herself appear larger than she was. Where was Roberts? She took the bag from Danzig, dumped it on the bed, and began sorting through the bills, looking for tracking devices.

"Y'all said, 'Raise up!'" said Danzig. He grabbed the other man, pulled him closer, and searched his face. It was the kind of gesture meant to imply that they were actively stamping this memory into their consciousness—a greedy, drunken gesture. Jackie had known men like them her entire life. She scooped the money back into the bag and checked the clock on the dresser. Where was Roberts?

Later, when Jackie looked back on this moment, she wondered if she'd missed something, some warning. Had shadows passed over the blinds? Had the floorboards on the balcony creaked?

She placed the bag of money on the ground. Danzig and Denver Mike, their tanned, stubbled faces still nearly touching, continued to talk incessantly. And then, without warning, the door burst open and men charged in. Jackie thought they were FBI agents at first, because of their dark clothes; she automatically dropped to the ground and covered her head. She didn't see guns, but she heard suppressed shots, deep and violent: *thoop, thoop, thoop, thoop.* Danzig and Denver Mike fell to the ground. The floor shook. Black blood pooled out from their heads. Jackie's world shrank down to a singular feeling—the desire to stay alive.

The next thing she knew she was being lifted by gloved hands. It was only then that she looked at the men's faces and saw they were all Asian.

They swung her around violently, pushed her against a wall, and duct-taped her hands behind her back. A pistol pressed against her temple. The men didn't speak much; when they did, it was in Chinese. She watched as one of them searched the floor for shell casings. Another man searched the dead men's clothes, finding a cell phone and scrolling through it, then taking pictures of its screen with his own phone. He took pictures of the dead men's faces, too. He had to lift Danzig's head and turn it to get the right angle. His phone made a camera clicking noise every time he snapped a picture. Then they dragged the bodies to the closet, smearing blood along the way. Jackie watched them struggle to stuff the men in, one on top of the other. The closet door wouldn't shut, and the man left it open.

One of the other men had pulled back the blinds and was looking out at the parking lot. His hand tapped against his thigh, like a nervous tic. Finally, he said something, and the others pushed Jackie toward the door, placing a jacket over her taped hands and marching her across the hot parking lot to a waiting SUV. There was a group of black men right across the street from her, but she was too scared to yell.

It was bright outside, and she squinted against the light. Tears streamed down her face. A driver stepped out of the vehicle, went to the cargo door, and opened it. She was forced to sit down on the bumper, and one of the men lifted her legs and pushed her in. The door slammed shut. She had two seconds alone, and then all four doors opened and the men piled in.

A man leaned back and wrapped silver duct tape around her head and mouth. Her shoulders ached from the pull of her hands behind her back. The tape didn't taste like anything, but it was wrapped so tight it made her drool. The car began to move.

She should have never been in that motel room, she thought—*stupid, amateur shit*. Why hadn't they killed her right then? The idea that they were going to try to sell her into some kind of sexual slavery passed through her mind. Her fear felt locked and permanent.

When they reached Ground Zero, they sat in the SUV for almost ten minutes. One of the men said something that must've been a joke, and the rest laughed. She willed herself to cry harder. She was incredibly thirsty, and it struck her as absurd that she might die wanting a drink. The men talked among themselves in hushed voices. She knew they were waiting for Semion to show up. When she closed her eyes she heard the peaceful drone of cars passing on the street.

Semion parked his white Range Rover—the same one she'd ridden in—right next to them. One of the Chinese men hopped out and greeted him. She could see their midsections but not their heads. The dull bass sound of male voices reached her ears, but she couldn't make out the words. She tried to concentrate. Somewhere in her mind, in the midst of all the chaos, she realized that the way to play Semion was to push against him. It wasn't going to work to claim love. It wasn't going to work to apologize. He needed to be abused. He was the type of man who could be swayed by abuse.

You're angry, she told herself, preparing like an actress. *You're furious. He fucked you. He forced you. Fuck him. Fuck him. Fuck him.*

The door opened. The light blinded her. The fear of death filled her up and she opened her mouth and let the words come out. The look on Semion's face—a disgraced, privileged face—inspired even more venom. *Fuck him. Fuck you. Fuck the world.*

He let her go.

Jackie ran directly from the parking lot to a gas station about six blocks away. Her lungs burned. She called Roberts from inside the station—surrounded by Day-Glo-colored snack food—and told him to pick her up. He showed up ten minutes later.

"What the fuck happened?" he asked.

"Where the hell were you?"

"I got lost!"

She stared at him for a moment. The man looked panicked. He needed a shave. His car smelled like cigarettes. She closed her eyes briefly, then opened them and fastened her seat belt. Roberts had turned in his seat and was looking out the back window. Jackie wanted to cry again, but she controlled herself. They pulled out onto the street.

"They're dead," she said. "They're dead, they're fucking killed."

"What happened?" Roberts said again. "Who killed them?"

She told him about the Chinese men, told him how they'd brought her to Semion and how he'd let her go.

"Why would he do that?"

"Because he got his money back." She watched Roberts to see how he took that news, then added, "And because he's soft."

"Lordy, fucking lord," Roberts said, banging on the steering wheel as he drove. "I swear, so help me, this is your shit! You did this! This is you! They are not paying me enough for this one, not even fucking close! Did you get your fingerprints all over the room? What did you tell them?"

She counted back from ten to zero, the way they'd taught her in anger-management class.

"I don't ever touch anything," she said, looking at Roberts like he was crazy. "And I said nothing. They had my mouth all tied up with tape. Semion showed up, took the shit off my mouth, and I said, 'Please let me go.' That's it."

"And the money?"

"It's gone. They took it."

Roberts stayed silent.

"Gone," she repeated. "For real." She closed her eyes for a moment, and violent images flooded in. Black blood on the floor, dead eyes looking at her. *This too will pass*, she told herself. *Bring calmness into this car. Compassion, empathy, calmness. Next time, make your own goddamn team—women only.*

Somewhere near Pinewood, they pulled into another gas station. Roberts searched her body for tracking devices. He touched her stomach, her legs; she felt disgusted, but she tucked in her bottom lip and nodded like he was smart, counting the days until she could be rid of him.

"They got the money?" he asked again, leaning back and looking at her. "Just like that?" He gave her a cop stare. The man seemed to believe he could tell—by simply looking at her—whether she was lying. They stood there for a moment. The parking lot radiated heat; a heavyset woman in a yellow tube top stared at them as she got into her car. Roberts's eyes filled with tears.

He's feeling bad because his friends just died, Jackie told herself. *Put yourself in his shoes. Hold his hand and walk with him.*

"We're right back where we started," she said. "You've still got the room wired up. He'll talk soon enough."

Roberts's shoulders slumped. "We gotta go move their fucking bodies," he said.

They went to a hardware store. Roberts bought a few lengths of zinc-plated chain, locks, two tarps, two rolls of duct tape, a pair of forty-five-pound dumbbells, a box cutter, some trash bags, bleach, scrub brushes, a huge pack of paper towels.

The motel room's door was unlocked. The yellow DO NOT DISTURB sign that Jackie had put on the doorknob was still there. Roberts pulled the bodies out of the closet; they had already started to stiffen with rigor mortis. The room smelled like feces. Roberts's face bunched up like he was crying, but no tears came out. Jackie felt strangely calm.

They laid the men on sheets, rolled them up like burritos, and wrapped them in tape. Roberts sat down on the bed, took out his phone, and used Google Maps to pick out a spot to dump the bodies. "We'll do it there," he said, pointing at a huge stretch of green parkland, east of Miami.

"What about all the blood?" asked Jackie.

Roberts brought out the box cutter. Bent over and breathing heavily, he cut out the stained parts of the carpet. Jackie watched him and wondered if he was beginning to crack. The room was a mess, and now the carpetless patches of the floor looked like a map of some lake district with a long canal where the men had been dragged. The blood hadn't leaked through at least, except in the closet, where Roberts worked it over with wet towels until it was just a brown smear. He put the ruined carpet and towels into trash bags.

It wasn't even 6:00 p.m. The sun was still up. They moved the truck first, pulling up right next to the door. Jackie's eyes settled on the small red stains that had already started to spread like hives on the sheets as they lifted the impossibly heavy bundles and set them onto tarps. After rolling them in the tarps, and watching out the window and waiting for the area to clear of people, they carried their bundles to the truck. Even with the heat, Roberts stood there shaking like he was cold. Huge dark shadows of sweat circled his underarms. He'd gone pale.

"I'll drive the truck. You follow me," he said.

"Stay the speed limit," Jackie said. "Try to calm down a little."

They took Highway 41 toward Naples. Jackie saw signs for airboat rides, gator parks, Buffalo Tigers. They stopped a few times along the way so Roberts could throw the men's wallets, their phone, their gun, and the bag of bloody carpet into different parts of the swamp. Finally, he chose a spot for the bodies.

It was swampland on both sides of the road. Cars kept driving past as they dragged the bodies away from the truck. Roberts looped a length of chain around each man, and then locked each bundle to one of the dumbbells. He wrapped his arms around the first man—Jackie thought it was Danzig—and walked straight out into the swamp with his shoes and pants on. About fifteen feet in, he dropped his burden. He returned and did the same with Denver Mike. The water wasn't deep; the blue from the tarps shined out of the black water like two blue flags. *It doesn't matter*, thought Jackie. *The gators will eat them.*

"Do you want to say anything?" she asked.

Roberts turned and looked at her like she was crazy. "No," he said. Then, lurching forward, he seemed to change his mind. "Jesus take these men back into your paradise," he said. "They were both good men and they're coming home."

"Amen," said Jackie.

The motel they'd been staying in for the past week, the Sunny Palms Inn, was nine miles north of the one the two men had been killed in. When they finally got back to it, after their trip to the Everglades, Jackie crushed two Xanax on the dresser, cut the powder into six small lines, and sniffed the first one through a rolled-up twenty-dollar bill. *Peace and calm in my heart.* Roberts had bought a bottle of rum and a six-pack of Coca-Cola. He turned on the television and found the local news. They waited for a report about a motel in Overtown, but it never came. Roberts was sullen and silent. He kept refilling his soft plastic cup with rum.

Jackie, letting the Xanax do its work, realized that she'd been so focused on Semion Gurevich that she hadn't really stopped to consider the larger situation. Her eyes shifted from the television to Roberts. She watched his torso grow and shrink with each breath. He had refused to tell her who'd hired him. *You don't know them*, was all he'd said.

She thought about something Denver Mike had let slip two nights ago, drunk in their motel room: "Someone wants to skip a step in the damn fish chain." There was a kind of logic to the statement. Semion Gurevich was clearly selling; she'd known that much right away. She'd known plenty of drug dealers. Her best guess was that whoever had hired Roberts was either buying dope from Semion or planning on stealing it. A lot of money had been spent on this little trip.

She sat there and studied Roberts and tried to decide the best way to proceed. *If you want something, ask for the opposite*, she told herself. She took a deep breath.

"I need to leave tomorrow," she said. She looked at her cell phone like it showed a message urging her to come home.

Roberts glanced at her but didn't say anything.

"You paid Harvey?" she asked.

"Yep," said Roberts.

"Good. So you'll give me a ride to the airport tomorrow?"

"We're not quite done here yet," he said.

Perfect, she thought. "Not done what?" she asked.

"I still might need you for a thing or two," he said.

He looked at her and their eyes locked. She stared at him like she wanted to let him know that it was okay for him to want her; she was there for him. He looked away. Nothing. *Gay*, she thought. *Definitively gay. Gay but lonely.*

"How long until I go?" she asked.

"You know you don't have to use that accent with me," he said.

"I like my accent. It makes me feel exotic," she said. "Fuck, you bore me sometimes."

"Look, you owe Harvey. Harvey owes me. I'm collecting my debt. I don't know what the hell I'm gonna need you for, but I might. I like to have my options open."

She apologized in a way meant to make him feel guilty.

"People saw me with them," said Roberts, changing the subject. "When their faces get up on the news, people are gonna say, 'There was the other dude, too, the bald one. There were three of them.'"

"And the beautiful girl, don't forget her," said Jackie.

"You sure you saw those Chinese dudes take pictures of their phone?" asked Roberts. "Taking pictures of all their calls? Their texts?"

She nodded her head. The image of the man turning Danzig's head popped into her mind.

"Who do you think those two were calling all week long?"

"They called you."

"They called me. Yes, they called me the minute they got here. Shit, they probably called me almost every day they were in town. 'Where's the liquor store?' 'Where's the Mexican restaurant?' 'Can you bring me some cigarettes?' So what do you think them Chinese boys wanted to do with that phone?"

"I don't know." said Jackie, playing dumb. "I know you don't have a phone under your real name, though."

"That's not the point," said Roberts. "The point is they know *something* about me. Someone gets curious enough, you never know what they can figure out with a ten-digit phone number. There are a million ways to pin a—"

Right then the phone he was holding began to vibrate. Roberts's face went white. "I told you," he said. The phone continued to vibrate. Jackie got off the bed and walked toward him. They both stared at the screen: *Unknown Caller*. She could smell rum coming off his breath. When the phone went quiet she put a hand on his shoulder.

"Don't worry, baby."

"Goddamn—I should've given it to you," said Roberts. "They already know you're in this, you get on—"

The phone began to vibrate again. "Answer it," he said, pushing the thing toward her.

She took it from him. "Hello?" she said.

A woman's accented voice on the other end answered: "Who's this?"

Jackie stepped away from Roberts, moving toward the window as though to look outside. "Can I help you?" she said.

"Put him on," said the woman's voice.

Roberts appeared to be in a state of panic. His head shook back and forth when Jackie looked at him.

"He will only speak to you," she said, "if he knows who is calling."

"Tell him it's Gloria."

"Last name?"

"Last name is Cunt. C-U-N-T. Put him on the phone."

Jackie smiled. She liked this woman. "Right away," she said.

She touched the speaker icon on his phone before she handed it to Roberts. "Gloria," she whispered.

"Hello?" he said.

"Everything good?" came the voice over the speaker.

Roberts winced, looked at the phone, switched it off speaker, and spoke into it. "Yeah, it's fine. Who? Nah, just a prostitute I'm going to beat with my belt when I hang up."

Jackie pointed at her own chest, raised her eyebrows. Roberts waved her away.

"Yeah, yeah, yeah. We'll see," he said. "I'll let you know. It might take some time, okay? Patience. Long game. Of course." He hung up.

"You didn't tell her about me?" Jackie asked.

"Why would I do that?"

"Is she your wife?" Jackie knew she wasn't, but sometimes she asked questions just to see how a man responded.

"Shit," he said, wiping at his forehead. He checked the phone, made sure it was off, and shook his head.

That was all she needed to see. She flopped back on the bed, feeling like she was finally on to something good.

"Are you lonely?" she asked Roberts the next night. "Not in a sexual way, but in a normal lonely kind of way?"

He stared at her. They were sitting in the motel room, Roberts at the desk, Jackie on the bed.

"Come on," he said, waving her away. "I don't want to do all this shit."

"I'm saying, just in a friendly way. I get lonely all the time, you know? I need to see people, be around people, just for dancing, talking. Otherwise, blah, what am I doing? Why am I here?" She paused for a moment, then asked, "Why are you keeping me here?"

"Because—and I'll tell you one more time—you owe Harvey. Harvey owes me. So, in a sense—and I'm not saying this as an antifeminist thing, so don't get all—but in a sense, I own you. And I may need you. I may very well still need your ass for something."

"I could fly back if you need me."

"Yeah, right."

The truth was she could leave at any time. She had her identification cards, credit cards. She came and went as she pleased, though she'd spent most of her days sunbathing by the kidney-shaped pool just outside the room. The worst that could happen was that Harvey would claim her debt wasn't erased.

Roberts had just returned from Semion Gurevich's apartment building. He had parked outside, just as he had the night before, and culled bursts of data sent via radio wave from the transmitters they'd hidden in the apartment's smoke detectors. It took him less than an hour to download a day's worth of recorded audio. The pictures Jackie had taken on her very first visit had allowed Roberts to plan exactly where he was going to place his little bugs. They were, as he liked to say, top-of-the-line NSA-level devices. Denver Mike had accompanied him to do the job. Danzig had stayed out front and watched the building, ready to call at the first sign of trouble. Roberts and Denver Mike had entered the building through the front door. Both men wore baseball hats, and kept their heads down. They checked in at the front desk. The doorman called up to Semion's apartment, and Jackie— Semion of course was unconscious at that point—had told the doorman to send them up. On the way in, Denver Mike carried a large bag that held two two-liter soda bottles that had been filled with pig's blood; on the way out, the bag—sagging heavily between the two men—carried Jackie.

Now, back in the motel room, Roberts was done talking. He turned back to his computer, raised his headphones, and continued to listen to the day's recordings. Sound waves played across his screen like electrocardiographs of Semion Gurevich's heart.

"What's he saying?" Jackie asked.

"It's just TV," said Roberts. "The man watches a lot of fucking TV."

It wasn't until the next night that Roberts sat up a little straighter. Jackie turned her eyes from the television to watch him rewind and listen to something again. He did this a few more times, then opened up a spreadsheet so he could fill in a few little boxes: TIME STAMP, SOURCE, CONTENT OF CONVERSATION. Semion had finally spoken.

"What is it?" she asked.

He turned, looked at her, clearly excited. "It's what God put me on this planet to do."

He stood up, unplugged the computer, and brought it into the bathroom with him. It was the first time he'd ever done that. She heard him begin to pee, loudly.

She reached into her pocket, pulled out a paper bindle, and poured the contents—three crushed Xanax—into his can of Coke. It wasn't a lot, but he didn't pop pills and she figured it would do the job. She swirled the can. He stopped peeing, started, stopped again. The toilet flushed.

"Go walk around the block," he said, when he'd come back out. "I gotta make a private call."

She left, not even trying to stay by the door to listen. It didn't matter. She'd get what she wanted in the next few hours.

"I'll take you to the airport tomorrow," he said when she came back.

"Finally," she said. "No lie, I'm gonna miss this trip. Best two-week vacation I've had."

"Twelve days," he said, bending over and taking out a double stack of hundred-dollar bills. "Eighteen thousand."

"What about the travel days?"

"I didn't say I'd pay you for that," he said, anger creeping into his voice.

"Shit, you take me here twelve days. I do all the work, get you into his house. You never even could've gotten in there without me!" She paused, waited a beat, continued. "I fucked him, you know that? You think I wanted to? I do all the heavy lifting, all the hard work. I still only make fifty cents to your dollar."

He didn't reply. She took the money and started counting it, pretending to be both upset with him and concerned with her payment. Roberts went back to the desk and sat down. She watched him sip his drink and refill it. Then he put his headphones back on.

He stayed awake longer than she expected. It was ten minutes after two in the morning when he slumped over on the bed, his computer sliding off his belly. She pulled his shoes off, studying his face, watching his chest rise and fall. Satisfied, she eased the computer from his hands. She set it next to him and sat watching him for another full minute. Then she brought his laptop to the bathroom and entered the passcode she'd caught him typing the day before.

On the desktop were the photos she'd taken of Semion's apartment. She clicked on one of them and was briefly transported back to that night. Then she closed it and clicked on the other files until she found the spreadsheet. Her eyes scanned the time stamps. She stepped back into the main room, checked on Roberts, confirmed he was still sleeping, and grabbed the headphones off the desk.

Back in the bathroom, she opened the latest audio file. After forwarding through most of it, she listened and heard what sounded like a physical confrontation. She could hear what sounded like a muffled gunshot, a loud thud, someone falling to the ground. Groaning. Two more suppressed shots. Then other men coming into the room. A voice said, "Move his fucking body to the shower. Moisey, Moisey, Moisey. No, no, come here Misha. Shh . . ." She heard Chinese words, things being moved around, and then the first voice again, speaking in Hebrew. She realized it must have been Isaak.

"So what?" he said. "It's fucking two hundred kilos, man! The bitch in San Francisco will buy the whole thing." Another voice said something, and Isaak replied, "So, you move here and we fucking split it eighty-twenty. You'll be rich. Retire in two years. Misha, don't be so fucking negative."

She felt sick. Had they just killed Semion Gurevich? She pictured kissing him, hugging him, his warm body, his breath in her ear. A drop of sweat dripped from her armpit and slid down her side. He was alive, and now he's dead. She almost cried, and then immediately stopped.

She stepped back into the bedroom and set the computer next to Roberts. He continued to sleep. She grabbed his phone from the desk, took it to the bathroom, swiped it open, unlocked it, and looked at his call history. He had called Gloria that evening, just after he'd asked Jackie to take a walk. Jackie entered the number into her own phone and saved it. *You never know what you can figure out with a ten-digit phone number.*

She looked through his text messages next. There were none from Gloria. Most of the messages were between him and Danzig, boring little remarks: *My phones dying. Bring lighter. Bullshit. Ha ahaa ahahaha. Denver says yo become a muslim.* It gave her a strange feeling to read the messages of a dead man. She thought of Semion again, saw his face in her mind, and pushed the memory out.

After cleaning the screen with her shirt, she flushed the toilet, and stepped back into the bedroom. Roberts didn't stir. She plugged his phone back in.

Then she lay on her own bed, took out her phone, and googled: *How much is one dose of MDMA.* It was 80 milligrams. She googled: *How many milligrams in a pound.* Her phone revealed the number: 453,592. She divided that by 80: 5,670 doses in a pound. She googled: *How many pounds in 200 kilograms.* She multiplied the answer by 5,670 and got 2,500,045 doses. She multiplied that by $20 and got $50,000,895.

Breathing slowly, she rechecked her math. It was correct. A shipment of Molly with a street value of fifty million dollars was coming to San Francisco.

Part 5

Part 3

Arthur Meehan, prisoner number E17073 at the Deuel Vocational Institution in Tracy, California, had set up the deal between Gloria Ocampo and Semion Gurevich. Gloria and Arthur had sold drugs and stolen goods to each other for almost twenty-five years; their relationship was professional, friendly, and mutually wary.

Arthur first mentioned this deal to Gloria on a call placed from prison, made on a smuggled phone. Someone, he explained, had approached him looking to unload a regular shipment of ecstasy. "Regular, meaning every damn month. Big, too. Thought of you right away." Gloria was suspicious, but she was willing to listen.

"Here's the thing," Arthur said. "You're gonna buy it from these Israelis, and then you're gonna sell it to another dude I know, Shadrack Pullman. You never heard of him?" At that time, she hadn't. She jotted his name down on a piece of paper.

Her eyes, like she was looking for a snake, moved back and forth over the floor in front of her as she listened. The deal, as Arthur explained it, didn't make sense. Why wasn't he setting his Israelis up directly with this other man, Shadrack?

"They'd never do a deal with a man like him," he said, when she questioned him. "They need a professional—someone like you." The phone cut out for a second. He had a way of speaking that made him sound country, like a cowboy.

"And you?" she asked. "What do you expect out of all of this?"

"Ten points on what Shadrack pays you."

"Have you lost your mind?" she said. "Ten percent? This is what we call a finder's-fee deal." She tapped on her knee with her hand.

"Look, you're gonna get this shit from these Jewish fellas, you're gonna hold it for a night, two nights, and then you're gonna flip it to Shadrack. You could damn near double the price. They're gonna want to do this every damn month. Shit, you should be happy I'm not asking for twenty-five. I'm handing you this thing wrapped up like a damn Christmas tree."

And how, asked Gloria, was she supposed to know that Shadrack Pullman wouldn't snitch if he got pulled in? She didn't know what kind of spine the man had. She didn't know anything about him.

"That's what I'm trying to tell you," said Arthur. "That's why you gotta pay me them points. The dude's gonna understand that you're working for *me*. He's gonna understand that speaking your name is as dangerous as speaking mine. And trust me, he knows how dangerous that is. The boy served time with me. He knows it like a cock knows the sunrise." Gloria stayed silent. "It's natural law," he added.

It sounded intriguing, she had to admit. Get it, hold it, double the price. Arthur told her to call the Israelis' man in

San Francisco, David Eban, to set up a meeting. He gave her a number and explained that when Eban answered the phone, she had to say, *Hello, I got your number from Uri.* He would ask, *And how is Uri?* And she had to answer, *Sadly, he's sick.*

"You gotta say it exactly like that," said Arthur. "He'll give you an address after that."

They had dinner at Harris's steak house. She left the meeting feeling impressed by Eban's intelligence—certainly a step up from the normal crowd. Over the next few years, she bought every shipment of MDMA that his partners brought to her. Each month, after the deal went down, she'd have one of her sons drop Arthur's 10 percent at a woman's house in the Sunset District. Depending on the particulars of the deal, Arthur's cut usually worked out to somewhere between forty-five and sixty thousand dollars.

It was a good arrangement. Everyone was making money. And it all worked smoothly until, without good reason, Arthur pushed himself further into the equation.

He would call occasionally to see how things were going. It was standard stuff: the man wanted to keep abreast of the situation. She would tell him every time that things were fine. On one of their calls, though, about a month before Raymond Gaspar showed up in San Francisco, Gloria mentioned that Shadrack was becoming a little eccentric. She didn't ask for help, didn't say it was a problem; she just mentioned it.

A few days later, Arthur called back. He told her he was going to send someone to check in on them. He said his man was going to straighten Shadrack right out.

"No, no need for that," said Gloria. "All I'm saying is that the man is strange. I don't need your help."

"The boy's just gonna look in on y'all, smooth things out," said Arthur. Gloria could hear the sound of prisoners shouting in the background.

She took a moment to formulate what she was going to say. This was the last thing she wanted. Finally, as firmly as possible, she spoke. "No, Arthur. We don't need him."

"He's a good old boy," Arthur said. "He'll be there in three weeks."

Gloria hung up the phone and sat staring at it. She knew what this meant. Wars didn't always start with cursing and screaming. They didn't always start with bullets flying. Sometimes they started calmly. *He's a good old boy. He'll be there in three weeks.*

He was preparing to move on her. It was obvious. He wanted to control the whole thing.

The next day she called Tom Roberts. She'd already used him a year earlier to figure out who David Eban was working for. Roberts broke in and bugged the man's Oakland apartment, followed him everywhere he went, dug through his trash, poked around on his computer, read his e-mail, and did God knows what else until he had it settled: David Eban's connection was a man named Semion Gurevich, a club owner. Gloria had looked at pictures of Semion on the Internet. He didn't look like a gangster, even in his flashy suits. He looked soft and sad.

Now she decided it was the perfect time to hear what Semion had to say for himself. Not that she would be calling him directly. But soon, if she was lucky, she'd be listening to him unwittingly telling her exactly what Arthur's plans were. Even if he did nothing more than mention Arthur's name, that in itself would tell her something.

She told Roberts she'd pay four thousand dollars a day, and sent him to Miami to bug Semion's apartment.

Gloria was sitting in her living room watching television when Roberts called.

"The shit has hit the fan," he said.

"Tell me." She raised the remote control and muted her celebrity dancing show.

"I swear to fucking God, so help me, it sounds like someone went into your boy's apartment and he had a—um—he had some kind of serious accident." Roberts always assumed his calls were being recorded. He spoke accordingly.

"What happened?" she asked. She shut her eyes so she could listen more closely.

"Your boy had an accident. I'll tell you more in person." His excitement made her feel annoyed. He sounded like a child. He dropped his voice to a lower register and continued.

"There's going to be a sale coming your way, too. It sounds like you could get ten times as many cases of wine for your party. At least two hundred—"

"Tom, do me a favor, please—listen—" She sounded out her words like a special education teacher explaining a complicated theory to a student. "Put the message in a folder, and I'll check it tomorrow. All this talk about wine—I'm not in a mood for wine, okay, sweetheart? Thank you." *Putang tanga*, she cursed him in her mind. Did he actually think she wanted his help interpreting things?

Later, when she listened to the audio he'd uploaded, she felt sick to her stomach. It was disgusting to hear someone get killed, to hear his gasps. Her ears perked up when they called her a bitch, though. *I am a bitch*, she thought. *The kind of bitch that has a microphone in your home. The kind of bitch that hears what you say.*

She let her mind process it all: Semion Gurevich was dead. He was dead and the Israelis were going to continue moving their drugs, only now they would be sending ten times more. Arthur's man, she felt certain, was coming precisely because of this increase. *Insulting*, she thought. *Send someone, then. Send someone and see what happens.*

Two days later, David Eban called and asked to set up a meeting. They went to Harris's, as always. Eban had lost weight and grown his hair out since the last time she'd seen him. His clothes sparkled. He looked wealthy. He kissed her on both cheeks when she came in. A few minutes later, he leaned forward and asked, "Do you want to buy more stuff?"

She acted confused.

"Ten times more," he said. "Between four and five hundred pounds." He seemed nervous, almost desperate. Gloria pretended to be surprised. She played it out like an actress, shaking her head, pursing her lips, then told him she'd have to think about it. But before the meal ended, she said, "I'll do it. We'll do it. It's on."

He told her the price. She didn't fight him on it. They shook hands across the table. Eban looked very pleased. They ordered another drink to celebrate.

"We'll be rich," he whispered.

Two days after that, she called Shadrack Pullman and told him to come to her office on Mission Street.

On the corner of Mission and Twenty-Third was a Laundromat. A stairway in the back led to a locked door. A camera pointed down at any callers. Twelve electronic poker machines stood inside, almost always occupied by Filipino senior citizens. The cost to play was a dollar a hand. The machines took credit cards.

In the back of that room, a second stairway led to another locked door, monitored by another security camera. Shadrack Pullman had never been invited to visit Gloria there before. He wondered if he'd done something wrong.

The door swung open before he reached it. A young Filipino man, wearing jeans and a sweater that made him look like a student, nodded and gestured for him to come up. When Shadrack passed through the threshold, the young man said, "Hands up," and motioned for him to put his hands on the wall. Shadrack did as he was told, and the man patted him down.

"Let me hold on to your phone," said the man.

Shadrack handed it over.

"Sorry, homey," the young man whispered as he slipped the phone into his pocket. Then he led Shadrack down a linoleum-floored hallway to an office.

Gloria Ocampo sat behind a plain wooden desk, facing the door. She looked like a lawyer in her glasses, beaded necklace, and suit. A stack of manila files sat on the desk, and a pair of file cabinets stood against the wall to Shadrack's left. The room was warm and smelled like cardboard. Shadrack stood blinking in the doorway.

Gloria looked up and smiled. "Pullman," she said. "You never visit anymore!"

He had never visited her at all. When she wanted to speak to him, or vice versa, she picked him up, drove him around the block, and dropped him back off. Until a few hours earlier, he hadn't even known she had an office in San Francisco.

She rose from the desk, walked over to him, and took his hands in her own. They stood facing each other like dancers. Shadrack's forehead became warm. He wasn't used to dealing with people in the light of day, and he certainly wasn't used to holding hands with Gloria and looking her in the face.

"Tell me everything," she said.

"Nothing to say. Everything's good. Shit, you know." He shook his head, gently freed his hands.

"Sit, sit, sit." She pointed at a chair.

Shadrack—after smoothing his pants and wiping his nose with his knuckles—sat. "You had me all scared, calling me in," he said. "I thought you were about to yell at me for something."

"Why would I yell at you?" asked Gloria, sitting back down behind her desk.

"Nah, just like yelling at me to change something."

"Well, now, see"—she pointed at him, raised her eyebrows —"you're not so wrong there. You're not so dumb as people say." Her accent made her sentences sound percussive. "Maybe you're smarter than they imagine." She smiled at him, lifted her chin. "So, tell me then, Shadrack, in an ideal world, what would I like to change?"

She'd raised the price last year. If she tried to increase it again, he'd have to argue. He didn't want to do that. He shook his head.

"Stop being so nervous, man," she said. "This is a friendly call. You're all"—she imitated a man holding his fists up, clenching her arms and shoulders, tightening her face like a child—"you're all tense. Relax."

Shadrack took a deep breath. He tried to relax.

"So tell me for real," she said, smacking her lips, "*For real, for real,* as my boys say, what would you change, if you were me? Not you. Me."

An idea occurred to Shadrack. He didn't like it. He sure as hell wasn't about to utter it. He reminded himself, as he had many times before, that the best way to deal with this woman was to play dumb.

"I don't know," he said, smiling. "I really don't. I'm clueless here. Everything's cool, you know. I wouldn't wanna guess in terms of what you would or wouldn't wanna do." He raised an arm, let it drop. "I trust you."

Gloria took her glasses off and rubbed the area between her eyes. Bass noise from the speakers of a passing car reached the third-floor window: *boom-boooom-boom-boooom.* Shadrack waited.

"How did we meet?" Gloria asked.

"How did *we* meet?"

"I'm asking you, how did we meet?"

"Arthur hooked us up." He couldn't avoid saying it any longer: *Arthur.*

"So?" she asked.

Shadrack stayed silent.

"I have an offer for you," said Gloria. "You're acting too scared to speak, so I'm going to make it simple, explain everything, and afterward, you can say yes, I like it, or no, I don't." She sat looking at him for a moment, and then continued. "Arthur is sending someone to look in on us. This man is supposed to arrive soon. I don't know when, but soon. Three times I said to Arthur: 'Don't send a man.' And three times he insisted. So what does it mean?" Gloria's gaze went from Shadrack's eyes to his lips, and then back up. The space between her own eyes furrowed sympathetically, as though she was about to deliver a painful prognosis. "It means he wants to replace you. I've known him for almost thirty years. I know how he thinks, and right now, he's sitting there locked up in his little cell, thinking: *My ten percent is not enough. I need the whole thing.*"

Shadrack shook his head involuntarily.

"He told me that rumors of your eccentricity are reaching him in Tracy," Gloria said. "I said, 'No, Shadrack is fine. We do business every month. He's reliable.' He tells me: 'I just want my boy to take a look at him.' I tell him again: 'No, no need, don't send anyone.' He says, 'I'm sending someone to help you deal with fucking Shadrack.' He wants to make a move."

"So maybe he wants to replace you," said Shadrack. His mouth had gone dry.

A hint of anger moved across Gloria's face, then transformed into a look of slight amusement. *A silly idea*, it seemed to say. She shook her head.

"I'll ask him," said Shadrack, trying to project calmness into his voice.

"Do that if you want," she said. "You're a free man in a free country, but I wouldn't if I were you." She rested her elbows on the desk and watched his reaction.

Her words sounded like a warning. Shadrack felt anger spread through his body. He wiped his forehead and cursed.

"No, no, calm down," she said. "Listen to me. My father used to tell me it's easier to walk in the dark if you close your eyes than it is to do it with your eyes open. You know what that means?" Shadrack shook his head. "It means that if you admit that you're blind, you end up taking the appropriate steps. Get it?"

Shadrack still didn't understand. Apparently sensing this, she changed tack. In a soothing voice, she asked whether they could agree that Arthur sending someone was a bad thing.

"Sure," said Shadrack. He flicked his hand up as though chasing a fly and nodded again. "But let me ask you a question," he said, pointing at her. "If he sends someone out, how do I know this dude's not going to push me out right away? Throw me on my ass?"

"You don't," said Gloria. "Nobody does. You never do, right? But I've made it clear to Arthur, I've told him again and again, that any act of aggression against you will be considered an act against me. Against my organization."

Shadrack didn't know whether to believe this or not. He warned himself not to feel flattered. *Listen to what she says*, he told himself. *Take it in, but don't give anything back.* He studied her face: she looked perfectly unbothered.

"One must take normal steps to protect oneself," said Gloria. She put her hands behind her head, elbows out, and leaned back. "If a man comes to your house, you check if he has a gun. If he has a gun, you turn him away. Do you have a gun? Maybe you'd be safer if you did. Look, at the end of the day, he's only sending one man, not an army. But you're playing with sharks now. You're not in Humboldt County anymore." She dropped her voice all the way down to a whisper. "We are about to be moving ten times more. It's a lot of shit. Arthur's not going to come in shooting. He's not going to come in and kill you. He's sending this man—probe, poke, sniff—see what he finds out, see if he can find an advantage, and then, once he knows, then he'll make his move."

Shadrack watched her, wondering what advantage she was pushing for.

She went on. "If Arthur wants to send someone to look in on us, under the false pretense that you and I"—she waved her hands back and forth in front of her as though drying her fingernails, pointed at him, then set them down gently on the desk—"that you and I have a problem with each other, then here is what I propose: instead of denying any beef, we should exaggerate it." She raised her eyebrows. He nodded. She continued, "Fine, we don't get along. We play this man—this rude interloper—off each other. Keep him engaged in petty conflicts." Shadrack's face showed concern, but she waved him off. "I have ways of handling men. Let me worry about that. But as soon as he arrives, we start *handling* him: give him drugs, keep him awake, don't let him sleep. We keep him busy, running this way, that way, and then—only then, when he's ready—we really begin to play him."

Shadrack sat silently, studying her. Her face remained serious, but underneath it, in her eyes, Shadrack could see that she enjoyed this stuff. It made her feel high. She loved it.

"Listen to me," she said. "If Arthur wants to put his nose in our business, then it's time for him to go. This ten percent deal is no good. Who pays for it? You do! No, no, no, no good. But you can't just push a man like Arthur out." She raised her hands from the desk, rubbed them together. "Let me ask you a question. What if the man that Arthur sent decided to rip us off?"

"Why would he do that?"

"I'm saying, what if it looked like he did? Couldn't we say, then: 'Sorry, Mr. Big Dick, but no more points, 'cause your man stole from us?'"

"And how the hell you gonna make it look like that?"

She squinted. "You make him do things that a man preparing a rip-off would do. Make him get a fake ID. Make him buy a plane ticket to Mexico. Make him buy guns. I don't know. Make him stop communicating with Arthur. Make him tell his family to move to a safe place. But finally, most importantly, the both of us—two separate camps—we both tell Arthur that his man stole our package. And even more to the point, if the Israelis have a problem with us pushing Arthur out, then we now have a reason. We have good cause. We can show them why we did it."

"So where would that leave me, exactly?" Shadrack asked. He couldn't hide his anger. "You want me to play Arthur? Next thing I know there'd be a contract on my ass! I'd wake up in the morning and find some Aryan Brothers sitting in my bedroom with condoms on their dicks and knives in their hands. Shit! You got no idea what you're talking about. *Cut Arthur out?* Nobody gonna cut Arthur out."

"Calm down," said Gloria. "Nothing happens to you. You're just being you. Normal you. Crazy Shadrack. Doing LSD, changing your cash into jewelry. Wearing dirty clothes. Not showering. Everything you're already doing. He can't kill you for that."

"And what about the man he sends?"

Gloria held her right hand up in the shape of a gun, dropped her thumb, and made a popping noise with her mouth. "Buried. Bottom of the bay. Never heard from again. He flew to Mexico with our shit. He's gone."

They sat staring at each other for a long moment.

"And so what the fuck am I gonna do? You want me acting all crazy? I'm not a damn actor."

"All you have to do is blame everything on me. Just blame me. Use all that anger that you feel in your heart, right this second, and push it on me. Ice cold, you can curse me up and down. Don't worry. I'll take care of it."

"Nah," said Shadrack, shaking his head. "I'm sorry. I gotta take a pass on this one." He put his hands on his knees as though preparing to stand.

"That's fine," said Gloria. "No hard feelings. But that means that you and me, we're done. I wash my hands of your dirty scent forever. I can't sell you anything. Deal over. No ten times, no nothing. You can go fuck yourself. Maybe you can go back to growing marijuana in Eureka. It'll make it easier for me. I'll just give your spot to Arthur's man." She sat there breathing hard. Her face darkened.

"You are one coldhearted lady. You know that?" he said. She smiled.

Four days later, Arthur called Gloria to give her final notice that his man was coming.

"His name's Raymond Gaspar," Arthur said. "He'll be there in less than two weeks. He's done some good work for me. He's my partner. You understand?" She could read the threat between the lines. "He's a good kid. Smart. I want you to welcome him with open arms. You can trust him. He'll help you deal with Shadrack."

Gloria thought about telling him, one last time, not to send anyone. But he'd already been warned. The fact that Arthur was sending the man right before the first big shipment had all but proven her case for her. He was making a move; she was sure of it.

Jackie Santos began watching Gloria as soon as she returned to San Francisco. The woman wasn't hard to find. She owned five different homes in the Bay Area, but she lived in a modest two-story house in Daly City.

One of Jackie's occasional boyfriends, a man named Johnson Lake, was a war vet. He'd been with the Special Forces in Afghanistan; he had that time memorialized above his heart with a tattoo that read: THE QUIET PROFESSIONALS. He had been honorably discharged for medical reasons after being arrested in Kabul carrying a pound of heroin. He avoided prison by making a single phone call to an associate at the

CIA. The associate had shown up within the hour and had the whole misunderstanding cleared up within the day. Johnson Lake returned to California with a beard and a nasty heroin habit. He told Jackie all of this in bed the first night they met, two years before her trip to Miami.

When Jackie presented him with the hypotheticals of the Gloria job, he said he could put together a team of three other soldiers in exchange for 50 percent of the take. It was painful, but she agreed to it.

She spent the next few weeks tracking Gloria. She watched the woman from her car, following her from place to place. She stared at doors and waited for them to open. It was a time characterized both by dullness and a desperate hunger. Jackie wanted to pull things off so badly that it felt like a physical craving. But what was the plan?

The truth was she didn't know. She would wait and watch, and see if an opportunity presented itself. For fifty million dollars' worth of Molly, it seemed reasonable enough.

On the twenty-third day of her surveillance, at 7:52 p.m., Gloria left her office and got into the minivan that normally drove her home. Jackie was prepared to follow the van south, to Daly City, but instead it circled around and headed in the opposite direction, toward downtown. It was almost two hours later than Gloria's normal drive home, and that, coupled with the change in direction, made Jackie's pulse quicken. This is what she wanted to see: change, variance.

She followed the van down Mission Street, staying a few cars behind. At Nineteenth, the driver pulled a U-turn, passed a parking spot, and backed into it. Jackie continued driving, and then double-parked. She turned in her seat just in time to see Gloria and the driver get out of their vehicle and buzz the front entrance of the Prita Hotel.

Jackie found a parking spot on Eighteenth, fixed her hair in the mirror, applied red lipstick, and walked toward the Prita. A black guy trying to sell her drugs said, "Wassup, mama? Outfits, outfits, outfits. I got two-for-ones." She ignored him. At the Prita, she buzzed the bell and ascended to the second door. It looked to her like a third world jail. Jackie pressed the second buzzer. Behind the front desk, a bulletproof box with a ticket slot on the bottom, sat an Indian woman. The smell of Indian food filled the air.

"How much for a room?" Jackie asked.

The female clerk stretched her neck to see Jackie. "Thirty-five," she said without smiling.

A guest sign-in sheet sat on the other side of the glass. Jackie could read it from where she stood. Gloria had signed in to visit someone named R. Gaspar, in room 32.

"Who's in thirty-two?" asked Jackie. "Is that Robert Gaspar?"

"We don't give out information," said the woman, shaking her head.

Jackie took out forty dollars from her back pocket, held it up for the woman to see, and then slid it through the slot. "There's a man named Gaspar that used to stalk me," she said. "I don't want to stay with him if it's the same one. He's dangerous."

The woman got out of her seat and took the forty dollars. "His name's Raymond Gaspar," she said.

"What's his date of birth?" asked Jackie.

The woman stood there. Jackie slipped another twenty through the slot. "He might be my stalker's brother," said Jackie. "Come on, woman to woman."

The woman looked through a box of notecards on the desk. "March twenty-second, nineteen eighty," she said.

After warning the woman not to mention anything, for her own safety, Jackie thanked her and left.

Later that night, she looked Raymond up on the Internet. A private investigator database that Roberts had installed on her computer revealed that the man had a criminal record, but it didn't give any details. She switched to the California Department of Corrections Inmate Locator Site and entered his name. He had been released from prison just that week. An almost narcotic feeling of excitement filled Jackie's chest.

She called in Johnson Lake for another set of eyes. She began following Raymond Gaspar, while one of Lake's men stayed on Gloria. She followed Raymond to Shadrack's house on Colby Street, and followed the two of them to the house near Dolores Park. After seeing a few other people enter the party, she joined a group and went in. She tried to listen as Raymond spoke to the people near the fire. The man was clearly high on something. When he kicked over a glass of wine, she helped clean the floor. The next day, she had Lake put a man on Shadrack, as well.

At night, when she went home to rest for a few hours, she had trouble sleeping. Her excitement felt like an infection. They were getting close. The shipment was coming. But that excitement had to be filtered through the drudgery of twenty-four-hour surveillance, and a near constant state of anxiety. But she couldn't stop. She learned to pee into a bottle—not an easy thing for a woman. She brought her meals for the day with her each morning. Her back ached from sitting so much. It was hard to stay awake. The days started to blend together.

She arrived on Gloria's block at 7:15 a.m. The man she was relieving, Johnson Lake's man, was parked three houses in front of her. He tapped his brake twice to signal his departure before driving off. Gloria typically left at twenty minutes past eight, and things proceeded as usual that morning. The tan minivan was parked in the driveway, as it always was. The driver came out first; he sat there alone for a while, maybe three minutes, with the engine running. Finally, Gloria emerged and stepped into the van. The driver backed out of the driveway and pulled away.

The moment Jackie turned her car on, she sensed something was wrong. It was like a vague premonition, something in the air. She sat there for a moment and considered whether she should follow them as planned or whether, today, she should just let them go. The van was disappearing around the corner in front of her. She counted to three and made up her mind.

When she rounded the corner, she was surprised to see the van sitting there, stopped in the middle of the street. Jackie stopped twenty yards behind it. Another car stopped behind her a moment later.

Nobody honked. They all just sat there.

Jackie watched as the door of the van popped open. The driver stepped out and began walking toward her. She still could have driven forward then, swung hard onto the sidewalk and made her way around them, but she didn't want to show her hand yet. It was a suburban Bay Area street; it wasn't illegal to be there. She decided to sit tight and feign innocence. She breathed in deeply and arranged her face into a look of friendly confusion.

The man wasn't Gloria's normal driver. Jackie had seen him coming and going over the last few weeks; he looked to be nearly sixty. He was skinny, and wore sunglasses. His cheeks were pockmarked. His pants were silky, and he walked with a friendly gait. Jackie looked in the rearview mirror and saw that a young Asian man sat waiting in the car behind her. Gloria's driver had reached her door. She lowered her window a few inches, smiled, and asked if she could help him.

The man returned her smile. As he did, the reverse lights on the rear of the van lit up. It was backing toward her. Now her car was truly pinned in. Her eyes went back to the man at her window.

"What's up?" she asked.

The man reached out and tried to open her door but it was locked. Jackie, in a panic, rolled her window up. The man removed his sunglasses and hung them from the top button of his shirt. Then he put both hands against the windshield and lowered his face to it. It was the kind of gesture a joking grandfather might perform for a child, but the effect was not the same. He smiled, and she saw that one of his front teeth was capped in gold.

She could ram the van, she thought, but she told herself that she could still act her way out of this. She held both hands up near her head in confusion.

"Open it," the man said. He produced a black pistol and tapped her window with it. It made a horrible sound, cold and hard: *tap, tap, tap.*

Everything blurred from there. The man, after looking all around to confirm they were unobserved, began screwing a silencer on to his gun. When he was done, he pointed it toward her head. She unlocked the door.

"What the hell is going on?" she asked, when he'd pulled it open. "What'd I do?"

"You're not police?" asked the man. He had a Filipino accent. His face looked genuinely concerned. He held the gun loose at his side now.

"No, I'm—what? I'm driving to work."

"Ah—and your work involves what?"

"I work at a school," Jackie said. "I'm a teacher."

The man used the gun to point at the watch on his left wrist.

"It's a little late to be teaching, right? Teachers go to school at seven thirty. It's after eight thirty already."

"I don't know who you think—" She willed authority into her voice. "It's not acceptable to go around and . . ."

"I've never met a teacher who follows a woman for days on end."

Jackie's mind went blank. "No?" she said.

He bent down so that his face was close to hers. The scent of cigarettes, coffee, and the soap on his skin drifted into her car. "I'm going to sit down in that seat," he said. He pointed at the passenger seat with his gun. "I'm sure it's a little mistake, a simple misunderstanding. You can explain everything, and then we'll have you on your way, back to your classroom. Please, don't do anything stupid." With that he closed her door and walked around the back of her vehicle.

She watched him in her rearview, and then turned and watched him approach the passenger side. She could still lay on the horn, ram the cars. But she didn't do anything. She couldn't. He opened the door and sat down.

"Good," he said. He leaned toward her and pressed the horn gently. The car behind them backed up.

"Drive back that way," he said.

"I have no idea what you think is happening," she said.

"It's fine—nothing—back up, back up," he said.

She had to turn halfway in her seat so she could see. The man with the gun stayed facing forward, a dreadful look hung on his face. As the car reversed, she spoke slowly, sounding out each syllable to emphasize her innocence: "I don't know who you think I am. Please, I'm begging you. I wasn't trying to follow you. If it seemed like I was, I apologize." She used her American accent. She sounded like a girl born and raised in California.

"Back in there," the man said, pointing at a driveway. "Back into it and then turn around. I'm sure it's fine. I guarantee you, no problem." He pointed his gun at the van in front of them. "But she wants to talk to you before the police are called. You know? Normal business. Go." He pointed toward Gloria's house.

Jackie, unable to stop her hands from shaking, steered the car back toward the house. Her chest clamped shut with fear.

"Please pull into this driveway," said the man.

Jackie turned into Gloria's driveway, the same one she'd been watching for weeks. The car that had been behind her parked on the street. The tan minivan pulled behind Jackie, boxing her in. Gloria sat in the driver's seat.

The man next to Jackie rubbed his forehead as though he had a headache. Jackie looked at his gun, imagined snatching it out of his hand, but couldn't bring herself to try. The front door of Gloria's home sprung open and a young man dressed like he'd been asleep came out. He was talking on a cordless phone. He walked right up to Jackie's window and looked in at her. He spoke Tagalog; Jackie couldn't understand him. She looked at her rearview mirror and saw Gloria speaking into a cell phone. They were talking to each other.

"This is so stupid," said Jackie. She shook her head and held her palms up.

"I know," said the man with the gun. His expression made him seem as annoyed as she was.

"I'm going to be late, and I'm fucking pissed," said Jackie. She banged on the steering wheel with the heel of her hand.

The man standing outside ended his phone call. He leaned down and studied Jackie's face for a moment, as though trying to recall if he'd ever seen her before.

"I have no clue what you want," she said, speaking loudly through the closed window. "This is insane." She ratcheted up her anger. "I'm going to call the police, I'm going to sue each and every one of you for false imprisonment, and I'm going to get really fucking pissed off if you don't let me go. You hear me?" She sounded genuinely aggrieved.

The man outside her window straightened up and looked around at the neighboring houses. He opened Jackie's door and motioned for her to get out. Jackie didn't move. The man in the passenger seat pulled her keys from the ignition and dropped them into her purse.

"Please. No sound. Silence. No talking," he said. He put his hand on her shoulder and pushed her out of the car. The man in the driveway had been joined by the other driver. They held their hands toward the front door of the house.

"Please," said the one in pajamas.

Jackie turned and looked at Gloria. The woman was watching everything from inside the minivan; the expression on her face remained flat. It appeared her thoughts were elsewhere. Jackie again considered screaming, but fear of being hit, or worse, kept her quiet. The street was empty. She walked toward the front door.

"This is beyond unacceptable," she said. "It's fucking bullshit. My father is a top attorney in San Francisco. Do you understand? Lawyer!"

"Please," the young driver said again.

The one in pajamas hurried ahead of them and held the door open. Jackie stepped into the house. The place smelled, not unpleasantly, like chicken porridge. The man with the gun pushed Jackie gently into the living room. Pictures of young children hung from the walls. She registered a bookshelf, a liquor cabinet. A doomed feeling spread over her. A moment later, Gloria stepped into the room.

"Hello," the older woman said. She said something in Tagalog after that, and the man with the gun frisked Jackie. He searched her roughly, untucking her shirt, pulling it up, and rubbing her back and belly. He circled her waistband with his fingers. She pulled away from him.

"This is fucking bullshit," she said, turning toward Gloria. "Ma'am, I don't know what you think—I have no—this—" She breathed in deeply. "Please, I'm sorry. I have no idea what you think happened."

Gloria waved for her to be quiet. The young driver walked into the room carrying Jackie's purse. He dumped its contents onto the table. Jackie heard loose change falling, heard her keys fall out. "Give me that!" she yelled. She started walking toward the man with the purse, but the one with the gun grabbed her arm.

"Jesus," she said. "What the fuck?"

"Shut up!" said Gloria.

The man at the table found her license and brought it to Gloria. Gloria took it and read the name aloud: "Candy Hall-Garcia." She said something about *Candy* in Tagalog and the men chuckled.

"You can't do this," said Jackie. "It's kidnapping. You could be in so much trouble. California does not—"

"Final warning," said Gloria. "Shut up. No speaking until spoken to."

The man searching through her purse handed Gloria her phone.

"Password?" Gloria said.

"I'm not—"

"Beat her until she says it," said Gloria.

The pockmarked man lifted his fist like he was going to hit her.

"Okay, okay, fine, Jesus: One-nine-eight-five."

She remembered too late that she'd been exchanging text messages with Johnson Lake. They'd used Gloria's name.

They'd texted about Raymond and Shadrack and John. A dark clarity settled over her. Gloria stood silently reading from the phone for a very long time.

The expression on her face, when she finally looked up, suggested icy hatred. She spoke a long sentence in Tagalog, and one of the men disappeared down a flight of stairs into the basement.

"Sit," said Gloria, pointing at the couch. Jackie sat.

"Move her car into the garage," Gloria said.

"I can pay you," said Jackie.

"The next time she speaks, I want you to break one of her fingers," said Gloria. "This one." She pointed at her own fourth finger. "Snap it."

She set a wooden chair in front of Jackie and sat down, pressing her hands together in front of her face like she was praying. The man with the gun stood by silently. Jackie, no longer able to maintain eye contact, glanced at Gloria every few seconds. The other woman didn't look away. She stared and stared.

Tears trailed down Jackie's face. She sniffled, quietly. The sound of a dryer tumbling clothes could be heard in a distant room. Finally, breaking the silence, the young man downstairs called up, "Okay!"

Gloria leaned back. She exhaled loudly, clapped her hands once, and pointed at the stereo. "Turn it on," she said.

The man in pajamas walked to the stereo and turned it on. The sound of a loud commercial filled the room. Gloria shook her head, and he changed the station. She shook her head again. When he found a station playing hopeful Christian rock, she nodded.

"Turn it up," she said. He did. "Louder," she said.

He made it very loud. The music blared from the speakers: *He will walk with you. He will sing with you. He will dance with you. He will battle for you.*

Jackie began sobbing quietly.

"Get up," said Gloria.

Jackie stood up and shook her head. "I told the police. They know I'm here."

Gloria stood and stepped closer, so that their faces were inches apart. "I told you I was going to break your finger if you talked," she said. "You're acting very stupid." She stared into Jackie's eyes. "Come on," she said.

The man with the gun grabbed Jackie by the shoulders. He was stronger than he looked. When they got to the stairs, he guided her down. She didn't resist. The music blared.

At the bottom of the stairs, the floor became gray concrete. The man pushed Jackie through a doorway into a large, fluorescent-lit basement. Random furniture cluttered the space. Boxes filled with toys and books sat on the floor. The other driver stood near the center of the room, where a metal beam stretched from the floor to the ceiling. A chair had been placed in front of the beam; on the ground, spread under the chair, was a painter's plastic drop cloth.

The young man held his hand out to the chair. "Please," he said.

A wave of uncontrollable crying swept over Jackie. She heaved for breath.

"Sit, sit, sit," said the man with the gun.

She was guided to the chair. The young man took a green garden hose and began wrapping it around her torso. He yanked on the hose and pulled it tight, then tied it behind her. It forced Jackie to sit straight.

Gloria spoke in Tagalog, and the older driver pulled his belt off. He stepped toward Jackie and used it to tie her head to the beam, so that the back of her skull pressed against the metal.

"Please," she said. "Please." The man tied the belt tight.

"I'm going to ask you one time," said Gloria. "Who you are with?"

"I'm not with anyone," Jackie said.

Gloria spoke in Tagalog and one of the men walked to the far side of the basement. He disappeared from Jackie's view. She heard him rummaging around in what sounded like a metal box. Muffled Christian music could be heard from upstairs. When the man reappeared, he carried small pruning shears. He handed them to Gloria. She stepped toward Jackie and snapped the shears open and closed in front of her face. They made an awful metallic cutting noise: *schink-schink-schink.*

"No," said Jackie. "Okay. I'm done playing."

"She's done playing," said Gloria, turning toward the man with the gun. Jackie's eyes went to him. He looked genuinely scared. Her own fear ratcheted up even further.

Gloria reached toward Jackie's face with the pruning shears and tapped her gently on the nose. She smiled coldly. "Final chance," she said.

"I'm on my own," said Jackie, crying. "I've brought in three other men. They work for me. They're not here, but we've been watching you, watching all of you—Shadrack, Raymond Gaspar, everyone. It's all stupid. So stupid. I'm sorry. I promise—" She breathed in deeply. "I promise it will never happen again."

"These are the men you've been exchanging text messages with?"

"Yes."

"And what is it you are looking for?"

"I'm trying to steal your shit," said Jackie. "It was stupid. I'm sorry."

"She's sorry," said Gloria.

Jackie looked at the man with the gun. He nodded at her, as though in encouragement.

"And how did you come to know about this shit you want to steal?" Gloria said.

"Roberts," Jackie said, pausing for a moment to cry. "Roberts. He brought me to Miami to help get him into an apartment. He didn't tell me about you, but I stole his phone. I looked on his computer. It's me. It's all me. Seriously, I've never done anything this stupid."

"Ah! Tom Roberts," said Gloria. "We spoke once on the telephone, didn't we?"

"Yes," said Jackie.

"I see," said Gloria. She nodded, cleaned her top teeth with her tongue. "Roberts. Call him," she said to one of the young men. "Tell him to come here. Tell him we have an emergency."

Gloria bent down near Jackie's face. "See? Honesty and respect, that's all we ask. We can't move forward if we don't learn how to be good to each other. Right?"

Jackie tried to nod.

"Can I get you some water?"

She nodded again, as much as she could.

When the water came, the woman poured it into her mouth. Then she patted her head and left her alone with the man with the gun. He sat down on a heavy armchair, pulled out his cell phone, and began playing a game. The stereo upstairs went silent. Jackie strained her ears, but besides occasional footsteps and muffled voices, there was nothing.

Her eyes grew heavy, and she let them close. The quiet beeping of the man's phone filled her mind.

At some point the Christian music came back. When she opened her eyes, Gloria was stepping into the basement. She was followed by the two young men and Tom Roberts.

Roberts's face changed when he saw Jackie: his mouth dropped open, and his head shook. Apparently, he hadn't expected to find her there.

"No, no, what is this?" he said, turning toward Gloria.

"You tell me," she said.

"What the fuck is this?" he said again, and then he turned to Jackie and asked the question with more anger. "Jackie, what the fuck have you done?"

"Your friend here has been following me," Gloria said.

"Oh, no, no, no—I didn't have anything to do with that," he said. Jackie stared at him. The man was panicking. His face was deformed and ugly with rage. He pointed at her. "I didn't know you were—what the fuck have you done? What'd she do?" He turned back to Gloria.

"That's it," said Gloria. "That's all we know."

Roberts looked back at Jackie. "You stupid bitch, you have no idea how much trouble you've gotten yourself into this time. What were you thinking?" He turned away again.

"I don't know anything about this girl," he said, raising his hands. He looked around wildly at the other men in the room. "Nothing. You're on your own on this one, Jackie. Fuck! Do whatever you need to do to her," he said, looking back at Gloria.

Gloria smiled thinly. She nodded at the younger driver. He stepped toward Roberts and held out a black handgun.

"Take care of it," said Gloria. "Show us you have nothing to do with it."

Roberts stood holding the gun for a moment. His shoulders slumped.

"No," Jackie said. "No, please." She tried to rock against the hose and belt, but they held tight. "Please," she said. "I can do so much for you. I can—"

Gloria put her finger to her mouth and hushed her. Jackie felt a strange sense of resolve take hold. She was stuck. This was it. The end.

Roberts's face looked somehow broken. His mouth frowned unnaturally. He muttered something as he approached her, maybe a prayer. He lifted the gun and pressed it against her temple.

"Oh my God, Jackie, I'm sorry," he said.

Jackie closed her eyes. A thousand sirens blared in her mind. She heard the sound of a click. Nothing happened. She opened her eyes. Roberts squeezed the trigger again. *Click.* The gun bumped against her head. He squeezed it again. *Click.*

"You need to have bullets in your gun," said Gloria.

The young man next to her held up a single brass bullet between his finger and thumb. The wave of panic that Jackie had been riding crashed. Language returned. She prayed: *Oh God, if you help me on this one, just this one, I will forever be your servant. Oh, Jesus Christ in heaven. Allah. Jesus. Buddha. Mom. Help me.*

The young man beckoned to Roberts with the bullet. Roberts, defeated, went to him. The young man took the gun, turned his back for a second, turned back, and pointed the gun at Roberts's head. Roberts stood there with his shoulders slumped. His back was to Jackie; she couldn't see his face.

The young man pulled the trigger. The gun clicked again. Gloria's men laughed. Roberts's body quaked.

"I wouldn't waste a bullet on you," Gloria said. "You're an imbecile, but if your disgusting white body was shitting blood on my basement floor you wouldn't be able to pay me back the money I gave you for your little Miami vacation. Sixty thousand, plus expenses. Look at me." He turned and looked at her. "You have forty-eight hours to bring that money back to me. Get out. Get the fuck out of here before I change my mind."

Roberts turned toward Jackie. His face showed pure animal rage, but it was shame, not rage, that he was feeling. He'd tried to kill her and failed. Every moment from his boyhood through right now, all of it, had been a failure. He wasn't going to go to hell. He was already in it.

"Go," said Gloria.

Roberts walked upstairs. The two young men followed him. The Christian music grew louder for a moment as they passed through the door.

Gloria walked to Jackie and untied the belt around her head. She brushed the hair out of her face. Then she put a hand on her shoulder, leaned down, and whispered: "Okay? Just us, now. No more playing around. No more games. You've seen me. You know my face. You've been following me. You know who I am." She stood staring at Jackie for a long time. "Tell me, it's you and four men and no one else?"

"That's right," said Jackie.

"And these men don't know that you're here with me right now?"

"No."

"And you hired the men? They work for you?"

"Yes."

"Do you sleep with the men?"

"No."

"They'll follow what you say?"

"Yes."

"Tell me about these four men," said Gloria. "Tell me everything about them."

Two days later, Raymond Gaspar was shot and killed in Hercules.

Gloria's young driver pulled the trigger. Shadrack shut his eyes when it happened.

He had gotten to the house an hour before anybody else. He carried in 5.6 million dollars in two separate bags, which he hid in the closet of one of the bedrooms. He set the plastic on the floor just like Gloria had instructed. Even as he did it, it hadn't seemed real. He kept telling himself that there would be some way out of it, that the killing would be called off.

The house didn't have any furniture. After Shadrack spread out the plastic, he walked around the place, looking at himself in the bathroom mirror and checking the refrigerator. It was empty. He lay down on his back on the living room floor. He stared at the ceiling and waited for everyone else to arrive.

The Filipinos got there first. Two of them came in together, the older one with the pockmarks and the younger driver. They smelled like they'd been smoking cigarettes. The driver had his gun out already and was screwing a silencer on to it. Both men were breathing heavily, like they'd run from the car.

"Where we doing it?" asked the young one. He seemed amped up. Shadrack pointed him toward the back room. He didn't know the men's names, and he didn't want to. They scared him.

John and Raymond arrived a few minutes later, right on schedule. The look on Raymond's face when he entered the house nearly broke Shadrack's heart. It was pale, sad, doomed, and weary. He looked like he knew exactly what was coming.

Shadrack had been around death before: he'd seen people stabbed and killed in Eureka; he'd had friends overdose on heroin. But he'd never been this close to it; he'd never been so much a part of bringing it about. The house seemed to shake for a moment when the gun went off.

Dark red blood pumped from the hole in Raymond's head onto the plastic sheet. His eyes stayed open, one arm bent up near his chest.

"Jesus, Lord forgive us," said Shadrack. He looked at John, who stood shaking his head. He looked like he was fighting back tears. The house, quiet as it was, seemed filled with noise.

The young man who'd shot Raymond bent down and poked at his body. "He's gone," he said. He checked Raymond's pockets, pulling out his phone, some money, and his license. He looked at the ID and tossed it to Shadrack. Raymond's face, in the picture, had a hopeful look. Then the young man found the key and the piece of paper that Gloria had given to Raymond, and held them out to Shadrack, too.

"Here," he said.

Shadrack was afraid to come close. The man must have sensed it. He straightened up and brought the key and the paper to him.

"The money's in the other bedroom," said Shadrack. He looked at the piece of paper. Handwritten on it was an address on Lemon Street, in Vallejo. The unit number had been underlined twice. Shadrack put the note and the key in his pocket.

"There a guard at this place?" he asked.

"Yeah," said the young man. "He knows you're coming. Just sign in, show him your license, and go to the unit. Just like always."

The older man came in and looked at the body. He spoke Tagalog to the younger one. "Are we good?" Shadrack asked. Nobody answered. "You better make sure that body don't ever get found," he said. "Unless you want Arthur coming for your ass."

Nobody said anything. "We good?" he asked again.

"All the money there?" asked the older man.

"Yeah, go on. Count it," said Shadrack.

In the other room, Gloria's men—two more had come in after the shooting—were taking the money out of the bags, looking it over, and counting stacks. When they finished they stood up straight, brushing the knees of their pants. The oldest one stepped forward and shook hands with Shadrack, putting a hand on his shoulder like he was comforting him. He shook hands with John, as well.

When they were safely in John's SUV, Shadrack said, "Man, the apple don't fall far from the tree with that lot, does it?"

"No, it doesn't," said John.

"They are a nasty bunch," Shadrack said.

"Give me that address," John said. "I'll put it in my little map, here."

Shadrack gave him the slip of paper. His hands were still shaking. John sat typing the address into his phone.

"They had the young kid do it, too," said Shadrack. He exhaled, then looked out the window at the stars in the sky. "Raymond was a good dude, man. Shit." John nodded. "I feel sick about it."

"His ass just got caught between a rock and hard spot," said John.

"I liked him, though," said Shadrack. "It gives you a damn pause, man, no joke. I mean, what the fuck we doing here?"

"He was a good kid," said John, shaking his head. "A good kid with bad luck."

At the storage facility, the guard stared at John's license for a long time before handing it back. He returned to his booth and raised the gate. John parked in front of the unit, a garage-sized one with a roll-down door. They sat for a minute, watching the area, making sure they were alone. The place appeared to be deserted.

"Give me that gun," said John. Shadrack opened the glove compartment, pulled out a handgun in a holster, and handed it over.

They unlocked the unit and pulled the door open. In the back of the space, pushed up against the wall, sat six plastic tubs—thirty-one gallons apiece.

"Pull that door closed," said Shadrack. "That is a lot of shit."

The tubs were sealed with packing tape. Shadrack pulled a knife from his pocket and flipped it open. He cut the tape at the corner of one of the tubs, pulled up the lid, and looked in: vacuum-sealed loafs of Molly stacked up in blue kilo packs. It was a beautiful sight.

"That's what I'm talking about," whispered Shadrack. "That's what the fuck I'm talking about."

John moved the SUV so that the back of it faced the door. They put the backseats down, loaded the tubs in, and covered them with a wool blanket. Shadrack pulled the door of the unit closed and locked it. The guard watched them from his booth as they approached. John held up a backhanded peace sign as they drove past.

"I wish you'd let me play some music," said Shadrack.

"Daddy told you he's gotta focus," said John.

"Oh come on, not this *daddy* shit again."

"Daddy coming home!" said John. "Daddy hungry!"

"Go to the damn drive-in, then!" said Shadrack.

"Shit," said John. He smiled and looked in the rearview mirror.

They traveled east on Lemon Street. It was twenty minutes past midnight; there were no other cars on the road. Dark warehouses stood on both sides of the street. Fences topped with razor wire appeared here and there. The streetlights cast an orange glow over everything. Fog had started to roll in.

Shadrack had just begun to say something—he'd gotten the first two words out, "All they"—when a violent *boom* interrupted him. The car jumped hard.

"What the fuck?" yelled Shadrack. "What happened?"

The men sat there in shock. Smoke was coming from under the SUV. When John pressed the gas pedal, the car made a terrible noise and didn't move at all.

"Shit!" said John. He was looking in the rearview mirror. Shadrack turned and looked that way: A black van with a red siren spinning on top had stopped fifteen yards behind them. A spotlight from the van lit them up.

John took the gun out of his pocket and handed it to Shadrack.

"We gonna shoot?" Shadrack asked. John tried to move the car again, but it was no use.

Two lights hit them from the front, then. Both men looked that way at the same time. The lights were attached to large guns, held by two hunched men closing in fast. They were right on top of them. John and Shadrack raised their hands. There was nothing they could do.

"Turn your phone on," said Shadrack. "Record this shit. This ain't no legal stop."

John was too scared to move. One of the men outside stepped to his window and smashed it with some kind of tool. Shattered glass fell in on them. A second later, Shadrack's window exploded, too. Guns pointed in through the broken windows.

"Open the back," said the man on John's side. They were dressed in black and had black balaclavas over their heads, but they were white men; Shadrack could see it around their eyes.

"Okay, okay," said John.

"Three, two—"

John leaned forward and pulled the latch for the back door. The man beside him raised a fist, and the spotlight on the van went dark. Shadrack could hear it begin to turn around. For a moment, he thought it might drive away, but then it backed up so that the rear ends of both vehicles faced each other. The back doors of the van popped open, and a third man jumped out. He pulled open the back door of the SUV. The men in the road held their guns pointed at John and Shadrack.

"Ten seconds!" said the man on John's side.

"They ain't cops," whispered John.

"Clear!" said the man in back.

"Careful," said the man on John's side. He looked in at both of them. "Wouldn't want to kill you."

The men in the road jogged to the van. John and Shadrack watched them in the side mirrors. They jumped in the back, the doors slammed shut, and the van took off.

"What the fuck was that?" asked Shadrack.

"They just took our shit," said John.

"What the hell happened?"

"We got jacked!"

"They hit us with a damn land mine!"

"I thought they were feds!"

"I thought they were gonna kill us!"

"Fuck me," said John.

They sat there for a few seconds, then unfastened their seat belts and stepped out of the car. Both of the front wheels sat bent out at an ugly angle. The fenders had been blown off.

"You better get rid of that gun," said John. "Cops probably gonna be here in a minute."

"You know who that was?" said Shadrack. "You know who masterminded that little operation?"

"No," said John.

"Arthur," said Shadrack. "I guarantee it."

Gloria knocked on the door, waited a moment, and then entered the room. Jackie, lying on the bed, pushed herself up. A small television played quietly on the nightstand.

They'd been holding her for the last three days. Except for being handcuffed to a chain locked to the bed frame, she'd been treated civilly. They fed her regularly, let her use the restroom. She'd even taken a couple showers. Still, she found herself in a constant state of fear. She was sick with it.

On the second night, Gloria had come into her room after midnight. She wore a white sleeping gown, something a grandmother might wear; it was loose, and looked expensive. Her face had a distant look to it. Jackie had sat up and waited for the older woman to say something. Gloria's breath had smelled strongly of white wine, and her eyes were bloodshot. Instead of speaking, she'd sat down next to Jackie and taken her sweaty hand in her own. Then she'd painted Jackie's fingernails with clear polish.

Jackie let her do it. What else could she do? When Gloria gestured for her other hand, the handcuffed one, she held it out. The older woman began to speak as she continued applying the polish. She said things that were supposed to sound soothing: *Don't worry, everything will be fine. You'll be okay. You'll see. Good, good, good.*

When she was done, she squeezed Jackie's hand, looked her in the eye, and asked if she was all better. Then she stood back up, said good night, and left.

They hadn't spoken about it since then. Jackie spent most of her time watching television or sleeping. Her mind had spun itself into a mess of repeated thoughts. She felt like she'd aged ten years in three days.

Gloria was in a pantsuit, now. "Good morning," she said. She went to the television and turned it off. Jackie tried to read her body language for any signs, but beyond a new perkiness, she didn't see anything. She sat up and let her feet rest on the floor. The room she was being held in had been, it seemed, a girl's bedroom; the colors, cream and peach, didn't speak of any boy having lived there.

"Did you eat?" asked Gloria.

"Yes, thank you," said Jackie.

And then she saw it: Gloria seemed happy. She stared at Jackie for a moment, smiling with her eyes.

"He texted," she said. She held up Jackie's phone and shook it like a baby's toy. "Shit is salt." She looked at Jackie meaningfully. "That's all he said: 'Shit is salt.'"

Jackie nodded her head. Gloria came to the bed and sat next to her. "You did it," the older woman said.

"They did it," said Jackie, feeling embarrassed.

"Yes, but you made them do it," said Gloria. "That's the secret of these things." She dropped her voice to a whisper. "*Make them do it.*"

"So?" asked Jackie, trying to find the most charming and beautiful version of herself. "Will you let me go?"

"That was the deal," said Gloria. She pulled out a key and unlocked the handcuff. Jackie rubbed her wrist. The possibility of escaping with her life began to seem real. She exhaled, and had to stop herself from crying.

Gloria had written the messages to Johnson Lake. She texted him from Jackie's phone, in Jackie's presence, showing the younger woman the messages before she sent them. Later, she made her call him. Jackie explained that she'd found out exactly when the package was coming. Lake pressed her for more, but she told him—acting breathless and excited—that she still had to confirm a few things.

When she hung up, Gloria, taking the phone back, said, "Well done."

Over the next few days, she sent a steady stream of texts to him from Jackie's phone: *Happening soon. Get men ready. Tuesday night. Pickup will be from a storage center in E Bay.* On the day the deal went down, Gloria made Jackie speak to him again. Jackie told Lake that her info was real, that she'd flipped one of Gloria's boys. She told him that she couldn't meet up with him because she had to stay with her source. To assuage his skepticism, she said, "If anything doesn't feel right, just pull back—but it feels solid to me." She put as much seduction in her voice as she could, realizing that she felt good doing it.

Gloria watched her talk, smiling, and then took her phone away again.

Later that afternoon, Gloria came back before sending the address. "Is that how you would phrase it?" she asked, holding the phone up for the younger woman to examine. Jackie read the message over twice, trying to project helpfulness, and told her it sounded right.

The message laid out all of John and Shadrack's movements for the night. It described the car, the men, the house in Hercules, the storage unit in Vallejo. It suggested that Lake's men hit them directly after they'd left the storage facility.

The soldiers trailed the car to Hercules first, setting remote-controlled C4 under the SUV's wheel wells while Shadrack and John were inside the house watching Raymond Gaspar get murdered.

But Gloria was playing the soldiers, too. The packages waiting at the storage facility in Vallejo had been fake. The vacuum-sealed packs contained nothing but salt.

The real stuff was sitting in Gloria's basement; it was going to be driven to Las Vegas in two days. She knew a man there she could sell it to. She'd even raised the price: $6.2 million.

$6,200,000 + $5,600,000 = $11,800,000.

Shadrack wouldn't suspect Gloria: in his mind, she would never send a bunch of white men to do a job like that. But even if he did suspect her, there was nothing he could do about it. He was outmatched, and he knew it. As soon as the next shipment came in, he'd be waiting to buy it. He might be more careful next time, he might even have to ask her for a loan, but he'd still buy it. The cycle would continue. The scramble would start up again.

As for Lake's men, Jackie would have to explain to them that she'd been played just like they had. What more could she do? She'd given them the same information she'd been given. You win some; you lose some. Gloria hadn't told Jackie that she was going to have the four men killed. They knew too much. But there was no point in explaining that. Not yet, at least.

Tom Roberts—now perfectly under Gloria's control—would handle the investigation of Raymond. He'd find the fake ID, the plan to move his mother, the ticket to Mexico. Gloria would bring all this information to Arthur, along with Shadrack's story about Raymond disappearing with the money. Shadrack would go along; he didn't have a choice. And what was Arthur going to do? Go to war over 10 percent? It occured to her that maybe he never knew the deal had become ten times larger. He might never find out. He'd get out of the hole—Gloria still had to pay off the prison guard she used for that—and find that everything in San Francisco had changed. The world moves fast. Hard to keep up, from prison.

It was a perfect situation. She just had to keep the men in Miami happy, and they'd start it all up again next month.

She smiled at Jackie again. "You know," she said, "I moved to America from the Philippines when I was twelve years old. I never went to school. Even here, I went straight to work; I washed dishes at an Indian restaurant in the Tenderloin for five years. And look at me now. I have a family.

I'm surrounded by people that love me. I have nine grand-children. I own property. I get awards from city hall for my community work. I pay my taxes. You understand what I'm saying?"

"I think so," said Jackie, even though she didn't. She concentrated on matching her breathing to Gloria's; when the older woman inhaled, Jackie did, too.

Gloria studied the younger woman's face for a long time. "We started off on the wrong foot, you and me," she said. "I'd be willing to bet that we had very similar lives, growing up." For a moment, her eyes seemed to fill with tears. "Too many problems in this world, you know? Too much hatred. Too much violence. When I was young, I was like you: beautiful. I only cared about dancing. It's all I wanted to do. Disco, you know—" She shook her shoulders. "Dancing, flirting, drinking, singing. Things change, though. Things happen. You can't dance every day. You have to make money, too."

Jackie nodded. Her nervousness faded. She couldn't help herself; she liked this woman.

"Women need to help each other," said Gloria, as though she could read Jackie's mind. "It's the most important thing. Men are dangerous. They ruin everything." She raised her eyebrows.

Jackie nodded her head. Her own eyes filled with tears. It was exactly what she'd been thinking.

"I have a job for you," said Gloria.

"What is it?"

"Someone told me that Shadrack Pullman didn't even pay with his own money. You know that? The five million, it came from a new partner of his. Some rich techie, an idiot, a white devil. He wants to pretend he's some kind of drug lord. So, we show him. We say, *Welcome to San Francisco*."

Jackie had a good guess who Gloria was talking about: Brendan Moss, the host of the party that Raymond and Shadrack had attended. She'd already started a file on him.

"The same little bird told me that Shadrack took a bag of jewels to this man," Gloria went on. "A big bag, left it as a deposit on the money." She counted on her fingers: "Diamonds, sapphires, emeralds, rubies." She dropped her hand. "All of it."

Jackie smiled.

"That's your thing, right?" asked Gloria. "Getting into men's apartments?"

That same morning, Gloria Ocampo's older driver, the man with the pockmarked face—Salvador Luis Macaraeg—arrived at the Wolf Point Yacht Club, in San Mateo. He parked the minivan on the south side of the lot and rummaged around in the glove compartment until he found some sunscreen. He dabbed a little on his nose, forehead, and the bald spot on the crown of his head. Then he got out of the van, looked around, and walked to the clubhouse to borrow a dock cart.

When he returned to the van, his nephew—the younger driver, Mario Ocampo—opened the back door, and together the two men lifted a 250-pound manhole cover from the back. The manhole cover was wrapped in a large black trash bag. Next, they opened the side door and pulled out a large green canvas Christmas tree bag. It was heavy, and they struggled to balance it in the cart at an angle. Inside the bag, wrapped in a blue tarp, which itself was wrapped in packing tape, was Raymond Gaspar's body. The manhole cover was going to sink it, and keep it sunk.

There wasn't a cloud in the sky. It was perfect weather. Salvador Macaraeg was a firm believer in doing his dirty work in the light of day. *Nobody sees you*, he liked to say. *You can do anything in the daytime*.

Together, the two men wheeled the cart through the front gate of the club and onto the dock. They wheeled it all the way to slip C-17, where the *New Moon*, a 26-foot Farallon Walkabout, was docked. Its diesel engine was already running. The captain of the boat, Chi Xingyou, a sixty-one-year-old fisherman, sat shaking his head disdainfully as the two men approached. He didn't like doing these jobs, but they paid him a thousand dollars each time, and, besides that, he didn't know how he was supposed to refuse a request from Gloria Ocampo.

He greeted the men with a nod as they carried the heavy bag onto the boat. A sunburnt white man accompanied by a blond woman walked by and waved; Chi Xingyou waved back, pasting a fake smile on his face and nodding his head uncomfortably. The two Filipino men returned to the cart and lifted the manhole cover out, straining and bent, breathing with their cheeks puffed out. They carried the thing onto the boat and set it near the bag. Then they opened the bag up and struggled to get the manhole cover inside, so that it rested on top of Raymond Gaspar's wrapped body. Salvador Macaraeg zipped the bag closed. It resembled a snake that had swallowed something too big for its belly.

Both men dragged the bag to the back of the boat's work deck. Salvador borrowed a pocketknife from the captain and began poking holes in the bag; when the time came, it would fill with water.

Mario told him to call him when he got back. He didn't like going on the boat; it made him seasick. He waved once, then took the cart and wheeled it back to the clubhouse. Chi Xingyou and Salvador began pulling in the lines and anchor chains. When everything was clear, Chi Xingyou went to the bridge, and they began motoring out. Salvador sat on the work deck and watched the view recede behind them. The bay was too shallow for this job, so they motored past the airport and under the Bay Bridge, passing Alcatraz on their right and crossing the Presidio Shoal. After piloting under the Golden Gate Bridge, they headed due west, out into the Pacific Ocean.

After forty-five minutes in open waters, Chi Xingyou killed the engine. The boat drifted and rocked on the little waves. The water, here, was a perfect shade of navy blue. The captain joined Salvador on the deck, and both men looked around. Except for a large tanker some distance west, there were no other ships in sight. Salvador took off his sunglasses and placed them in a cup holder. He moved toward the Christmas tree bag, and the captain joined him. They didn't speak as they bent and strained and lifted the heavy thing up, rolling it over the back of the boat and into the water. Afterward, the captain went back to the bridge and closed himself in. In the water, the bag—straining between the downward pull of its contents and the upward push of trapped air—looked like it might float. Salvador watched as it slowly began to fill with water, until finally, without spectacle, it sank under the surface of the sea.

ACKNOWLEDGMENTS

During the writing of this book I was helped in innumerable ways: people fed me, housed me, gave me socks, gave me shoes, took me into the jungle, read my book, answered my questions, told me when I'd gotten off track, encouraged me, gave me ideas, edited the book, designed the cover, and inspired me again and again. I sincerely want to thank my agent Charlotte Sheedy. Thank you to Morgan Entrekin, Allison Malecha, Deb Seager, Charles Rue Woods, Judy Hottensen, Julia Berner-Tobin, Paula Cooper Hughes, and everyone at Grove Atlantic. Thank you to Jordan Bass, Walter Green, Eli Horowitz, Eric Rosenblum, Jason Schwartz, Jason Blaylock, David Hoffman, Jane Rogers, Chesa Boudin, Kent Lam, Amelia Hassani, Jason Richman, Andrew Koltuniak, Barbara Poldino, Uncle Jimmy, Brigid Hoffman, Ali Nelson, Becca Nelson, Nigel Philips, Tim O'Brien, Nate Thayer, Phearith Tit, Mey Sopheakdei, Kris Kelder, Nick Berry, Andrew Tsui, Stacey Crevello, Sarah Lannan, Simon Evans, Bear Korngold, Willow Schraeger, Shem Korngold, Violeta Garcia, Billy McEwan, Megan Winters, Avi Lessing, Dante Ortiz, Ashley Ortiz, Kent Simpson, Ben Roberts, Basho Mosko, Brendan

Morse, Nathan Burazer, Gina Macaraeg, Ed Loftus, Stevie Infante, the BMFB's, Jet Martinez, Kelly Ording, Maggie Otero, Jonathan Holland, Heather Hickman, Dan Johnson Lake, Carlos Garcia, Alexis Georgopoulos, Brendan Francis Newman, Ezra Feinberg, Caroline Paul, Wendy McNaughton, The Center for Fiction, Tomo Yasuda, Pat Harmanci, Cem Harmanci, Kerim Harmanci. Mostly, thank you to Reyhan Harmanci, who helped and inspired me in every way, without her I couldn't have done it.

RIP to Lucas Goettsche.